DARING DUCHESSES
They'll scandalise the Ton

Back in society after becoming widows, three duchesses dare to contemplate the wicked delights of taking a lover…

Except they haven't bargained on the gentlemen who rise to the challenge being *quite* so gloriously devilish!

SOME LIKE IT WICKED
December 2012

SOME LIKE TO SHOCK
January 2013

Also read Sophia's story
SOME LIKE IT SCANDALOUS
November 2012 Historical *Undone!*

AUTHOR NOTE

Welcome to the third story in my *Daring Duchesses* trilogy—I do hope you read the eBook, featuring Sophia and Dante, SOME LIKE IT SCANDALOUS, which is the introduction to the mini-series and features all of my heroines and heroes for the stories.

It has been tremendous fun writing about these three daring ladies and the three gentlemen who attempt to tame them. They fail, obviously, but fall in love with them anyway—their *Daring Duchesses* just wouldn't be as adorable if they weren't daring!

I really hope that you enjoy reading about them too.

Have fun!

SOME LIKE
TO SHOCK

Carole Mortimer

MILLS
BOON

First published in Great Britain 2013
by Mills & Boon, an imprint of Harlequin (UK) Limited.
Harlequin (UK) Limited, Eton House, 18-24 Paradise Road,
Richmond, Surrey TW9 1SR

© Carole Mortimer 2013

ISBN: 978 0 263 89799 9

Harlequin (UK) policy is to use papers that are natural, renewable and recyclable products and made from wood grown in sustainable forests. The logging and manufacturing process conform to the legal environmental regulations of the country of origin.

Printed and bound in Spain
by Blackprint CPI, Barcelona

Carole Mortimer was born in England, the youngest of three children. She began writing in 1978, and has now written over one hundred and fifty books for Harlequin Mills & Boon®. Carole has six sons: Matthew, Joshua, Timothy, Michael, David and Peter. She says, 'I'm happily married to Peter senior; we're best friends as well as lovers, which is probably the best recipe for a successful relationship. We live in a lovely part of England.'

Previous novels by the same author:

In Mills & Boon® Historical Romance:

THE DUKE'S CINDERELLA BRIDE*
THE RAKE'S INDECENT PROPOSAL*
THE ROGUE'S DISGRACED LADY*
LADY ARABELLA'S SCANDALOUS MARRIAGE*
THE LADY GAMBLES**
THE LADY FORFEITS**
THE LADY CONFESSES **
SOME LIKE IT WICKED†

The Notorious St Claires
**The Copeland Sisters*
†*Daring Duchesses*

You've read about *The Notorious St Claires* **in Regency times. Now you can read about the new generation in Mills & Boon® Modern™ Romance:**

The Scandalous St Claires:
Three arrogant aristocrats—ready to be tamed!
JORDAN ST CLAIRE: DARK AND DANGEROUS
THE RELUCTANT DUKE
TAMING THE LAST ST CLAIRE

Carole Mortimer has written a further 150 novels for Mills & Boon® Modern™ Romance, and in Mills & Boon® Historical *Undone!* **eBooks:**

AT THE DUKE'S SERVICE
CONVENIENT WIFE, PLEASURED LADY
SOME LIKE IT SCANDALOUS†

Peter, all my love as always.

Chapter One

❦

May, 1817—London

'May I offer you a ride in my carriage, Genevieve…?'

Genevieve turned sharply to look at the man standing beside her at the top of the steps leading down from St George's Church in Hanover Square. The two of them had just attended and acted as witness at the wedding of mutual friends.

It was not the gentleman's tone which surprised her, but the question itself, when her own carriage and maid were clearly waiting at the bottom of the steps in preparation for the drive back to her home in Cavendish Square.

There was also the fact that she was Genevieve Forster, widowed Duchess of Woollerton, and the gentleman at her side was Lord Benedict Lucas, known to his close friends and enemies alike as merely Lucifer. There was a difference in their social standing, the two of them having only been on nodding acquaintance before today, which should have dictated he refer to her as your Grace rather than by her given name…

'Genevieve?'

She felt a quiver of awareness travel the length of her spine at the husky intensity of Lucifer's voice, even as she realised he was looking down at her with enigmatic coal-black eyes, with one equally dark brow raised in mocking enquiry beneath the tall hat he had placed upon his head upon leaving the church.

Lucifer…

How well that name suited this particular gentleman, with his midnight-black hair curling softly over the collar of his black superfine and eyes so dark a brown they also appeared black. His cheekbones were high besides a sharp blade of nose and sculptured mouth that occasionally curved in sensual appreciation, but was more often than not thinned in haughty and unapproachable disdain above the firmness of his arrogantly angled jaw.

Aged one and thirty, Lucifer was but six years older than Genevieve, but the depth of emotions hidden behind those glittering black eyes spoke of a gentleman much older than his calendar years.

Part of the reason for that, Genevieve and all of society knew, was the tragic way in which his parents had met their deaths ten years ago. Lucifer had found the couple murdered at their country estate and their slayer had never been found or brought to justice.

Which was perhaps also the reason Genevieve had never seen Benedict Lucas wearing anything but black over his pristine white linen, all perfectly tailored, of course, to emphasise the width of his shoulders, muscled chest, lean hips and long legs in black Hessians. It was attire which should have given him an air of somberness, but on this gentleman only added to his air of danger and elusiveness.

An elusiveness, if Genevieve's assessment of his offer was to be believed, which Benedict Lucas was now suggesting she might be allowed to breach by travelling home in his carriage with him...?

A suggestion, if Genevieve were to accept, which was so very much in keeping with her declaration a week ago to her two closest friends, Sophia and Pandora, that as widows recently returned to society after the required year of mourning, they should each of them take a lover, before the Season ended. It had been a brave and *risqué* suggestion on her part, Genevieve knew, and made more out of bravado than intent on her part; her painful and humiliating marriage to Josiah Forster had resulted in a physical wariness on her part in regard to all men.

She moistened her lips. 'It is very kind of you to offer, my lord, but—'

'Surely a lady as…daring as you cannot be feeling nervous at the idea of travelling alone in my carriage, Genevieve…?'

That quiver of awareness turned to one of alarm at Lucifer's use of the word *daring*, for that was exactly the same term she had used a week ago, when talking to Sophia and Pandora in regard to their taking of a lover. It had been a conversation she was aware one of Lucifer's two closest friends had overheard—and perhaps repeated…? It was most ungentlemanly of him to have done so if that should turn out to be the case.

Her chin rose as she looked up at Lucifer with guarded blue eyes. 'I was not aware that

I had ever behaved in a manner which any might consider "daring", my lord?' Nor was she at all sure she would ever be able to do so. Bravado with her two close friends was one thing, acting upon that bravado something else entirely.

Besides which, Benedict Lucas was a gentleman whom all of the *ton* talked of in hushed voices, if they dared talk of him at all. A man of deep and violent passions, he was known to have vowed ten years ago that he would find the person who had murdered his parents, no matter how long it took him to do it, and that when he did he would kill the man himself rather than trust to the justice of the law.

Lucifer was also known as one of the finest shots in England, as well as a superior swordsman, skills he had honed and perfected during his years spent in the army, which meant that he was more than capable of carrying out such a threat.

'Or perhaps you have heard otherwise, my lord?' she challenged at his lack of reply.

Benedict might have laughed at how little that expression of haughty reproach suited Genevieve Forster's impishly beautiful face. Almost. Except laughter, amusement of any kind, was not something which had come easily to him this past ten years. Instead, his mouth now curled into a hard and mocking smile. 'Not particularly, Genevieve.' He continued to use her given name deliberately, having noted her earlier discomfort. 'But I am sure it is not too late for you to remedy that particular omission, if you so choose…?'

There was no denying that Genevieve Forster was a very beautiful woman; her abundance of curls beneath her blue bonnet was the colour of flame and her mischievously twinkling eyes the colour of periwinkles. Her nose was slightly snub above full and sensuously pouting lips, her complexion that of peaches and cream. And although tiny in stature, almost daintily fragile, the swell of her breasts, above the low neckline of her blue gown, appeared full and lush.

To Benedict's knowledge she had been married for six years, and widowed for one. She was without any male relatives, except for her stepson, the current duke, a gentleman who was several years older than Genevieve, and it was known that the two were not close. Her two closest female friends were also currently engaged in relationships which he knew took them from Genevieve's side.

Not that Benedict had ever been known to

prey on unprotected females, but as a widow of five and twenty years, that term hardly applied to Genevieve Forster. A public acquaintance with her would do well as a foil for his own movements over the next few weeks, in his capacity as a spy for the Crown, with the added bonus that her beauty and vivacity would also ensure that Benedict enjoyed that acquaintance.

'Unless, of course, you feel it would be *too* daring to travel alone with me in my carriage...?' he now challenged softly.

Genevieve bristled at what she considered to be a slur upon the independence she had tried so hard to acquire since her widowhood a year ago. She was also well past the first flush of youth. She was a duchess, and a widow, and as such she could, and would, now behave as she pleased.

Neither would she give the arrogantly mocking Benedict Lucas the satisfaction of thinking her a coward. 'Not at all, my lord,' she assured him frostily. 'If you will just give me a moment to dismiss my own carriage?'

'And your maid?'

Her spine stiffened at this further challenge. 'And my maid,' she conceded coolly after several seconds' thought.

'Shall we…?' Benedict Lucas offered her his arm to escort her down the steps.

Genevieve's cheeks were pale and her heart was beating a little too rapidly in her chest as she placed a gloved hand lightly upon that muscled arm and allowed Benedict Lucas to escort her down to her carriage, whereupon he excused himself to stroll across to engage in conversation with his own coachman as he waited for her to join him.

'Are you sure, your Grace?' May, Genevieve's maid for the past seven years, had given a wide-eyed glance in the direction of the dark and dangerously attractive Lucifer upon being informed of Genevieve's intention to ride home in his carriage with him.

'I am very sure, yes,' Genevieve stated more firmly than she felt. May knew better than most how horrific Genevieve's marriage to Josiah Forster had been.

Her maid looked unconvinced. 'I've heard such tales about that particular gentleman—'

'That will be quite enough, thank you, May.' Genevieve had also heard 'tales' about Lucifer, and all of them wicked. But what else could she have done when he had challenged her so obviously?

Run as far away as was possible, came the instant and emphatic answer!

No, she would not, could not, continue to live in the way she had been forced to live during her marriage to Josiah, frightened of her own shadow most of the time. No matter how much the thoughts of being alone with any gentleman made her pulse flutter and her stomach clench with nausea!

Besides, what could Benedict Lucas possibly do to her in his carriage in broad daylight…?

'Is that really necessary, my lord?'

Benedict smiled at Genevieve Forster as she sat across the carriage from him, those blue eyes wide as she watched him pulling down the blinds on the windows. 'Do you not find the sun a little…overbright?' he drawled derisively.

She studied him for several long seconds. 'It is a little…intrusive,' she finally conceded abruptly.

'Exactly.' Benedict's gaze continued to meet hers as he pulled down the last of the blinds. 'This is much cosier,' he murmured appreciatively.

'Much.' The coolness of her smile was belied by the telltale rapid beating of her pulse in the slenderness of her throat. 'Tell me, were you as surprised by today's wedding as I?'

'No,' he answered unhelpfully; the confidences of the bridegroom were exactly that, confidences, and they would remain so.

'Do you think—?'

'No.'

Genevieve Forster arched red-gold brows. 'You have not heard my question as yet.'

Benedict gave a hard smile. 'It is not necessary when I have no intention of discussing the private business of today's bride or groom.' His gaze moved to the firm swell of her breasts as she drew in a deep breath. 'That is a very pretty...necklace you are wearing.'

'I— Thank you.' Her gloved fingers instinctively moved to touch the sapphire as large as a robin's egg nestling between her breasts. 'It was a wedding gift,' she added stiffly.

'Obviously your husband was a gentleman of discerning tastes,' Benedict murmured softly. 'Both in his wife and the jewellery he bestowed upon her.'

'You may choose to think that if you wish, Lucas.' Genevieve's voice had hardened to ice.

The sharpness of Benedict's narrowed gaze returned to her face, easily noting the twin spots of colour that had appeared in her cheeks and the angry sparkle in those beautiful blue eyes. 'The duke was not a gentleman of discerning tastes…?' he said slowly.

'He was not a gentleman at all!' she snapped scathingly. 'And, might I say, Lucas, that if you invited me into your carriage with any intention of furthering our acquaintance, then I believe I must tell you that, by introducing the subject of my late husband into our conversation, you have failed utterly!'

Benedict's brows rose at the directness of her statement. 'Your marriage was not a happy one?'

'Obviously not.'

Genevieve Forster was proving more of a distraction than Benedict would ever have guessed before engaging in conversation with her.

'You did not find becoming a duchess suitable…compensation, for the duke's deficiencies as a husband?'

'I did not.' Genevieve's mood was not in the least lightened by the glint of humour she was sure she could now see in the darkness of Benedict Lucas's eyes. 'A word of caution, perhaps, for the next time you find yourself alone with a lady, might be not to mention the woman's dead husband!'

'If I have offended—'

'I am not offended, my lord, I am merely bored by this conversation.' She turned to raise the blind beside her before looking out at the street below.

Benedict sat back in stunned silence for several long seconds, as he acknowledged he had never encountered a woman quite like Genevieve Forster before. For all that he was always discreet, Benedict had known a number of women intimately this past twelve years. Women he had desired physically, but had no interest in knowing in any other way, let alone any of the private details of the lives they had led before he met them.

His intentions towards Genevieve Forster had been equally dispassionate, in that it had been his intention to use a friendship with her, as he had others in the past, as a shield to his appearance in society. Benedict usually made a point of avoiding attending any of society's balls and parties, and it was only when it was required, in his role as agent for the crown, that he deigned to accept any of those invitations.

For Genevieve Forster to so firmly express

her own lack of interest in continuing their acquaintance was galling, and yet somehow intriguing, at the same time. 'Is there not some way in which I might redeem myself?' he cajoled softly.

An irritated frown still creased her creamy brow as she turned to look at him. 'I should tell you that I was married for six unhappy years and have spent the last year in mourning for a husband I thoroughly detested. As such I seek only adventure and fun in my life in future.'

Benedict had known of the huge difference in ages between the duke and his wife, but until now he had not been aware of the circumstances of Genevieve's marriage to Josiah Forster. Now that he did, he could not help but wonder in what manner that marriage had been so unhappy. 'And you believe me to be incapable of providing that adventure and fun?' He arched dark brows.

'Adventure of a kind, perhaps,' she acknowledged in measured tones. 'After all, you are known as the dangerous and elusive Lucifer.'

His brows rose. 'Am I?'

'Oh, yes.' She nodded derisively. 'But fun?

No, I do not believe so, my lord.' Her smile was coolly dismissive.

Benedict's irritation increased at that easy dismissal. 'How can you be so sure of that without having spent any time in my company?'

'I have spent the time of this carriage ride in your company, my lord.' She eyed him haughtily.

'And?'

She shrugged. 'And that has been quite long enough to assure me that the differences in our natures would not suit.'

Benedict's frustration with this conversation, with this woman, grew by the minute. 'Will you be attending Lady Hammond's ball this evening?'

She gave an elegant shrug. 'I am undecided as yet between attending the ball or enjoying a private supper with the Earl of Sandhurst.'

'You are thinking of supping with Charlie Brooks?' Benedict sat forwards on his seat.

Those blue eyes widened defensively at his obvious disdain. 'The earl is not only charming and affable, but also as handsome as a Greek god.'

The Earl of Sandhurst was all of those things. He was also known to be one of the biggest lechers in London. Which no doubt perfectly suited Genevieve's immediate plans for indulging in 'adventure and fun', following marriage to a man so obviously lacking in those attributes, a man she had bluntly stated she despised.

Could it be that Benedict's own chagrin towards Sandhurst was irritation at being told he 'did not suit'? Maybe a little, he conceded irritably. But really, to be passed over for that lightweight Charlie Brooks, of all men!

'I have an engagement earlier in the evening, but the two of us could have a private supper together later tonight if that is what you believe you would find adventurous and fun?' he heard himself offering.

'I think not, but thank you for asking,' Genevieve refused coolly.

'Why the hell not?' Benedict snapped.

'Well, for one thing, I do not appreciate being informed I would have to take second place to your other engagement earlier in the evening.'

'It is a business appointment!'

She shrugged those delicate shoulders. 'Then I wish you more success with it than you have had with me.'

Lucifer glared. 'You are being unreasonable!'

Genevieve gave him a pitying glance. 'I am sure that there are many women who would appreciate your interest, my lord, but following so soon after my unhappy marriage, I believe I require something a little more... romantic than you appear to be currently offering.'

'Romantic!' He stared at her as if she had completely lost her senses.

Genevieve glanced out of the window. 'It would seem we are arrived at my home, Lucas.' She gave him a vacuous smile as she collected up her reticule in preparation for leaving the carriage. 'Thank you for the carriage ride, my lord, it has been most...enlightening.'

He scowled darkly. 'There are many ways in which to have fun, Genevieve,' he drawled softly. 'And I believe, if you were to reflect, that you would realise that I have a much better...understanding of them than Sandhurst.'

She raised her brows. 'Perhaps one day I might consider comparing that...understanding, and so decide for myself if that is so, but not today.'

Lucifer frowned darkly. 'You are being extremely naïve in believing you will only be asked to enjoy "adventure and fun" with one such as Charlie Brooks.'

Genevieve was having fun right now, if truth be told. She had been very young when she married Josiah, with little opportunity to flirt with other men before that marriage; but even so, she had absolutely no doubts that she had now piqued Benedict Lucas's interest by refusing to be in the least attracted to his dark and brooding good looks.

She might indeed be as naïve as Benedict Lucas had just accused her of being in regard to the behaviour of the gentlemen of the *ton,* but she was not stupid, and a man such as he would obviously see no challenge whatsoever in the easy conquest he had so obviously believed Genevieve might be to his lazily arrogant charms. It was, she acknowledged with wonder, quite deliciously enticing to know that she had aroused the interest of such a dangerous and elusive gentleman...

She gave a shrug. 'As I said, I wish to be wooed a little before I would ever consider taking any gentleman as my lover.'

'Sandhurst—'

'—sent me flowers and chocolates earlier

today. Accompanied by a beautifully worded card.' She smiled at the memory.

'Only because he is hoping to entice you into sharing his bed later this evening!'

'I am aware of that, of course,' Genevieve acknowledged with a cool inclination of her head. 'But Sandhurst hoping for such an outcome to the evening will not make it so.'

Had Benedict ever felt such frustration and anger with a woman before? He could not remember doing so. Indeed, he rarely if ever allowed himself to express strong emotions of any kind. Which was not to say he did not feel them, only that he chose not to reveal those emotions to others. 'I fail to see anything in the least romantic in Sandhurst plying you with flowers and chocolates, and prettily worded cards…' his top lip curled up with distaste '…for the sole purpose of expecting you to go to bed with him immediately after the two of you have dined privately together.'

Genevieve eyed him mockingly. 'And would you not have expected the same from me, without benefit of flowers and chocolates and prettily worded cards, if I had agreed to meet you at Lady Hammond's ball later this evening?'

He snorted his impatience. 'If that is so,

then at least I have been honest in my intentions.'

She gave him a pitying glance. 'Perhaps too much so...?'

His nostrils flared. 'You are an extremely aggravating woman, Genevieve!'

She gave a surprised laugh. 'Now that truly is honest, Benedict.'

Those black eyes glowered across the carriage at her. He gave an impatient shake of his head. 'You will find me at Lady Hammond's ball later this evening if that should be your choice.'

She gave another cool inclination of her head. 'I will keep your gracious offer in mind. Now, if you would not mind...?' She glanced pointedly towards the carriage door, leaving Benedict with no other choice but to alight from the carriage before turning to offer Genevieve his hand as she stepped down beside him. She gave him another cool nod before turning to gracefully climb the steps to the front door of her home, which opened immediately for her entrance before closing firmly behind her.

All, Benedict noted broodingly, without so much as a backwards glance in his direction...

Chapter Two

'Has Sandhurst displeased you in some way?'

Benedict turned to raise dark, questioning brows at the short and rotund gentleman who had joined him as he stood beside the crowded dance floor in Lady Hammond's ballroom. 'And why should you think he has displeased me?' He spoke loudly to be heard over the noisy chatter and laughter of the three hundred or so members of the *ton* squeezed into the candlelit ballroom, the bell-like laughter of one person in particular catching his ear.

'Possibly because you have been glowering at him for the past several minutes?' Lord Eric Cargill, the Earl of Dartmouth and Benedict's godfather, chuckled wryly.

Benedict deliberately turned his back upon the couples dancing. 'I was merely trying to understand in what way Sandhurst might possibly be perceived as resembling a Greek god,' he drawled dismissively.

'Oh?' The earl's surprised grey brows shot up into his thinning hairline.

Benedict gave a self-derisive smile. 'Not for my own edification, you understand.'

'Ah.' The older man nodded in obvious relief, before then giving a slow shake of his head. 'No, I am afraid I do not understand in the least?'

'No reason why you should,' Benedict dismissed briskly, having no intention of confiding that the reason for his own interest was currently dancing in the other man's arms!

The earl eyed him piercingly for several minutes before obviously dismissing the subject as being unimportant. 'If I had known you were to be here this evening, then I would not have bothered to come myself.' He grimaced. He had served as a colonel in the army for many years, and was now spymaster for the Crown under the guise of a minor ministerial post, but was no more a lover of society balls than Benedict.

'And in doing so you would have also have

deprived my Aunt Cynthia the pleasure of attending, too,' he drawled mockingly. The earl and countess had become his aunt and uncle by long association, the couple having adopted him as their own since the death of his parents, their own long marriage sadly childless.

'There is that to consider.' The earl chuckled, brown eyes twinkling merrily. 'But, much as I intend to enjoy her expression of gratitude later this evening, I am not sure even that is worth the tedious hours I have already suffered tonight in the line of duty!' His eyes narrowed as he turned to look at the couples still dancing. 'Who is the beautiful young woman currently dancing with Sandhurst?'

'I believe it to be the Duchess of Woollerton.' Benedict had no need to turn and look across the room to know the identity of that 'beautiful young woman'.

Eric Cargill gave him a cursory glance. 'I was not aware that Forster had taken a wife?'

'Perhaps I should have said the widowed Duchess,' Benedict corrected lightly.

The earl's brows rose again. 'That young beauty is the child-bride Josiah Forster's kept shut away in the country from the moment he had married and bedded her?'

Benedict winced at the crudeness of his uncle's statement. 'So it would appear.'

'I had no idea…' the older man murmured appreciatively.

'You really should try and get out and about in society more, Dartmouth,' Benedict drawled.

His godfather grimaced at the thought of it. 'I have deliberately engaged the services of people such as yourself so that I have no need to do so.'

Benedict had joined the army not long after his parents were murdered, venting his anger and frustration upon Napoleon's armies for seven years, only resigning his commission after the Corsican had been safely incarcerated on the Isle of Elba—at least, all of England had believed him to be safely incarcerated! Benedict had returned to the army only briefly after Napoleon's escape, before the tyrant was once again defeated and this time placed on the more isolated island of St Helena.

Benedict had then found the tedium of civilian life did not suit his inner restlessness in the least. His godfather's offer of a position, working for him as one of his agents for the

Crown, had helped to ease that restlessness, if not completely alleviate it, this past two years.

It could not be completely erased until Benedict had learnt the identity of the person who had slain his parents and dealt with them accordingly. Something his position as one of the Earl of Dartmouth's agents allowed him to continue to pursue privately, and without anyone suspecting he was doing so.

Except when it came to attending evenings such as this one, which was when Benedict usually used a show of interest in a particular woman to act as a shield to the real reason for his presence. Much as Benedict abhorred the crush of such events as this one, he appreciated that they were the perfect opportunity in which to receive or give information.

It still rankled with him that Genevieve had firmly refused any intention of becoming that current interest earlier today. Even more so, when, having arrived an hour or so ago, he had thereafter been forced to observe Sandhurst's more-than-obvious pursuit of her, as well as Genevieve's laughing responses to the other man's no doubt heavy-handed flattery.

Genevieve herself was a vision in cream silk and lace, with pearl droplets adorning her fiery-red curls, her eyes a deep blue and her lips a rosy peach against the creaminess of her complexion. More pearls encircled the delicacy of her throat and her creamy shoulders were left bare by the style of her gown.

'—have not seen any sign as yet of the Count de Sevanne—Benedict, are you even listening to me?'

Benedict turned from once again observing Genevieve as she danced elegantly around the ballroom with Sandhurst, to find the earl frowning up at him for his inattentiveness. He determinedly shook off that complete awareness of Genevieve Forster's beauty, as he instead gave the appearance of concentrating on discussing the French count, who was the reason for his own and Dartmouth's presence here this evening. Napoleon might have been subdued, but there was no reason to suppose he would remain that way. Nor was he England's only enemy.

Benedict gave the appearance of concentrating on his uncle's conversation, because, even as he and Eric Cargill continued to talk softly together, his own attention wandered time and time again to Genevieve Forster, especially when she and Sandhurst left the dance floor together some minutes later in search of refreshment.

Or, knowing Sandhurst, the privacy in which to deepen their dalliance, in one of Lady Hammond's more secluded parlours...

Genevieve, having earlier today sent word to Charles Brooks that she had decided to attend Lady Hammond's ball rather than join him for a private dinner, had been fully aware of having Lucifer's dark gaze upon her since his arrival at the ball an hour or so earlier. Reason enough, she had considered, to encourage and accept Charles Brooks's attentions when he had arrived immediately after Lucifer and instantly made his way to her side before commencing to flirt with her outrageously.

A flirtatiousness Lucifer did not in the least appreciate, if the tight clenching of his jaw, and the dark glitter of his eyes as he continued to observe Genevieve beneath hooded lids, was any indication.

Genevieve had not felt so giddy with excitement for years. If ever...

Josiah Forster, a man almost forty years her senior, had offered for Genevieve halfway through her first Season, an offer which her brother had been only too pleased to accept on her behalf. The man was a duke and Genevieve would become his duchess, Colin had argued when she had protested at the idea of marrying a man so much older than herself.

It had been a fairytale wedding, with all of the *ton* there to witness the union. And if Genevieve had quaked in her satin slippers at thoughts of becoming the wife of the elderly and obese Duke of Woollerton, no one would have guessed it as she floated down the aisle, a vision in satin and lace, nor at the wedding supper later, as she had stood at the duke's side, smiling and greeting their guests.

It had only been later that evening, during the carriage ride to the Woollerton estate in Gloucestershire, that Genevieve's nerves had got the better of her at thoughts of the night ahead.

A night which had been every bit, and more, the nightmare Genevieve had feared it might be, Josiah making no allowances either for her youth or her lack of experience.

She shuddered now just at the memory of the horrors she had suffered that night, and that had only been the start of those fearful years of incarceration as Josiah Forster's wife.

A prison Genevieve had only escaped upon his death.

Consequently this was the first London

Season that Genevieve had been allowed to enjoy for seven years. And, as such, she intended to enjoy every moment of it!

And how better to do so than to know that the attentions of the handsome, blond-haired and blue-eyed Charles Brooks, whilst flattering in themselves, were made even more so because they obviously irritated the usually disdainfully detached, black-haired and black-eyed and enticingly wicked Lucifer?

It was heady stuff indeed to be the centre of attention of two such handsome gentlemen after so many years of being secluded away in rural Gloucestershire. Her husband had supervised her time and pursuits with the intensity of a hawk about to swoop on its unsuspecting prey, with the administration of suitable punishment if she did not do exactly as he wished.

Even now Genevieve could not repress the shiver of revulsion at the memory of Josiah's treatment of her on their wedding night. She shut down those thoughts immediately as she determinedly returned her attention to the more welcome attentions of Charles Brooks. His fingers lingered overlong against her gloved hand as he handed her one of the glasses of champagne he had just acquired for the two of them.

'To us, my dear Genevieve.' His eyes gleamed down at her appreciatively as he gently touched his glass against her own.

'A wholly inappropriate sentiment, Sandhurst,' Benedict Lucas drawled dismissively even as he plucked the champagne glass from Genevieve's gloved fingers before turning to place it on the silver tray carried by one of Lady Hammond's footmen, with a muttered comment for him to 'dispose of this'. 'Our dance, I believe, Genevieve?' He looked down the length of his nose at her, arrogant brows raised over eyes that gleamed with challenge.

To say Genevieve was astounded by his interruption would be putting it mildly. And she was furious at Lucifer's highhandedness in removing her glass of champagne in that peremptory manner, so much so that she seriously considered refusing to go along with his fabrication; he had not so much as attempted to even greet her this evening, so how could he possibly claim this as being 'their dance'!

Benedict, having easily read the light of battle which had appeared in Genevieve's expressive blue eyes, now took a firm hold of her arm before striding determinedly away from the other man.

A move she certainly did not approve of as

she tried to free herself from the firmness of his grasp. 'How dare you, Lucas!'

'I dare because Sandhurst had introduced a little concoction of his own to your champagne in order to make you more…compliant to his advances,' he muttered disgustedly as he continued to walk in the direction of the ballroom.

Her arm stiffened beneath his hand, her face paling as she glanced back to where Sandhurst stood glowering after them. 'What did you say…?'

Benedict spared her an impatient glance between narrowed lids. 'A mere "thank you for your timely rescue, my lord" will do.'

'You are talking utter nonsense.' She eyed him impatiently as she was forced to take two steps to his one in order to avoid tripping and falling.

'Am I?' He gave a derisive shake of his head.

'Of course you are.' Her cheeks now bore an angry flush. 'Just because I so obviously prefer the attentions of a gallant gentleman such as Sandhurst is no reason—' She broke off her tirade as it was met with a disparaging snort from Benedict. 'It is obvious from your behaviour that *you* are not a gentleman at all!'

'And you, my dear Genevieve, have tonight proved that you are a mere babe in arms when it comes to men such as Sandhurst,' he assured grimly. 'Once the champagne had been consumed and the effects of the concoction had reached their desired effect, you would then have found yourself more than willing, indeed eager, to retire somewhere more private for whatever debauchery Sandhurst had in mind for the two of you this evening!'

She gasped. 'You are merely saying these wicked things about Sandhurst in order to alarm me! Or, more probably, in an effort to make me think more highly of you,' she added with dismissive disdain.

Benedict's mouth firmed. 'I very much doubt it is possible for you to think any less of me!'

'And I am sure that I might manage it somehow!' Her eyes sparkled with her anger.

He gave a humourless smile. 'No doubt.'

She nodded, red curls bouncing against her nape. 'And how would you even know about such "concoctions", if you were not familiar with or had used them yourself?'

Benedict's breath left him in a hiss, a nerve pulsing in his tightly clenched jaw as he came to an abrupt halt in the cavernous hallway of

Lady Hammond's London home before turning to face the infuriated Genevieve. 'I assure you, madam, I have never needed to use such underhand practices as that in order to persuade a woman into sharing my bed!'

Her little pointed chin was raised stubbornly as she met the dangerous glitter of his dark gaze. 'And why should you think Sandhurst might, when he—'

'Is in possession of the handsomeness of a Greek god,' Benedict completed disgustedly. 'I agree with you, Genevieve, he should not need to do so. Unfortunately, your Greek god has grown weary of the chase, and those flowers and chocolates you received earlier today would have been his first and last "gallant" gesture. Sandhurst now prefers that his courtship be less…protracted and the woman willing to bed him as quickly as possible, along with any number of his less savoury friends, so that he might watch and so add to his own entertainment.'

Genevieve's gaze wavered uncertainly at this graphic description of debauchery. Could Benedict Lucas—Lucifer—be telling her the truth? Had Sandhurst really put something in her champagne in order to render her willing to do unspeakable things, with both him and his friends? It sounded highly unlikely to her innocent ears, but at the same time she had to admit, much as the *ton* loved to gossip about Lucifer, she had never heard them question his honesty.

Had Genevieve been taken for the fool this evening by Sandhurst?

Could her silly flaunting of Sandhurst's attentions under Lucifer's arrogant nose have resulted in her not seeing what was directly in front of her own?

After all, what did she really know of Charlie Brooks, except that he was an earl, and a charming and handsome rogue? And a gentleman the marriage-minded mamas of the *ton* preferred that their innocent daughters avoid.

Genevieve had assumed the latter was because Sandhurst had made it perfectly clear that he had no serious intentions in regard to marriage. But her assumption might have been wrong, and in fact those young innocents may well be kept out of Sandhurst's reach for fear they might suffer the ruin and disgrace Lucifer had just described to Genevieve so vividly.

Benedict knew exactly the moment that Genevieve began to accept that his claims in regard to Sandhurst might have some truth to them. Her face became even paler, her eyes flashing a dark and stormy blue, her full and enticingly delectable bottom lip trembling slightly.

He forced himself to relax some of the tension in his own shoulders. 'Come now, Genevieve, there has been no real harm done,' he cajoled. 'No one was hurt. I succeeded in rescuing you before you had chance to drink any of the champagne, and so both you, and your reputation, remain unsullied.'

If anything, her eyes grew even more stormy at his assurances. 'And you think that should be an end of the matter?' Her voice was deceptively soft.

Benedict eyed her warily. 'Is it not?'

'Not in the least,' she bit out with a scathing determination.

A determination Benedict readily admitted to finding slightly unnerving. 'Genevieve—'

'I believe you said this was our dance, my lord?' she prompted lightly.

He blinked at the sudden change of subject. 'It is almost over...'

'Then we will stand and talk together until the next one begins.' She tucked her little gloved hand into the crook of his arm. 'Unless, of course, you fear your own reputation might suffer if you were to be seen escorting a lady who left the ballroom with one gentleman and returned on the arm of another?' She arched challenging brows.

'I have no interest in what others may or may not think of me.' Benedict stared down at her impatiently.

'Then perhaps you do not dance?'

He gave a humourless smile. 'I believe I am right in saying that my tutors saw to my being well versed in all of the social graces, as well as the education of my mind.'

'Then perhaps it is that you do not care to dance with me?'

Benedict knew he would enjoy nothing more than to hold Genevieve in his own arms after watching her for the past hour or more, as she was twirled about the ballroom by one gentleman or another, so allowing Benedict the freedom to admire her beauty and grace. To know that even now his own body responded, hardened, just looking at the delicacy of her bared throat and the soft swell of her breasts.

'I have every intention of dancing with you, if only to show the cats of the *ton* that you have not left Lady Hammond's home with Sandhurst as they all no doubt expect you might have done,' he concluded tersely. 'But first I would like your promise that you will stay well away from Sandhurst and his disreputable cohorts in future.'

She looked up at him through the long sweep of her lashes. 'And why should you care one way or the other what I choose to do in future?'

'You ask the most damnable questions!' Benedict glared his impatience. 'Perhaps it is that one of your closest friends married one of mine earlier today, and as such I feel a certain responsibility— What?' he demanded as Genevieve smiled.

'It is very sweet of you to feel protective towards me.'

'Sweet?' Benedict gave a pained wince. 'I am certain *that* is not a sentiment anyone has ever dared to level at me before this evening!'

Those blue eyes glowed with mischief. 'Perhaps other people do not know your kindness as I now do?'

'You do not know me, either, Genevieve,' he bit out impatiently. If she did, then she would know that at this moment Benedict's feeling towards her were almost as disreputable as Sandhurst's, inasmuch as he would enjoy nothing more than to drag Genevieve off to some secluded spot where he might make love to her!

She gave his forearm a conciliatory pat. 'Do not worry, Lucas, your secret is perfectly safe with me.'

Benedict scowled even as he stiffened warily. 'What secret?'

'Why, that you are not really the big dark Lucifer at all, but more like one of those darling little cherubs seen in a Rubens's painting.' Her eyes were wide with innocence.

'I am like—! You— I—' Benedict found himself spluttering with an inelegance totally contrary to his normal cool control. 'You are daring to liken me to one of those sickeningly chubby little cherubs?'

Genevieve barely managed to contain her laughter at Lucifer's obvious disgust. 'Well, you are not in the least chubby, of course, and you do not have golden hair…'

'I assure you, madam, you are wrong in thinking there is any resemblance whatsoever between myself and a fat cherub!' He glared his displeasure. 'Genevieve…?' He eyed her suspiciously as she could no longer contain her laughter.

'If you could only see the indignation upon

your face!' She continued to chuckle huskily, her eyes gleaming with unholy glee.

'You were teasing me…?' He gave a disbelieving shake of his head.

'Of course.' Genevieve nodded, still smiling as she realised from his reaction that it was not something which occurred very often in regard to this particular gentleman.

Her teasing had also succeeded in distracting his attention away from her earlier remarks in regard to Charles Brooks; that gentleman had certainly not heard the last from her on the subject of his daring to attempt to make a fool of her.

If her years of being unhappily married to Josiah Forster had succeeded in doing nothing else, then it was to instil in Genevieve an appreciation for the freedoms of choice she now enjoyed as his widow. Charles Brooks had attempted to circumvent that freedom this evening with his machinations and it was not something Genevieve intended to easily forgive, or forget.

'It is past time we danced, I believe.' Benedict Lucas did not wait for her reply before sweeping into the throng of other couples braving the noisy and crowded dance floor.

He danced divinely. His imposing height

made him at least a foot taller than Genevieve, the muscled length of his body mere inches away from her own as they danced the daring waltz together, one of his hands firm against the back of her waist so that he might guide their steps about the dance floor, the other lightly clasping her gloved fingers, with Genevieve's hand resting lightly against the broadness of one of his shoulders in his beautifully tailored black evening jacket. He smelt divine, too—a clean and yet earthy smell that was a mixture of sandalwood and some exotic fruit, and which led Genevieve to wonder how she could ever have found Charles Brooks's pretty good looks and overpowering cologne in the least attractive.

So entranced was Genevieve by the combination of Benedict's undoubted height and strength, and that deliciously male smell invading her senses, that it took her some minutes to realise the two of them were being openly stared at by the majority of Lady Hammond's guests, the conversation in the room having died down to the softness of a whisper behind open fans.

She glanced up at the lean strength of her dancing partner's tightly clenched jaw as Benedict's attention seemed to be fixed upon something over her left shoulder. 'We appear to be attracting a certain amount of attention,' she murmured softly.

His jaw became even tighter. 'Yes.'

Her lashes lowered on to suddenly warm cheeks. 'Do you have any idea why that is?'

'Yes.'

She winced. 'Do you think—can it be because of my earlier error in judgement, with regard to Sandhurst?' Having only just rejoined society, Genevieve had absolutely no desire to behave in any way that might cause her to be immediately ostracised.

'No.'

'Well?' she demanded sharply as he made no attempt to add to that unhelpful statement.

He breathed out impatiently. 'I believe the reason we are being so closely…observed is because it must be ten years or more since I have bothered to dance with any lady at one of these tediously boring balls.'

'Really?'

Benedict glanced down at Genevieve as he heard the curiosity in her voice. 'Yes. Really,' he snapped his irritation, both at the *ton*'s speculation at the phenomena and Genevieve's obvious pleasure in the fact. 'Does it please you to know that every member of the *ton* present this evening is now speculating as to why I should have chosen to dance with the Dowager Duchess of Woollerton?'

'Yes.'

He frowned darkly at her candour. 'Why?'

She shrugged slender shoulders. 'Because it is...the fun we discussed earlier today.'

'Genevieve—'

'Lucifer?' Her eyes glowed deeply blue beneath the long sweep of her dark lashes, an entrancing dimple having appeared in her left cheek, as she continued to look up at him.

Benedict stared down at her in frustration for several long seconds. 'Oh, to hell with this!' he finally rasped his impatience as he came to an abrupt halt in the middle of the ballroom before placing his hand firmly beneath Genevieve's elbow. His expression was one of grim determination as he escorted her from the dance floor.

Genevieve looked up at him curiously. 'Lucifer—'

'My name is Benedict, damn it!' A nerve pulsed a steady and rapid tattoo in the tightness of his jaw.

'But everyone calls you Lucifer...?'

'Rarely to my face,' he assured grimly.

'Oh.' A delicate blush coloured her cheeks.
'I had not realised...'

'And now you do.' Benedict was only too
aware of the name by which the *ton* referred to
him privately, but no one else had ever dared
to address him in that way directly.

'Where are we going?' Genevieve demanded as Benedict collected her cloak from
Lady Hammond's attentive butler.

'As far away from here as is possible,'
Benedict answered tersely as he placed her
cloak about her shoulders before taking his
own cloak and hat.

Having observed Eric Cargill in conversation with the Count de Sevanne whilst he was
dancing with Genevieve, the older man gave
Benedict a nod in confirmation that he had received the information they needed. Benedict
now saw no reason why he should prolong this
tortuous evening any longer. Nor did he think
it a good idea to leave Genevieve here alone.
For a woman aged in her mid-twenties and a
widow after six years of marriage, Genevieve
seemed extremely naïve when it came to an
awareness of the licentious behaviour of certain gentlemen of the *ton*.

Himself included...

Chapter Three

Genevieve was a little surprised at having her evening brought to such an abrupt and unsatisfactory end. Although, after her error in judgement earlier, perhaps it was for the best if she left now in order to retire and regroup so that she might 'fight another day'.

Besides which, if she did have to leave the ball earlier than anticipated, was it not better that she do so in the company of one of the most sought-after gentlemen of the *ton*?

'You did not say where we are going, Benedict?' Genevieve was careful to use his given name this time, having had no idea, until he'd corrected her, that it was simply not done to refer to him as Lucifer to his face. 'Benedict?' she prompted again as he made no effort to answer her as the two of them stepped from Lady Hammond's town house into the dark of the early-summer evening.

'Perhaps because I have not decided as yet.' He looked down at her, his face appearing all sharp and dangerous angles in the moonlight. 'Your reckless behaviour this evening would seem to imply you are seriously in need of a man constantly at your side to keep you from becoming embroiled in scandal.'

She gave a soft gasp. 'That is unfair.'

'In what way is it unfair?' Lucifer arched his dark and arrogant brows. 'If not for my intervention earlier, I have no doubts you would even now be in a position where you were completely at the mercy of Sandhurst's plans for you.'

Much as Genevieve hated to admit it, she now believed that to have been the case too. 'Is it really so wrong of me to want—to yearn—for fun and excitement?'

Benedict frowned as he saw the tears glistening in her beautiful blue eyes. His frown deepened as he recalled Eric Cargill's comment of earlier, in regard to Josiah Forster having kept his 'child-bride…shut away in the country from the moment he had married and

bedded her'. 'Was your marriage so very unhappy?'

'Tortuous,' she confirmed flatly.

A 'tortuous' marriage which had lasted for
six years, followed by another year of mourning the husband she had not loved. That meant
that this was perhaps the first opportunity
Genevieve had had for a very long time in
which to enjoy all that a London Season had
to offer. 'Did Forster treat you unkindly?'

Her shudder of revulsion was answer
enough. 'I will not talk of it, Benedict. It is
just— It is so long since I was able to attend
and enjoy parties and balls such as this one,'
she confirmed his earlier summation.

'Some would say that you were fortunate in
having done so,' Benedict drawled, affected,
in spite of himself, by the deep yearning he
could see in those expressive blue eyes.

'The "some" who have always been free to
enjoy such things, perhaps,' Genevieve conceded wistfully.

'Unlike you?'

She sighed. 'I have said I will not talk about
any of that.'

His eyes narrowed. 'What on earth did you
find to do in the country for all of those years
of exile?'

'You are very determined!' Her little chin rose as she looked up at him. 'Truth be told, I mainly plotted and planned ways in which I might dispose of my husband!'

Benedict found himself stunned into silence for several minutes, before he then gave in to the urge he had to laugh at the bluntness of Genevieve's statement. And neither was it the first time that this red-haired minx of a woman had reduced him to laughter with her outrageous candidness.

She arched a red-gold brow. 'I hope you do not suppose for one moment that I am jesting?'

No, Benedict could see by the earnestness of Genevieve's expression that she was completely serious. His own humour lessened to an ironic tilting of his lips. 'What did Woollerton do to earn such a fierceness of emotion?'

Her shadowed gaze dropped from meeting his dark and probing one. 'I cannot, will not, talk of his cruelties to me.'

Benedict's humour faded completely in the face of Genevieve's obvious distress. He had not known Josiah Forster personally—that gentleman had been a contemporary of Benedict's father rather than himself—but he had never heard any gossip in regard to cruelty by the other gentleman. Which was not to say it had not existed; the *ton* had a way of keeping the worst of its excesses behind closed doors. Certainly, keeping Genevieve's beauty and vivacity of nature incarcerated in the country for so many years could be called a sin in itself.

Benedict frowned down at her bent head, the hood of her cloak throwing her face into shadow. 'Name one thing which for you represents this "adventure and fun" you speak of.'

She raised long lashes, her eyes now twin pools of hurt. 'So that you might laugh or ridicule me?'

'I had it more in mind to gauge whether or not I might see fit into escorting you in the endeavour of your choice,' Benedict conceded drily.

Her eyes widened. 'Really?'

'Really.' Benedict sighed, sure that he was making a mistake by indulging Genevieve in this way, but finding himself totally unable to refuse the appeal of the unhappiness he had brought to those deep-blue eyes by speaking of her dead husband.

Genevieve looked up searchingly into those dark satanic features, but could find no amusement or mockery in his eyes. Indeed, Benedict Lucas wore an expression of resignation rather than amusement. 'I have always longed to visit Vauxhall Gardens in the evening in the company of a gentleman,' she answered huskily.

His dark brows rose. 'You are assuming, if I were to agree to take you there, that I will behave as that gentleman?'

She looked up at him uncertainly. 'Are you saying you would not?'

He breathed deeply. 'No. Although I do wonder how it is you have survived these past six weeks of the Season without falling into some sort of scandal or another!'

'Possibly because, until these past few days or so, I have had Sophia and Pandora to advise me when someone or something is not quite… suitable,' she allowed ruefully.

And, as Benedict was only too aware, this past week had seen both her close friends becoming entangled in relationships with his own friends Dante and Devil.

Genevieve looked up at him almost shyly. 'Perhaps I am now to have a fallen angel to watch over me?'

'It will be for one evening only,' Benedict warned firmly, not sure he particularly cared for being referred to as a 'fallen angel'. 'I do not have the time, nor the inclination, to be continually available to rescue you from your own lack of insight into a gentleman's true nature.'

'But you will spare me this one evening?'

Benedict found himself unable to resist the excitement he could see glowing in those deep-blue eyes. At her thoughts of being allowed to visit Vauxhall Gardens, not at spending the evening with him specifically, he reminded himself firmly. 'If that is what you wish, yes.'

'Oh, it is!' She smiled up at him. 'Oh, thank you, Benedict. What shall I wear, do you think? Perhaps—'

'Did you listen to anything I just said, Genevieve?' Benedict made no effort to descend the steps to where their carriages now waited, the one to return Genevieve to the safety of her home, and the other to take Benedict to his club where he could overindulge in the strong liquor he currently felt so desperately in need of. 'I will agree to escort you to Vauxhall Gardens, but only on the understanding that in future you will think more before embarking on this quest for "fun and adventure".'

'Could we both wear masks, do you think, so that we are not recognised? It would be so much more fun!'

'Genevieve!' he thundered impatiently.

'Yes, Benedict?' She looked up at him with guileless blue eyes.

He gave a pained frown. This woman was a troublesome minx and he rued the day that he had made the effort and stirred himself to speak with her.

Benedict also had reason to question how it was that he had so completely lost sight of his original plans to use this woman's company as his foil in society. He now appeared to be going where Genevieve led rather than the other way about! His mouth thinned. 'We will visit Vauxhall Gardens tomorrow evening, if you are available?'

'I will ensure that I am.' She nodded.

'We will stroll about the grounds and arbours for an hour or so, before returning.'

'What of the masks, Benedict?'

He breathed his impatience with her single-mindedness. 'We will wear masks if that is what you wish.'

'Oh, it is!' She glowed up at him.

He looked down at her reprovingly. 'I should warn you, there is no guarantee that the masks will conceal our true identity.'

She arched her brows. 'And is there some-one in your life at present who might find reason to…object to your being recognised out and about with me?'

Benedict raised his brows. 'Would it matter to you if there were?'

Would it matter to her? Yes, Genevieve believed that it would. She had absolutely no doubts that Benedict had saved her from Sandhurst's clutches this evening, and that, despite what he had said to the contrary, he would, if necessary, rescue her again if the need should ever arise. Obviously, in view of this kindness, Genevieve did not wish to be the cause of any discomfort in Benedict's own personal life.

She looked up at Benedict through thick lashes. 'Is there someone who might object?'

He glowered down at her. 'As it happens, no, there is not. Which is not to say,' he continued firmly as she would have spoken, 'that I intend to babysit you for more than a single evening.'

Genevieve nodded. 'Tomorrow evening.'

'Tomorrow evening,' he echoed wearily. 'Now allow me to see you safely delivered to your carriage so that I might be on my way in mine.'

'Are you going anywhere fun?'

She seemed to be obsessed with that word, Benedict acknowledged frowningly. Possibly because fun was something which had been sadly missing from her own life to date? Indeed, Genevieve behaved more like a newly come-out débutante than a widowed duchess of five and twenty. Because of Josiah Forster's cruel treatment of her? Benedict feared so.

But despite her husband's cruelties, Genevieve still possessed a naïveté in regard to men that was wholly appealing. His expression softened as they reached Genevieve's carriage and he turned to tap her playfully on the end of her enchanting, slightly uptilted nose. 'Nowhere that you might follow, little one.'

Her eyes widened. 'Are you going to a house of the *demi-monde*? Or perhaps a brothel? I have long—'

'Please do not say you have "always longed to visit" one of those two establishments, too!' Benedict groaned in protest.

'No, of course I have not.' She looked up at him reprovingly. 'That would be most improper. I have merely wondered…'

'I am not on my way to either a brothel or a house of the *demi-monde*, Genevieve.' Benedict scowled down at her. 'Neither would I discuss it with you if I were.' He gave a disgusted shake of his head at the impropriety of this conversation. 'Indeed, most ladies of my acquaintance would scream in shock at the mere mention of either establishment in their presence, let alone choose to discuss such things themselves.'

'Are you implying that I am not a lady?'

No, Benedict was not saying that at all. How could he, when it was perfectly obvious that Genevieve was very much a lady, from the top of her pearl-adorned red curls to the dainty satin slippers upon her feet. It was only that she was a type of lady, forthright and yet endearingly vulnerable at the same time, whom Benedict had never encountered before today. Indeed, he currently found himself in a position of having no idea what Genevieve would do or say next to surprise him.

'Your enthusiasm for life is...refreshingly different, to say the least,' he conceded gruffly.

'And at worst...?' Genevieve looked up at him suspiciously, sure that Benedict was mocking her in some way, but as yet unsure how. But no doubt she would have plenty of time to give thought to that before he accompanied her to Vauxhall Gardens tomorrow evening!

He gave a derisive smile. 'At worst your behaviour is such that you are likely to get your pretty fingers, and other parts of your anatomy, well and truly burned!'

Her cheeks warmed. 'By you?'

He drew in a sharp breath. 'I am too old, in experience if not in years, and far too jaded in spirit, for one such as you to flex your delicate little claws on, pet.'

Her gaze became searching on Benedict's harshly hewn features and she knew that she liked and trusted Benedict, despite how experienced or jaded he might claim to be. He was perhaps both those things, but he had also shown a kindness and concern for her this evening which said he was, despite everything, a man of honour.

She smiled up at him warmly. 'I shall very much look forward to seeing you again tomorrow evening, Benedict.' She moved up on tiptoe to kiss him lightly upon one rigidly tensed cheek before turning to step into her carriage and instructing her driver to move on, a smile curving her lips as her last view of Benedict showed him scowling darkly in his displeasure.

Her smile widened as she thought of their visit to Vauxhall Gardens.

'I believe I told my butler to inform you that I am not at home?' Genevieve stood up to glare coldly at the gentleman who presented himself uninvited in the gold salon of her London home the following afternoon, her hands clutched tightly together so that he should not have the satisfaction of seeing how they trembled at his unexpected appearance here.

This morning had, predictably, been a busy one for her, with visits from both admiring gentlemen bearing more flowers and chocolates and many of the ladies who had been present at Lady Hammond's ball yesterday evening. Most of them were calling out of curiosity in regard to the time Genevieve had spent in the company of the elusive Lord Benedict Lucas, to the degree that he had danced with her when he had not taken to the dance floor these past ten years—a fact which secretly thrilled Genevieve.

None of those ladies who had called knew Genevieve intimately enough to ask her the question direct, of course, but their curiosity was none the less tangible and highly entertaining to Genevieve.

The gentlemen who had presented flowers and bonbons had been even more pleasant, even if Genevieve was aware that those calls were being made because Lucifer's interest had somehow succeeded in making her the latest fashion.

But her visitor of this afternoon was most unwelcome.

'Obviously your butler was mistaken, because here you most certainly are,' William Forster, the tenth Duke of Woollerton, mocked drily as he glanced in the direction of the obviously uncomfortable and apologetic butler standing in the doorway behind him.

'You may go, Jenkins.' Genevieve gave the elderly man a reassuring smile before returning the coldness of her gaze back to her unwanted visitor.

The same man had been Genevieve's stepson for the duration of her marriage to his father, and at nine and twenty and in possession of fleshy good looks, William bore a startling resemblance to his sire. Nor had William ever made any secret of his disapproval of his father's choice of Genevieve as his second wife. It was perhaps the only thing upon which the two of them had ever agreed; Genevieve had not been happy in his father choosing to marry her, either.

William now looked down the length of his supercilious nose at her. 'It has been brought to my attention, by several of my acquaintances, that you have been cutting a swathe in society this past six weeks or more.'

'Have you dared to spy on me?' Genevieve's eyes flashed angrily, her cheeks flushing with temper; she had spent enough years being bullied by this man and his father to know she did not intend to suffer those same bullying tactics as Josiah's widow.

'It cannot be called spying, when the whole of the *ton* has been witness to your outings with those other two silly ladies these past weeks!'

'I believe you are referring to the Duchesses of Clayborne and Wyndwood.' Genevieve frowned, still uncertain as to the reason for William's visit today, because there must assuredly be a reason for him to have bothered himself in coming here. 'Neither of whom can be considered in the least silly.'

'That is surely a matter of opinion?' he drawled disdainfully. 'Nor is it of importance.' He gave a dismissive wave of his hand. 'How can it be, when it is your own…behaviour with Lord Benedict Lucas, which is now in question.'

Genevieve's chin rose defiantly. 'By whom, might one ask?'

'By me, madam.' He looked at her coldly.

'And by the Earl of Ramsey. You are acquainted with that gentleman?'

Genevieve blinked, having no idea what the earl had to do with her, or where this conversation was going. 'I believe we have been introduced, and have met by chance a time or two in recent weeks, yes.'

William nodded. 'He was also present at Lady Hammond's ball yesterday evening. A fact which you were no doubt unaware of, when all of your own attention was so firmly fixed first upon Sandhurst and then Lucas.'

In truth, she did not remember seeing the Earl of Ramsey at the ball yesterday evening, occupied as she had been. Nor did she understand why she should have done so. 'I am sure this is all very interesting, William, but—'

'Tell me, has Lucifer been more successful than my father in parting your silky thighs without benefit of a wedding ring?'

Genevieve paled at his crudeness. 'Why do you insist on reducing everything to the level of the gutter?'

'Perhaps because that is where I have always considered you belong?' William gave a scathing and humourless smile. 'I do not believe I ever made a secret of my lack of understanding as to why my father ever bothered himself to marry a young woman without fortune or position.'

'As I never made any secret of the fact that it was always my dearest wish he had not! That I wished to be free of the both of you!' Genevieve's hands were now clenched so tightly at her sides she could feel her nails digging into her palms through the lace of her gloves.

He eyed her pityingly. 'You may thank your worthless brother for that particular predicament.'

Genevieve stood as tall in her satin slippers as her five feet and two inches would allow. 'My brother has been dead these past six years, sir.'

'By his own hand,' William Forster dismissed in a bored voice. 'A coward's way out, I have always thought.'

'Neither you, or your thoughts, hold the slightest interest for me, sir.' Genevieve looked at him coldly. 'And if Colin chose to take his own life, then it was your father's lies and deceit that made him do so.'

Having only met Josiah Forster on two occasions before her brother, Colin, also her guardian, informed her of his offer for her, Genevieve had at first refused to even consider it. But she had been aged only eighteen and her brother had been deeply in debt because of his addiction to gambling. It was a debt the duke had promised to pay once Genevieve became his wife. Even knowing that, Genevieve had found the whole idea of being married to a man as old as Josiah Forster repugnant. But Colin's entreaties had eventually prevailed and Genevieve had duly married her duke and returned with him to Woollerton Hall for their honeymoon period.

She gave a shudder as she once again recalled her wedding night. A night of fear, and humiliation, which had only grown in intensity as the days, weeks, and months had passed and Josiah's cruelties towards her had intensified.

Nor had he ever made good on his promise as a gentleman to pay Colin's gambling debts once Genevieve had become his wife, and so had left her brother at the mercy of the men to whom he was so deeply in debt.

Was it any wonder that, feeling responsible as he did for both Genevieve's obvious unhappiness in her marriage, and his own unbearable circumstances, Colin had visited the duke one last time to ask for his help and had again been refused, before then choosing to hang himself from one of the trees in the woods at the back of Woollerton Hall?

William Forster now looked at her as mercilessly as his father had always done. 'Your brother was weak, as well as a fool, in not demanding my father's promise to him in writing before your wedding.'

'And your father was not a gentleman, or a man of honour.'

'Honour?' William laughed derisively. 'Why should my father stir himself to honour anything he might have said to your worthless brother, when he had already sampled your charms and found them wanting?'

Genevieve welcomed the pain as her nails now pierced the palms of her hand through the lace of her gloves, 'I wish for you to leave my home.'

'Not until I have said what I came here to say.'

'You will leave my home now!' Genevieve shook with the anger that now consumed every part of her.

'And who is going to make me? Your elderly butler?' William challenged confidently. 'Or perhaps your new lover?' His cold grey gaze roamed over her with a familiarity that made Genevieve cringe. 'From all that I know of Lucifer, he is not a man to trouble himself in regard to any woman he takes as mistress.'

'I am not his mistress!' Genevieve's eyes glowed a fiery blue in warning.

'Yet,' William bit out harshly. 'And it is my intention that he never will be.'

'And what business is it of yours, sir?'

'For better or worse, you are my father's widow.' Those pale grey eyes raked over her with dislike. 'And tomorrow morning will see the announcement of my betrothal to the Earl of Ramsey's only daughter, the wedding to take place next month. A marriage which will be beneficial to both our families.'

'Perhaps it behoves someone to warn that poor girl of exactly what sort of family she is marrying into— Take your hands off me!' Genevieve gave a pained gasp as William moved to take a tight grip of one of her wrists before twisting her arm painfully behind her back, causing her to arch her back in an effort not to allow their bodies to come into any sort of contact.

'I have no intention of releasing you until I consider this conversation to have been settled to my satisfaction.' William thrust his face very close to her own, the warmth of his breath brushing against Genevieve's throat, and causing her to quiver with revulsion.

'What do you want from me?' she gasped softly.

'Ramsey is…something of a prude, and as such I do not believe he would appreciate it if my father's widow, the woman who was my stepmother, and is now the Dowager Duchess of Woollerton, were to become involved in a sordid affair with the man the *ton* calls Lucifer. Therefore, I advise that you cease your relationship with him before such a possibility occurs.'

'It is not for you to dictate to me whom I should or should not take as my friends,' Genevieve refused determinedly.

'I thought you might say that.' William sneered at her bravery. 'But you may rest assured, Genevieve, that if in the next month you should do or behave in such a way which might interfere with my own marriage plans, then I will personally make sure that you regret that behaviour. Am I making myself clear?' His voice was as hard with cruelty as his father's had always been.

'God, how I hate you!' Genevieve choked, wishing this conversation over, most of all wishing this man's presence gone from her home, and the memories he had brought with him. Memories of her wedding night, followed by Josiah's numerous cruelties to her. Of the times she had tried to escape him by running away, only to be brought back and beaten by the very same man who now twisted her arm so painfully.

'The feeling is mutual, I assure you,' William sneered. 'Nevertheless, you will do as I say and immediately break off this scandalous friendship with Lucifer.' He gave her arm another vicious twist before pushing her roughly away from him, studiously straightening the leather riding gloves he wore as Genevieve stumbled to regain her balance at the same time as she clutched her bruised arm.

How Genevieve hated this man and his father for what they had both done to her. For what William was still trying to do to her.

And she hated him even more for his confidence that she would again do as he had instructed.

'Leave,' she managed to choke out.

'I will go when I am good and ready.'

'You will get out of my house now!' She refused to so much as sway on her feet until after William, with one last mocking smile in her direction, strode confidently from her salon and her home.

At which time Genevieve's legs would no longer support her and she fell down on to the carpet, her wrist and arm hurting so badly that she sobbed tears of pain and humiliation, knowing that the peace she had acquired this past year, her belief that she was finally rid of Josiah, and his equally as cruel and unpleasant son, was completely shattered.

Chapter Four

'...and Sheffield had only been gone but a few minutes when Lord Daniel Robson arrived in company with Billy Summersby. They are both of them so very sweet. And the Earl of Suffolk, a gentleman who has never paid me the slightest attention before now, also presented his card and expressed a wish to take me riding with him in the park early tomorrow morning. It is all your doing, of course, Benedict, because none of those gentlemen had given me so much as a second glance before your own noticeable attentions to me yesterday evening.'

Benedict had been listening to Genevieve prattle on like this for almost the past hour: as soon as she had greeted him in her gold salon, for the whole of the carriage ride from her home, and during this boat ride across the Thames to Vauxhall Gardens. All of it nonsense, and not at all what he had come to expect from her. Indeed, it was the fact that Benedict never knew quite what to expect when in Genevieve's company which had given rise to his feelings of anticipation of their meeting this evening. Only to have those feelings dissipate when she immediately began to rattle on like this the moment they were alone together.

'Genevieve...'

'—I really should thank you—'

'Genevieve.'

'—for my current popularity with so many fashionable gentlemen of the *ton*—'

'Genevieve!'

Her chatter ceased, as she instead looked up at Benedict in the moonlight through the two slits for her eyes in the golden mask she wore over the top half of her face. She wore an evening cloak about her shoulders which prevented him from seeing the gown she wore. 'I am sure I was only—'

'I am well aware that you have "only" chattered incessantly this past hour, so much so that I could not get a word in edgewise,' Benedict drawled his impatience. 'And I am curious to know the reason for it.'

She blinked. 'I thought to amuse you with news of my gentlemen callers today…'

'You thought no such thing.' Indeed, Benedict had found himself becoming less and less amused the more he heard of the visits of Genevieve's many admirers. 'What else has happened today that could have turned you into such an empty-headed ninny?' he prompted shrewdly.

Genevieve would have taken exception to such a description if she had not known it was perfectly justified; she was prattling on like so many of those empty-headed ninnies in society that she most despised. Her only excuse was that she was not fully recovered from William Forster's visit to her this afternoon. Or the threats he had made to her.

So much so that she also inwardly trembled at her own daring in keeping to her original arrangement to go to Vauxhall Gardens with Benedict this evening.

Her initial instinct had been to do as William had asked—demanded!—by sending her apologies to Benedict, but she had thought better of it almost immediately and refused to continue to be bullied by such a hateful man as William Forster. Her rebellion had been helped by the fact that she and Benedict would both be wearing masks, so that no one could say for sure whether or not it was the two of them at Vauxhall Gardens!

Truth be told, Genevieve was also loathe to give up the idea of spending time in Benedict's company, despite the risk of incurring even more of William's displeasure.

But there was no doubting that her enjoyment of an evening spent in the company of the most eligible and sought-after gentleman in London, at Vauxhall Gardens of all exciting places, had been severely curtailed by William's issue of more threats to her physical well being if she did not obey him. To the point that she had begun to chatter nonsensically the moment she found herself alone in Benedict's company.

And he looked so splendidly handsome in the moonlight, too. A black evening cloak thrown elegantly over his usual black attire and snowy white linen, and the unadorned black mask that covered the top half of his face beneath his top hat, only added to his usual air of danger and mystery.

She forced a smile to curve her lips. 'Why

on earth should you imagine that anything might have happened?'

'Perhaps because I have come to know you a little these past two days?' His mouth was a firm line beneath that mask. 'And the Genevieve I have come to know, whilst lively in her conversation, does not prattle.'

'Whilst I find the first part of your comment flattering—'

'It was not intended to flatter, Genevieve, it is merely a statement of truth,' Benedict assured harshly.

She avoided looking into that glittering black gaze. 'No. Well. You are partial to the truth, I take it?'

'Always.'

Genevieve gave a slight shiver at his uncompromising tone, at how ruthlessly that tone implied Benedict would deal with anyone who did not give him that truth. 'Could we not just enjoy the boat ride, Benedict? Everything looks so romantic in the moonlight that I am sure—' The resumption of Genevieve's nervous chatter came to an abrupt halt as Benedict—*Lucifer*—placed his mouth firmly against her own.

Silencing her.

Stunning her.

Warming her as those firm and sensual lips moved over and against hers in slow exploration. His arms moved about the slenderness of her waist and Benedict drew her into the heat of his firmly muscled body before deepening the kiss, sipping, tasting, gently biting her lips before soothing with the hot sweep of his tongue.

Genevieve's initial surprise was not, as she had always feared would happen, followed by revulsion at having a man kiss her. Instead, after that first shock, Genevieve found herself shyly returning those gentle kisses as she clung to the width of Benedict's shoulders, her own lips parting instinctively to allow the kiss to be deepened.

She was leaning weakly against that hard and muscled chest by the time Benedict raised his head to look down at her with glittering black eyes. 'What else happened today, Genevieve?'

'I—' Genevieve pushed against his chest to distance herself even as she blinked in an effort to clear her head of the effects of that astonishing—and totally unexpected—kiss. 'It was most unfair of you to attempt to use seduction in order to attempt to force my cooperation, Benedict.' She looked up at him reproachfully.

His eyes narrowed behind the unadorned black mask. 'Seduce you into telling me what exactly, Genevieve?'

She gave a pained frown as she realised her mistake. 'Into telling you nothing,' she dismissed lightly, 'for there is nothing to tell.'

'Genevieve.'

'Will you please desist from constantly repeating my name in that reproving manner?' She bristled irritably as she straightened her gown unnecessarily, still flustered by that kiss. 'I am not a naughty child to be spoken to in that tone.'

Benedict bit back his own impatience, totally aware that Genevieve was now using anger so that she did not have to answer his original question, something he was unwilling to allow her to continue to do. 'If I considered you a child, of any description, then you would not be here with me now. Nor would I have kissed you,' he added harshly, also aware that having intended to use the kiss only as a means of silencing Genevieve, he was now the one who was left uncomfortably aroused, his shaft a hot and throbbing ache inside his breeches.

A blush warmed her cheeks. 'No, of course you would not. I— It is only that—' She drew in a shaky breath. 'Perhaps we should continue with this conversation once we are safely arrived at the gardens?' She gave the boatman sitting in front of them a belatedly pointed glance.

Another excuse for delaying their conversation, Benedict guessed easily. And one that succeeding in making him even more curious as to what might have occurred to put Genevieve in this state of nervous tension. A curiosity that would have to wait as he saw they had almost reached their destination. 'Very well,' he conceded tersely. 'But I advise against you using the intervening time in which to make up some excuse,' he added sternly, standing up as they had now reached the quayside, collecting up the picnic basket and stepping out of the boat before turning to take Genevieve's gloved hand and aid her own step on to dry land. 'What have you done to your arm…?' he prompted shrewdly as he saw her wince as he clasped her hand.

Genevieve continued to look down at where she was stepping rather than at Benedict. 'I caught the sleeve on my robe on the door han-

dle of my dressing room this morning and
wrenched my arm.'

'Careless of you.'

'Yes.' She added nothing more, knowing
this man was too astute for her comfort. Because he was Lucifer. A man many of the *ton*
feared. And none dared cross. Because Lucifer
was a man who remained emotionally aloof,
even from those women lucky enough to become his mistress.

Lucky enough...?

Yes, Genevieve realised she now considered
any woman who attracted, and held, Benedict's attention, to be very lucky indeed. But,
painful as her own arm still was—and becoming more so as time passed rather than less—
Genevieve also knew that William's visit to
her earlier today had now placed her in even
more of a dilemma, and one that had nothing to do with her own physical well being.
There was also Charlotte Darby, the Earl of
Ramsey's daughter, to consider.

As far as Genevieve could recall, Charlotte
Darby was a young lady of only twenty or so,
reasonably pretty, and no doubt starry-eyed
in regard to her forthcoming marriage to the
present Duke of Woollerton.

Except William Forster, like his father before him, was not a man any young and innocent girl should marry with starry-eyed expectations. How could he be, when Genevieve knew him to be a man vicious by nature?

Genevieve shuddered in revulsion just thinking of another young innocent being exposed to that viciousness. No, Charlotte really should not be allowed to marry William Forster and made to suffer as Genevieve had once suffered.

'It was not my intention for you never to talk again…' Benedict drawled drily as, having paid and entered the gardens, and walked some distance down one of the lantern-lit gravel pathways, Genevieve remained lost in thought. Perhaps that same something that had preoccupied her earlier?

She gave a guilty start, before turning to look about them. 'Oh, how lovely!' Her blue eyes glowed through her mask as she looked about her at the many arbours and pathways leading from this one, all of them lit by dozens of lanterns placed in the trees, with the sound of music playing and fountains gurgling in the background, amidst the laughter and chatter of all the other people currently enjoying the gardens.

Benedict had deliberately chosen to arrive at the gardens after darkness had fallen, knowing that Genevieve, at least, would appreciate the romance of the glowing lanterns to light their way. After his own response to kissing her earlier, Benedict was no longer sure he appreciated the privacy offered by so many of the tree- and shrub-enshrouded arbours, several of which were already providing that privacy if the soft murmurs and pleasurable groans he could hear were any indication!

Genevieve seemed totally unaware of those less proper activities as she tucked her gloved hand trustingly into the crook of his arm. She looked up and gave him a glowing smile as they continued to walk down the pathway crowded with other revellers. 'This is all so perfect, Benedict. And just as I imagined it might be! Can we go and listen to the band playing at the colonnade? And see some of the beautiful fountains? And then could we—?'

'You are rattling on again, Genevieve.' Benedict gave a weary shake of his head, grateful that his two closest friends could not see him now. Indeed, he thanked heaven Dante and Devil were at present too occupied in the pursuit of their own respective ladies to interest themselves in Benedict's own activities, otherwise he doubted he would never hear the end of this hellish evening he had brought upon himself!

For hell it now most assuredly was, when Benedict was so physically aware of Genevieve; her cloak had parted, and the lamplight now revealed the full swell of her breasts above the pale gown she wore, her lips a full and tempting pout beneath her golden mask, and his nostrils were being assaulted by the delicate floral perfume she wore.

All of which was succeeding in making him feel more inclined to drag Genevieve into the privacy of one of the shadowed arbours, before kissing her once again—more than kissing her!—rather than continuing to stroll innocently about the gardens with her as had been his original intention.

'I am only excited to be here, Benedict, with one of the most handsome gentlemen in England.'

Benedict's eyes narrowed behind his own mask. 'If you are hoping, by flirting with me, that you will succeed in diverting my attention from your unanswered question of earlier, then I am afraid you are going to be disappointed.'

She shot him an impatient frown. 'You are unflatteringly single-minded, Benedict!'

He eyed her mockingly. 'Unfortunately for you, yes, I am.' He nodded unapologetically. 'So…?'

Genevieve drew in a deep breath before answering him reluctantly. 'It really is nothing of importance…'

'Then be so kind as to share this "nothing of importance" with me.'

She sighed. 'If you must know, I received a visit from my stepson earlier today.'

Benedict eyes narrowed. 'William Forster?'

'Yes.'

'And?'

'And we have never liked each other,' she dismissed heavily.

'If that is the case, then why did he bother himself to call upon you?' His eyes narrowed as he felt Genevieve's uninjured hand tremble slightly where it rested in the crook of his arm.

'We are related by marriage, and I am now his father's widow, thus making me—'

'I am aware of the relationship, Genevieve,' Benedict put in evenly. 'But William Forster has never struck me as a man who bothers himself with any sort of politeness if it is not beneficial to himself.'

She looked up at him sharply in the moonlight. 'You are personally acquainted with that gentleman?'

'By reputation only.' Benedict grimaced. 'But it is a reputation that does not in the least endear him to me,' he added grimly as he recalled the tales he had heard whispered at his clubs of the present Duke of Woollerton's activities; unlike Benedict, William Forster was known to be a frequent visitor to some of the seedier brothels and gambling dens of London, his taste questionable at best and disgusting at worst!

Genevieve appeared to relax slightly. 'I have never found his...character to be in the least appealing either. But the connection is there, so I fear we must both put a polite face on things. Indeed, William called to inform me that tomorrow the announcement of his engagement will appear in the newspapers, along with his wedding next month, to the Earl of Ramsey's daughter.'

'With the intention of inviting you to the wedding?'

'Lord, I hope not!' The words left Genevieve's lips before she had chance to stop them, her cheeks warming as she instantly found herself the focus of Benedict's narrowed black gaze. 'That is…' She took her hand from the crook of his arm as they stepped aside to avoid another group of revellers. 'I believe William visited me only so that he might inform me that, upon his wedding day next month, I am to officially become the Dowager Duchess.'

'Indeed?'

'Why else would he have called to see me?'

'I was hoping you might tell me that…?'

Genevieve had absolutely no intentions of confiding anything to Benedict with regard to William Forster. Indeed, her memories of the beatings he had enjoyed inflicting upon her at his father's behest so distressed Genevieve that she could not bear to think of them now. For fear, she knew, that if she did so she might break down completely. Which would never do in the company of such an astute and single-minded gentleman as Benedict Lucas. 'There is nothing to tell. He called to see me, told me of his marriage and then left.'

'Nothing else…?'

'Could we not just enjoy our walk through the gardens now, Benedict?' she prompted somewhat agitatedly.

'Rather than continue to talk of William Forster?'

She shot Benedict an irritated glare. 'And cease talking of anything!'

'I am willing to forgo further conversation about William Forster for the moment—'

'That is very generous of you!'

'—but not so in regard to what answer you gave Suffolk earlier today in regard to his invitation to ride with him in the park tomorrow morning.'

Genevieve's eyes widened. 'So you *were* listening to me earlier?'

'Every prattling, nonsensical word,' he confirmed drily.

Genevieve frowned her displeasure. 'You are being unkind, Benedict.'

'But I am not a fool,' he assured firmly. 'And for me to allow you to go riding alone with Suffolk in the park tomorrow morning, or any other time, without cautioning you that you will more than likely find yourself mounted in another way at the first convenient grove of trees would be very foolish of me indeed!' His face appeared all dark and satanic angles in the moonlight.

'Are all eligible gentlemen of the *ton* of a certain age as…devious and set in their pursuit of pleasure?'

'I have no idea.' He shrugged. 'I can only

warn you of what I know of men such as Sandhurst and Suffolk.'

'And in doing so you are seriously in danger of overstepping the bounds of our newly formed friendship.' She eyed him primly.

Benedict gave a humourless smile. 'Was the kiss we shared earlier not also "seriously overstepping the bounds of our newly formed friendship"?'

Genevieve clutched her cloak more tightly about her as a gentle breeze rustled through the trees. 'We did not share a kiss—you took one!'

'Strange you should think that,' he drawled derisively: 'When I distinctly remember the parting of your lips so that we might deepen the kiss?'

Genevieve's cheeks flared with embarrassed colour even as she looked about them self-consciously to see if anyone might have overheard their conversation; luckily everyone else strolling the pathways seemed intent only on their own pleasure. 'I admit I was momentarily too taken back to do anything other than respond, but that does not alter the fact that you were the one to instigate the kiss.'

Benedict chuckled huskily. 'Or that you are hoping for me to "instigate" another one, perhaps even more than a kiss, before this evening is over?'

Genevieve had no idea whether she was hoping or dreading such an occurrence, although her response to his earlier kisses was daringly reassuring of the former, to say the least! 'You really are the most insufferable, conceited—' She broke off as he gave another chuckle. 'I fail to see what is so funny, Benedict!'

'Why, you are, my dear Genevieve.' He eyed her derisively. 'For believing, for one single moment, that I will allow myself to be diverted, even by thoughts of making love to you under the moonlight at Vauxhall Gardens, from knowing the answer you gave Suffolk in regard to the two of you riding in the park tomorrow morning.'

If not for the fact that she was wearing delicate silk slippers, and would no doubt have caused herself pain on the gravel pathway beneath those slippers, Genevieve would have stamped her foot in temper at this gentleman's unshakeable—and equally as infuriating!—single-mindedness.

As it was she could only scowl at him—a completely wasted scowl, when Benedict could not even see it behind her golden mask.

'If you must know, I turned down Suffolk's invitation for tomorrow morning.'

'I am glad to hear it.' He nodded grimly.

'But I am seriously considering accepting for the morning following that one,' Genevieve finished triumphantly. 'I only refused for tomorrow because I felt sure I would not wish to rise so early in the morning, after what will probably be a late night this evening.'

Benedict stared down at her in frustration, again wondering how it was that a woman of such experience could be so worryingly naïve in regard to the gentlemen of the *ton*. Suffolk was both a handsome rogue and notorious for his exploits in the bedchamber and no doubt fully intended to seduce Genevieve the moment the two of them had reached a place he considered private enough for that seduction to take place!

Unless, of course, that was the appeal the invitation held for Genevieve?

Benedict's mouth firmed. 'And would I be right in supposing, that an early ride in the park, alone with a handsome gentleman, is yet more of that "adventure and fun" you hunger for?'

Genevieve eyed him impishly. 'Suffolk *is* very handsome, is he not?'

Benedict bit back his impatience with the habit Genevieve had of latching on to the least important of his comments. 'He holds no appeal for me, of course.'

'Of course.' She chuckled softly.

'But I can see how his golden good looks might…hold appeal for some women,' Benedict concluded.

'I believe you might apply that to any woman with red blood flowing in her veins,' she corrected ruefully.

'Maybe so,' he continued firmly.

'What do you have in the basket, Benedict?' she prompted with a teasing glance at the basket he still carried.

In truth, Benedict had forgotten all about the damned picnic basket during their sometimes-heated conversation; indeed, Genevieve seemed capable of making him forget most things.

Such as the very reason he had first approached her, his idea to use her as a shield for his activities for the Crown apparently forgotten, or rather dismissed, once he became better acquainted with this often exasperating and yet beautiful and enticing woman…

'Benedict…?'

He sighed. 'The basket contains our supper and a blanket upon which we might sit and eat it.'

'Oh, how wonderful of you to think of doing something so romantic!' Her eyes glowed with her pleasure even as she threw her arms about his neck to hug him tightly before stepping back self-consciously, her gaze no longer meeting his. 'Might we go into one of the secluded arbours? Oh, please, Benedict!' She looked up at him pleadingly.

'If that is what would make you happy.' Benedict was still too taken aback by the unabashed warmth of Genevieve's hug to even think of denying her.

He was not a man that people hugged. At least, not without invitation. And, despite what the *ton* might think in regard to his sexual exploits over the years, those invitations had been few and far between. Genevieve, with her warmth and exuberance for life, had not even considered waiting for him to make such an invitation, but had merely acted with her impulsiveness of nature.

'Oh, I believe I should like it above all things!' She smiled up at him glowingly now.

And Benedict, fool that he undoubtedly was—and despite having claimed otherwise only minutes ago!—found he wanted to give Genevieve, at least for tonight, exactly what she wanted…

Chapter Five

'Is this the time in the evening when the gentleman would usually make indecent advances?' Genevieve enquired carefully as she knelt up on the blanket to pack the remains from their picnic back into the basket. In the light of the lanterns hanging from the surroundings trees they had both removed their masks, their cloaks also discarded in the gentle warmth of the summer evening, the sound of a band playing and other people talking and laughing just a low hum in the distance.

Benedict drew his breath in sharply before answering her. 'It is to be hoped, Genevieve, that if I were to make advances, either now or at some time in the future, that I would wish for you to consider them to be at least halfway decent!' He sat beneath a tall oak tree, watching her, his arm resting across one of his bent knees.

She laughed softly. 'And fun?'

There was that word again. Fun. It was not a word, or a condition, which Benedict was accustomed to think of in regard to his own life. 'As I have already told you, I am much too old to indulge in such nonsense as fun, Genevieve.'

'Pooh,' she dismissed irreverently. 'You are surely only three or four years older than I?'

'I believe it is six.' He grimaced. 'In years, at least. In experience...' he shrugged '...that is quite another matter.'

She lifted a hand to gently touch the hard contours of his cheek with her fingertips as she looked at him searchingly. 'You have known much sadness in your life, have you not? During your years in the army and—and in other ways?'

He frowned darkly. 'You are referring to my parents' deaths? Then no more so than you, I believe?' he added at her nod of confirmation.

'Maybe so.' She grimaced, as she allowed her hand to drop away. 'But I at least can draw comfort from knowing that my parents died together in a carriage accident, and that—that my brother, Colin, chose to take his own life.' A look of sadness now shadowed her face.

'And your husband?' Benedict prompted softly.

That sadness was instantly replaced by coldness. 'Did not die soon enough in my estimation!'

'Genevieve!' Once again Benedict found himself shocked into laughter by her outrageous candidness.

'I only state the truth, which is what you say you prefer.' She gave another sigh as she turned to sit with her back towards Benedict, nor did she offer any resistance as Benedict moved forwards to gently pull her back so that she now rested against his chest. 'I often imagined placing one of Josiah Forster's own pillows over his face and suffocating him in his sleep and was only prevented from doing so because I was unsure whether or not the doctor, when he came to examine the body, would be able to tell the cause of death. Much as I disliked my husband, I did not consider the taking of his life to be worth relinquishing my own to the hangman's noose!'

Benedict was too stunned by Genevieve's honesty this time to even attempt a rebuke.

He was aroused by the way her bottom was now nestled against his erection, her thighs touching both of his, those red curls resting against his waistcoated chest, the full swell of her breasts visible to him above the long-sleeved, gold-coloured gown she had earlier revealed she wore beneath her cloak.

Just as he had been moved by the gentleness with which Genevieve had touched his cheek moments ago...

'What a vengeful little minx you are...' He twirled one of her red silky curls about his finger.

She glanced up at him. 'I believe you are the one who is reputed to still be seeking vengeance for past wrongs?'

'Perhaps.' Not only was Benedict 'reputed to still be seeking vengeance' for the murder of his parents, but he had vowed that he *would* find the person, or persons responsible, before he even considered making any sort of life for himself. Hence the years he had spent in the army fighting for his king and country, and this past two years working for the Crown, neither of which allowed for the sort of settled personal life his two closest friends now seemed to be seeking.

Genevieve gave an inelegant snort. 'And if I

were truly a vengeful person, then I am sure I would have saved myself much heartache and stabbed my husband through his black heart on our wedding night!'

And there, Benedict felt sure, was a tale that would be worth the knowing, but not one he wished to force Genevieve into revealing this evening. Not when this conversation had already caused her to lose so much of that happy glow which had lit her face only minutes ago. A happy glow which Benedict found he was very much enjoying being a part of.

He moved slightly, so that he was no longer sitting behind Genevieve, but at her side as he drew her down to lay slightly beneath him. 'This, I believe, is the appropriate time in the evening for the gentleman to make indecent advances,' he murmured throatily before his head lowered and his mouth claimed the parted pout of Genevieve's.

Genevieve had wondered if she might have imagined the pleasure she had experienced as Benedict had kissed her earlier; she had certainly felt none of that pulse-pounding joy when the duke had kissed or touched her.

No! She would not think of her husband now, or the horror of their wedding night.

This, here and now, might be the only joy in a man's arms she would ever know.

And, as Benedict kissed her, gently at first, and more deeply, hungrily, Genevieve knew she had not imagined a single thing about her response to his earlier kisses. That, despite the past, she actually enjoyed being kissed by a man as excitingly, disturbingly sensual as Benedict Lucas!

Her arms moved up tentatively to allow her fingers to caress the muscled width of his shoulders, as his hands cradled her cheeks. His tongue swept slowly, erotically across her lips, parting their softness as he groaned low in his throat before his hunger returned to deepen the kiss.

He kissed her long and druggingly now, causing the pleasure to course hotly through Genevieve's body, radiating outwards, until every part of her felt as if she were on fire with an aching need that caused her to arch up against Benedict, her breasts swollen and aching against the hard friction of his chest, the softness of her thighs moving sinuously, pleadingly, against the hard and throbbing length of his hard arousal.

'Oh, yes, Benedict…!' She wrenched her mouth from his, groaning her need for him to never stop as his lips moved to the sensitive column of her throat and his hand moved slowly along the flatness of her abdomen before cupping the fullness of her breast and squeezing gently through the soft material of her gown. 'Benedict!' She gasped as that pleasure now radiated fiercely from her breasts down to between her thighs, heating them and making her long for so much more. 'Benedict, please…!'

He groaned. 'We should stop before this goes any further.'

'No!' Genevieve's lids flew wide, her eyes feverish as she surged up with surprising strength before turning, so that Benedict was now the one who lay upon the blanket, looking up at her as she lay half across him. 'We will not stop, Benedict.' Her eyes glittered down at him heatedly. 'Can you not see that I need this? That I need you?'

Benedict had been taken by surprise by her sudden refusal to end their encounter. He saw the determined glitter in her eyes and could only watch in mute fascination as she reached behind her to unfasten the buttons at the back of her gown before allowing the material to fall away from her breasts, revealing that she wore only a thin chemise beneath, her breasts showing firm and plump.

He licked his lips in anticipation of experiencing the succulent taste and feel of them. Even so... 'Have I not warned that you are in danger of finding your wings well and truly singed in a situation such as this one?'

'I already burn, Benedict,' she assured him huskily, holding the darkness of his gaze with her own as she pulled that last covering away from her breasts before leaning forwards to place those breasts enticingly close to his parted lips. 'I burn, Benedict!' She sounded both distressed and fascinated that this should be so.

Her words and her bared breasts were an enticement, a veritable feast—Benedict had no willpower left with which to resist!

Genevieve gave a low and keening moan at the first touch of Benedict's parted lips against the heated tip of her breast, followed by yet more groans as he lathed her swollen nipple with the soft, moist rasp of his tongue before opening his lips wider and drawing the ripe and aching tip deep into the heat of his mouth.

Eyes closed to absorb and enjoy every particle of this, the first pleasure she had known in a man's arms, Genevieve's fingers became entangled in the heavy thickness of Benedict's black hair as she held him to her, shivering, quivering and burning with need. She felt his hand move beneath the hem of her gown to push the material aside, allowing those caressing fingers to travel along the length of her leg to the opening of her drawers between her thighs. 'Do not stop...!' she pleaded as those long and sensitive fingers came to a halt at the opening. 'Touch me there too, Benedict? Give me the pleasure, *all* the pleasure, I have only ever dreamed existed until tonight, here with you!'

Benedict could not resist or deny a woman as beautiful and responsive as Genevieve, when she asked. And so utterly revealingly...

Benedict had no doubts left and no longer just suspected, but *knew* that whatever her marriage to Josiah Forster had been, it had held very little in the way of happiness or pleasure for Genevieve. The sort of pleasure Benedict now dearly wished to share with her...

He claimed Genevieve's other nipple into the heat of his mouth, to the rasp of his tongue, as his fingers moved assuredly through the slit in her drawers, seeking out the heated folds as he caressed her there, his fingers moving higher and seeking out the hard and throbbing little nubbin above as he touched her with a slow and sensuous rhythm.

She was so deliciously responsive there, her neck arching, her groans becoming more rapid and uneven, and she cried out her pleasure as Benedict continued to caress her with the soft pad of his thumb, entering her with one finger, and then two, thrusting slowly, deeply, into that hot and moist channel.

'Benedict…? What is happening?' She gasped suddenly, her eyes wide when he glanced up at her. 'Oh.' Her eyes widened even further, her body tensing even as Benedict felt the first contractions of the muscles as she began to climax.

Genevieve felt consumed with heat as a pleasure unlike anything else she had ever known—could ever have imagined!—pulsed through her hotly, sweeping everything but Benedict from existence, as those waves of pleasure took her even higher as an intensity of pleasure that was almost pain ripped fiercely through her.

'Oh, yes, again,' Benedict encouraged gruffly, his face now bearing the fierceness of a conqueror as he looked down at her. 'And again…!' he insisted as those ripples of pleasure surged from deep inside her to take her over that edge to a third, shattering climax.

Aphrodite. Venus. Diana.

As Benedict held Genevieve cradled against his side, her head resting on his shoulder, her gown still gaping open and revealing breasts once again covered by the thinness of her chemise, he very much doubted that even one of those beautiful and sensual goddesses had ever been as responsive to a man's caresses as Genevieve had just been to his. So open, so honest, in her pleasure that Benedict now felt humbled, privileged, to be the man with whom Genevieve had chosen to share such an uninhibited response.

Although, as she lay silent and still in his arms, her body still racked by the occasional aftermath of trembling sensation, he was unsure if she now felt as comforted in that knowledge.

'Genevieve...?' he finally prompted gruffly when he could stand her silence no longer. 'I did not hurt you? Or your sore arm?'

She breathed out a shaky breath. 'Not in the least. And I was so lost to—to pleasure, that I completely forgot my arm was sore,' she added self-consciously. 'That was—it was perfectly, utterly, delicious. But—'

'But?'

'But you did not find your own release.'

'No.'

'Do you now wish me to—?'

'No.' Benedict held her still at his side as she would have moved up on to her knees.

'No…?' She sounded surprised, even slightly startled. 'But are you not in some discomfort? Do you not wish me to—?'

'No,' Benedict assured again ruefully as he turned so that he might once again look down at her as he gently cupped one of her cheeks. 'I am content, Genevieve, completely satisfied, in the knowledge that you found pleasure.'

'Oh…'

'Does it surprise you to know that a man may enjoy giving you pleasure so much that he feels no need for that release himself?' Benedict looked at her searchingly.

Everything about Benedict was a surprise to Genevieve. Before she had met him, spoken with him, she had heard such tales whispered of Lucifer's cold aloofness amongst the *ton*, and especially so in regard to women and his relationships with them; anyone less aloof than Benedict a few minutes ago, as he caressed and gave her such pleasure, Genevieve could not imagine!

'Yes,' she answered him with that honesty she knew he now expected from her.

He smiled quizzically. 'You have not found the other gentlemen you have…known…to be so easily satisfied, I think?'

'Other gentlemen?'

Benedict gave a terse inclination of his head. 'Your previous lovers.'

'Oh. Oh, yes.' Genevieve turned her gaze away from meeting that coal-black one. 'No, I do not believe that they were.'

Other gentlemen? Genevieve might have spoken so casually a week ago, to her friends Sophia and Pandora, as to the benefits of them all taking a lover, but there had been no man intimately in Genevieve's life, other than the hateful Josiah Forster, and now the man now lying beside her. But she did not need to have known any other lovers to realise that Benedict was both an experienced and generous one.

She faced him bravely. 'If you really do not require me to see to your own needs—'

'I do not,' Benedict drawled ruefully.

Her cheeks warmed. 'Then perhaps it is time for us to leave?'

'If that is what you wish.'

She avoided his gaze, her throat moving as she swallowed. 'I think it would be for the best.'

He looked down at her intently. 'Genevieve, you are not regretting what just happened?'

'Not for a moment!' Her eyes were wide with sincerity as she turned back to him. 'You must believe me when I tell you it was—your lovemaking was the most pleasurable thing I have ever known in my life.'

Benedict laughed softly at the earnestness of her expression. 'My ego is not so fragile, love, that you need ever feel you must flatter and pet me—'

'But I assure you it is not flattery, Benedict.' She gave a firm shake of her head. 'Indeed, this evening has been a revelation—I have enjoyed your lovemaking so much that I fear you may have ruined me completely in regard to—to lovemaking with anyone else,' she added huskily.

A frown darkened Benedict's brow at the thoughts of Genevieve making love with other men. A perfectly natural reaction, he immediately assured himself, when Genevieve lay still half-undressed and satiated beside him. Tonight, making love to a woman as responsive as Genevieve had been extremely satisfying, but he must not allow that satisfaction to cloud other issues in his life; he still had his work to do for the Crown, and he was no closer in his search for his parents' murderer now than he had been when he left the army two years ago.

He nodded abruptly. 'As you say, it is time we left.' He stood up and turned away to collect their discarded masks so as to give Genevieve the time, and privacy, in which to straighten and refasten her gown.

They spoke little as they packed up their things and retied their masks, or as they walked back to take a boat to the other side of the river, where Benedict's carriage was waiting to take them home, both equally as lost in their own thoughts as they travelled back through the darkened streets to Genevieve's home.

'Was your visit to Vauxhall Gardens with a gentlemen as enjoyable as you had hoped it might be?' Benedict prompted softly after walking with Genevieve to her door.

'Very much so.' She nodded, her lashes lowered on to the warmth of her cheeks. 'Especially so when that gentleman chose to behave so indecently.'

Benedict chuckled huskily. 'How could any man, gentleman or otherwise, possibly behave in any other way when in your beautiful and charming company?'

Genevieve looked up to give him a reproving glance. 'Now who is become the flatterer?'

He raised mocking black brows. 'Have you never heard it said that Lucifer is given to flattery?'

'Not that I am aware, no.' She smiled ruefully. 'But then I believe I spent the evening with Lord Benedict Lucas and not with Lucifer.'

His mouth twisted derisively. 'Are you sure about that?'

'Very sure.'

He frowned at her certainty. 'How so?'

'That is easy to answer, my lord.' Her smile widened. 'The rakish and decadent Lucifer would never have refused my offer to give him satisfaction.'

Benedict drew his breath in sharply at the acuity of Genevieve's words; Lucifer would most definitely not have refused the pleasure that had been offered to him with Genevieve's lips and hands. 'I believe it is time you went inside, Genevieve; the wine we drank with our supper seems to have filled your pretty head with yet more nonsense.'

'Now *that* is Lucifer.' Her eyes danced with mischief as she added, 'Unlike Benedict, I believe he enjoys nothing more than being arrogantly condescending to lesser mortals.'

Benedict's brows lowered. 'You talk as if they are two different people?'

'Possibly that is because I believe that they are.' Genevieve nodded.

'And which of those two gentlemen do you prefer?'

'I have no preference.' An endearing dimple appeared in her cheek as she smiled. 'Lord Benedict Lucas is handsome and charming, and Lucifer rakish and wicked. Both are deliciously attractive and I do believe the excitement is in not knowing which of the two will appear at any given moment.'

Benedict gave an exasperated shake of his head. 'Nonsensical chit.'

'Perhaps that is what you find so...interesting about me?' She gave him one last mischievous smile before turning and entering the house, the butler softly closing the door behind her, leaving Benedict with the knowledge that there was more, so much more, to Genevieve than that 'beautiful and charming' woman he had alluded to earlier...

Chapter Six

'Why are you sitting here alone in the dark?'

Genevieve rose sharply to her feet to stare across at the man silhouetted in the doorway to her private parlour. As stated, she was alone in the room, in the darkness, with the curtains drawn across the windows, the candles alight in the hallway behind him the only illumination. Even so, Genevieve would know that voice and silhouette anywhere. 'What are you doing here, Benedict?'

'I believe I asked my question first.' He made no effort to enter the parlour, but continued to loom dark and dangerously in the doorway.

Genevieve gave an abrupt shake of her

head. 'I must have forgotten to light the candles...'

'Forgotten?' Benedict repeated slowly.

'Yes. I—I had a headache earlier and the sunlight hurt my eyes, nor had I noticed, with the curtains drawn across the windows, that it had become dark.'

'I do believe you are babbling again, Genevieve.'

'And you are intruding upon my privacy!' Her eyes flashed in the semi-darkness at his obvious mockery.

'Yes.' He nodded slowly. 'Which is most interesting, when your butler informed me that you were not at home.'

She shot him an impatient glance. 'We both know that it is commonplace for such an excuse to be given when one does not wish to receive visitors—'

'Again,' Benedict continued as if she had not spoken. 'I called to see you yesterday morning, and was told the same thing,' he added hardly. 'Again this morning. And again just now. And on every one of those occasions I have had no doubts you were very much at home.'

Genevieve drew in a sharp breath. 'But, as I have just said, in no mood to receive visitors.'

'Just certain visitors, or all?'

She was not fooled for a moment by the mildness of Benedict's tone, knew him well enough to sense the seething displeasure beneath that calm politeness. 'I told you, I have had a headache—'

'For two days?'

'For as long as I have known you, as it happens!'

'Better,' he murmured appreciatively.

She shot him an irritated glance. 'How is it you managed to find your way in here, Benedict, when I distinctly left instructions I was not to be disturbed?'

He shrugged those broad shoulders. 'I waited until the butler, having dutifully delivered my dismissal, returned below stairs, before I then quietly let myself back in the house to seek you out.'

Her eyes widened. 'In other words, you broke into my home.'

'The door was unlocked.'

'That is no excuse for your arrogance—'

'I will be back in just a moment...' He stepped back into the hallway, coming back into the room just seconds later with a three-pronged candelabra which allowed that coal-black gaze to look at her critically. 'Have you been crying?' he probed shrewdly.

Yes, Genevieve had been crying. She seemed to have done little else for the past two days.

'Genevieve…?' Benedict prompted softly at her continued and uncharacteristic silence, deeply concerned by how fragile she appeared in a pale peach-coloured gown, her eyes very big and deeply blue in the pallor of her face. 'I hope you have not been upset because of what happened between the two of us the other evening?'

'No! No, Benedict,' she repeated more calmly as he raised dark brows at her vehemence. 'That evening was, and will remain, one of the most perfect and memorable of my life.'

'Then why have you been crying?' Benedict stepped further into the tiny parlour before placing the candelabra down on a small side table next to one of the armchairs on either side of the unlit fireplace. 'And why have you shut yourself away in your own home, turning visitors away at the door and not venturing out yourself?'

Her eyes widened. 'How could you possibly know I have not been out and about this past two days?'

'I made it my business to know,' he answered unapologetically. 'Just as I know that you have allowed one visitor to call, at least.' He looked down at her through narrowed lids. 'Sophia Rowlands. No doubt she came to inform you of her impending marriage to my friend Dante Carfax?'

'Yes.' And Genevieve was happy for both Sophia and Pandora, felt nothing but admiration for her two friends, because they were both obviously brave to try marriage for a second time. But with her two closest friends now totally absorbed in their new husband or husband-to-be, Genevieve did not feel it right to confide her own present unhappiness to either of them, with regard to William and his rough treatment of her when he had called two days ago. Not that she ever had told Pandora and Sophia the details of her marriage to the elderly Josiah Forster anyway, but they had at least known, and sympathised with the fact, that she admitted to it having been a less-than-happy one. With those two ladies' own happiness now assured, Genevieve did not feel she could confide in either of them with regard to the continued cruelty of the hated William Forster.

She schooled her features into ones of calm composure. 'I am very pleased that both Sophia and Pandora have found happiness at last.'

Benedict allowed himself a wry smile. 'But you have, nevertheless, still been crying.'

'But not because of Pandora and Sophia's obvious happiness!' she defended herself indignantly. 'And how dare you first force your way in here, only to then insult me because my red nose and sore eyes are evidence of the tears I have shed?'

Much, much better, Benedict acknowledged inwardly; he could deal much more ably with a spitting and angry Genevieve than the pale and sad-looking woman he had found when he first entered the parlour. Nor was he convinced that the intimacies they had shared at Vauxhall Gardens two evenings ago were not partly responsible for those tears...

He frowned darkly. 'I should like to extend my apologies if my behaviour at Vauxhall Gardens in the least offended you.'

'Why, when I have told you—when I have expressed my—' She gave an impatient shake of her head, red curls bouncing. 'An apology is not necessary. How could it be, when you must know how much I enjoyed our…intimacies?'

Benedict had thought often of the intimacies he had shared with Genevieve these past two days: during the restless night's sleep which had followed, when the throbbing ache of his own arousal had made a complete nonsense of his assurances to Genevieve that it was not necessary for him to attain his own physical release, and yet again the following morning after being turned away at her door.

He had even thought about their night at Vauxhall Gardens over lunch at his club and during a meeting with Eric Cargill later that afternoon to discuss how best to use the information received from their French count. This had been followed by another restless night of very little sleep. And the frustration this morning when he was once again refused entrance to Genevieve's home, despite knowing that Sophia Rowlands had not received that same refusal.

To have returned this evening, following another unsatisfactory day when he had thought far too much of Genevieve, only to be told once again that she was 'not at home' had just been too much.

Hence his having decided to just walk in

once he was able to do so without any of Genevieve's household staff being any the wiser; he was, after all, an agent for the Crown, able to move with both stealth and speed when the situation warranted it. He had decided that this situation warranted it.

His expression softened now as he looked down at Genevieve. 'Your nose is not red nor your eyes looking sore— What is it?' he demanded as Genevieve drew her breath in sharply when Benedict reached out to take a light hold of the slenderness of her wrist, her face having now turned a sickly grey. 'Genevieve—'

'Please, Benedict…!' she groaned as she tried to release even that light grip of his fingers from about her wrist. 'You are hurting me!' Tears glistened in her eyes.

Benedict released her immediately. 'What is it, Genevieve? Can it be that your bruised wrist is still paining you?'

'I am sure it is getting better.' She attempted to smile dismissively.

'Show me.' He held his hand out towards her, palm turned encouragingly upwards.

'No!' There was pure panic in those expressive blue eyes now as she put her hand behind her back.

'Genevieve…'

'I have told you, it is nothing.'

'Then allow me see that for myself,' he insisted firmly.

Her lashes lowered and for several long seconds she looked down at the hand Benedict still held out to her, before slowly, very slowly, lifting her own hand with the other and placing it lightly in his.

Benedict shot her a searching glance before slowly unwrapping the bandage he discovered still covered her wrist. 'Who did this?' he growled harshly once the swelling, and lividness of the purple-and-black bruising about her wrist, was revealed to his angry gaze.

Genevieve winced at the harshness of Benedict's tone. 'I told you, I caught the sleeve of my robe—'

'This was not done by wrenching your arm on a door handle.' He appeared every inch Lucifer at this moment, his expression coldly angry as he looked down at her.

Not angry towards her, Genevieve accepted, but towards whoever might be responsible for causing her injury. But to answer him truthfully would, Genevieve had no doubts, cause Lucifer, and not Lord Benedict Lucas, to appear on the doorstep of William Forster's Lon-

don home before this day was over, for the sole
purpose of inflicting suitable punishment for
the other man's offence against her. An outcome Genevieve might wish for, but could not
allow to happen. Not because she did not believe Benedict perfectly capable of besting the
other man. Or because William did not fully
deserve the retribution Benedict would inflict
on her behalf! But she knew William far too
well. Knew of his viciousness of nature, both
verbally and physically, a viciousness that
Genevieve had no doubt would include telling lies about her if it suited his purpose. As,
in this case, it surely would.

The worsening condition of her arm, rather
than its easing, was the very reason that Genevieve had chosen to hide herself away these
past two days. Waiting, hoping for its recovery, before she dared to face the eagle-eyed
Benedict Lucas again.

She gave a shake of her head. 'As I explained to you the other evening—'

'I believe we have already discussed my
feelings in regard to being told untruths?' His
voice was dangerously soft.

Genevieve moistened her lips with the tip
of her tongue. 'It looks much worse than it is.'

'Somehow I very much doubt that,' Benedict bit out harshly. 'Now tell me how this happened—I will not be answerable for the consequences if you attempt to lie to me again, Genevieve!' His eyes glittered darkly in warning, a nerve pulsing in his tightly clenched jaw.

Genevieve winced at the anger she could see in his glittering black gaze. 'It is not so very painful.'

There was a knot of anger lodged in Benedict's chest and a cold fury inside his head, both making it impossible for him to see any further than the bruising and livid bruises about Genevieve's tiny wrist. Such a slender and delicate wrist, to have been treated so cruelly. 'These are fingerprints, Genevieve.' He placed his own fingers gently about her wrist in demonstration. 'A man's fingerprints,' he added grimly as his own fingers touched the exact same places where those bruises appeared more vivid.

Genevieve's mouth now felt so dry she had trouble swallowing, let alone forming an answer, knowing that Benedict's own strength lay not in subjugating a woman, but in seducing and pleasuring her, and so rendering another man's physical bullying totally unacceptable to him.

And she could not bear it, if Benedict were to confront William, for him to learn the ugly truth of her marriage from that hateful man. Nor did she have the courage as yet to tell him of that marriage herself. Perhaps one day, if he were to ask, but not yet. Not yet!

She gave a shake of her head. 'The fact that the…discomfort is worse now than the day I caught—when the injury first occurred,' she quickly amended as she saw Benedict's frown darken, 'does seem to imply that I have done more than just bruise the skin,' she conceded huskily, having found little rest or sleep these past two nights as the discomfort of her wrist and down her arm seemed to increase by the minute.

'What did the doctor have to say?'

'I have not sent for the doctor—'

'Why not, when your arm is obviously so painful to you?' he demanded incredulously.

It had simply not occurred to Genevieve to send for the doctor to examine her arm, because one had never been called to see her in the past when Josiah had ordered William to beat her for one misdemeanour or another.

'Never mind,' Benedict bit out harshly as he saw the uncertainty in her expression. 'My own doctor will be sent for immediately.'

'And what will I tell him?' Genevieve looked distressed again. 'How will I explain my…my injury to him…?'

Benedict's eyes narrowed. 'Honestly, it is to be hoped.' He crossed to the fireplace to ring the bell for Jenkins. 'Although I somehow doubt that any doctor worth his salt could possibly mistake the reason for those bruises.' His mouth thinned. 'I only hope that he will not jump to the conclusion that I am the one responsible for them— Ah, Jenkins.' He turned to the surprised butler as he appeared in the doorway, offering no explanation for his presence there, despite the older man having only minutes ago refused him entrance, instead briskly issuing his instructions and the directions to the doctor's place of residence.

'Poor Jenkins,' Genevieve murmured as soon as the bewildered butler had departed to send for the doctor.

'Poor Jenkins, be damned.' Benedict gave a disgusted snort as he began to restlessly pace the parlour, his hands gripped tightly behind his back. 'If the man had allowed me entrance yesterday you might not have been in pain for as long as you so obviously have.'

'He received his instructions from me—'

'I already know what instructions he has

received from you.' Benedict eyed her impatiently. 'We will talk of this again once the doctor has examined you and you are hopefully in less discomfort than you are now.'

Much as Genevieve knew Benedict should not be here, that it would be better for him if he did not become embroiled in the unpleasantness between herself and William Forster, she nevertheless felt better than she had for the past two days. Less…vulnerable. As if just Benedict's presence made her safer. Made her *feel* safer.

Even if she knew she was not…

And now that her initial shock had passed, and part of the truth of her injured wrist revealed at least, she had time, whilst they waited for the doctor to arrive, to look her fill of Benedict. To really look at him.

He appeared tired, the lines beside his eyes and mouth somehow seeming deeper, grimmer, as if he had not rested for the past two days or nights either. Oh, not because of her— Genevieve did not fool herself into believing that she was in any way important to Benedict's life. He found her amusing, they had shared…intimacies, but Genevieve did not fool herself that she meant any more to him than that. Just as she knew it was now Benedict's inborn sense of responsibility that made him demand his own doctor be sent for to examine her wrist and arm.

And it did hurt so very much. Unbearably so. An aching, nagging throb, which had prevented her from achieving any rest or calmness of mind or body this past two days and nights.

In the past William had always made sure that he hit her where no one would be able to see the bruises. Always hard enough to hurt and humiliate her, but never enough to break anything or for those bruises to be visible to others. Genevieve was not sure she had been so lucky this time.

A fact Benedict's doctor confirmed some half an hour later, after examining her thoroughly and declaring that she had broken a small bone in her wrist, before giving her something to take for the pain and then bandaging it tightly and giving her a sling to put about her neck to take the weight off her arm. The easing of the constant pain, brought about just by that simple act, was enough to cause Genevieve to sigh her relief as she relaxed back in one of the armchairs by the fireside whilst Benedict walked downstairs to personally see to the doctor's departure, closing her eyes in the first relief of pain she had known for some time.

Benedict took one look at Genevieve when he returned a few minutes later and knew that she had fallen asleep. A deep and untroubled sleep, it was to be hoped, the lines of pain smoothed from her beautifully delicate face, those long dark lashes fanned out upon the paleness of her cheeks.

Benedict wished that his thoughts could be as untroubled, but they could not. Not until he knew who had inflicted this injury upon Genevieve. What man had dared to treat such delicacy of body and nature with such brutality as the doctor had told him would have been necessary to bruise her so badly and break the bone in her wrist?

It was incomprehensible to Benedict that any man could ever find reason to harm such a gentle and beautiful soul as Genevieve, and not just physically, but to the degree that the light of excitement and joy she found in life had been completely erased from her expressive eyes.

One thing was certain, Benedict did not intend leaving this house until Genevieve had told him the name of the man responsible.

* * *

Genevieve sensed—knew, as she began to awaken from her deep sleep, that she was not alone. That there was someone in her bedchamber with her. Not just in her bedchamber, but actually in her bed.

Her stomach gave a sickening lurch at the thought that it was Josiah. The husband she despised. The husband she feared. And she could not bear it. Had to get away. To escape—

'Everything is well, Genevieve.' A gentle hand was placed soothingly against her cheek. 'No one shall harm you whilst I am here.'

Benedict!

It was Benedict who lay beside her, not Josiah. Thank God. Josiah was long dead. And Benedict...

Benedict should not be in her bedchamber, let alone lying on her bed with her!

Her eyes opened wide to candlelight and she found herself looking up at Benedict as he bent over her, such an expression of concern upon his wickedly handsome face it made her heart ache. 'Why are you still here?' Her voice sounded hushed in the semi-darkness of her bedchamber.

He gave a rueful smile. 'Waiting for you to awaken, of course.'

'And how did I get here?'

'I carried you.'

A frown creased her brow at her lack of memory of having been lifted into Benedict's arms and being carried to her bedchamber, let alone being placed in her bed. She also noted that Benedict had removed his black superfine and loosened the neckcloth at his throat; it was to be hoped that he had not undressed her too! 'What time is it?'

'Almost two o'clock—'

'In the morning?' Her eyes widened even further. 'But you cannot—you must not be here with me, in my bedchamber, in the middle of the night, Benedict!'

'And yet here I am…'

Yes, here he was. And much as Genevieve knew he should not still be here, of the scandal that would ensue if anyone were to know of the presence of Lord Benedict Lucas in her bedchamber in the middle of the night, let alone the repercussions she might expect from William Forster if he were ever to find out, she felt glad, happy, to know that Benedict had stayed here with her.

Which was a danger in itself, when she had strived so hard this past year of her widowhood to be independent and unafraid, two things she had never been allowed to be whilst she was Josiah Forster's duchess. She could not, must not, rely on anyone else for that independence or lack of fear. Comforting as it was to know—to feel Benedict's protection of her, she *had* to manage alone.

She gave a tight smile. 'And now that you are assured of my well being you must depart for your own home.'

'Must I?' He raised one dark and arrogant brow as he looked down at her.

'I believe so, yes.' Genevieve turned away to throw back the bedcovers with the intention of rising from the bed, thankful that she was still wearing the gown she had on earlier, only to find it impossible to sit up with her arm secured in the sling about her neck. 'Bother.' She scowled as she struggled to even sit using just one arm.

'Here, let me.' Benedict swung his legs down from the bed before standing up. Four strides took him round to the other side of the bed before he placed an arm beneath Genevieve's uninjured arm and helped her sit, then scowling down at her as she would have risen to her feet. 'The doctor instructed that you are not to exert yourself or remove your arm from the sling for at least the next few days.'

She gave him an impatient glance. 'I do not believe that included my needing to use the chamberpot!'

'No.' Benedict grinned at her spirited response, happy to be able to do so; there had been an uncharacteristic air of frailty about Genevieve earlier, with only the occasional glimpse of her usual vivacity, something he had not cared for at all. 'Would you like me to assist you?'

'Certainly not!' Two bright spots of embarrassed colour heightened her cheeks as she rose to her feet.

'You might find it a little difficult to manage on your own with the use of only one arm.'

'I am sure I shall manage somehow, thank you!'

'As you wish.' Benedict stepped back.

'You will take that smile from your lips, Benedict,' she instructed pertly, shooting him one last reproving glance as he refused to do so, before she walked quickly across to the adjoining dressing room and closed the door firmly behind her.

* * *

Benedict's teasing grin disappeared the moment that door closed. He gave thought to Genevieve's panic as she had begun to awaken, as if she feared seeing who lay on the bed beside her...

Did Genevieve fear *him*?

Had their lovemaking two evenings ago put her in fear of him, after all? She had claimed not earlier, had told Benedict that she considered that evening as having been the most perfect and memorable in her life.

So if Genevieve did not fear him, then whom did she fear? The obvious answer was the same man who had broken the bone in her wrist. A man who had perhaps been her previous lover? Perhaps one who had not been pleased to see himself replaced with Benedict? It would certainly explain Genevieve's reluctance to talk about this other man to him.

But as far as Benedict was concerned, there was no excuse, no reason on this earth, why any man should ever physically hurt a woman. In Genevieve's case, a woman who was so tiny and delicate she had no chance of being able to physically defend herself against even the smallest show of brute strength.

A brute strength which, in this case, had resulted in her wrist being broken. Benedict was determined to know this other man's name, either from Genevieve herself, or by some other means...

Chapter Seven

Genevieve was feeling more than a little disgruntled when she returned to her bedchamber some long minutes later, having had more of a problem than she could possibly have realised dealing with her ablutions with only one useful hand. Even now she was unsure of whether or not her gown was tidy—or even decent!—at the back.

'I will have the man's name, Genevieve.'

She faltered slightly as she looked across the bedchamber, not because of Benedict's demand but because he had made himself comfortable in her absence and was now stretched out upon her bed, with several pillows supporting his head and shoulders, his black hair tousled. He had removed his neckcloth completely, with several buttons of his shirt unfastened to reveal a glimpse of the dark curls that covered his chest.

Genevieve wished she could avert her gaze, but unfortunately instead found herself mesmerised by such blatant male sensuality. 'You look as tired as I, Benedict,' she spoke in self-defence.

His mouth twisted derisively. 'It is after two o'clock in the morning.'

'A time when you, and no doubt many of your friends, often begin the evening's activities rather than end them!'

'True,' he acknowledged unrepentantly as he lazily crossed one booted foot over the ankle of the other to look at her uncompromisingly between the highly polished tips of those boots. 'The man's name, Genevieve.'

'Is there a particular reason for your own... fatigue?' Once again she ignored his question, having no idea how to answer him now any more than she had earlier. 'Perhaps you have made some progress on your own quest in regard to your parents'— Benedict?' Her eyes widened in alarm as he swung his booted feet impatiently to the floor and sat up.

He was so very, very *male*!

Clothed in his usual elegant finery, with

his dark and dangerous looks, Benedict was enough to make every female heart in a room pound the moment he entered it. But here and now, with his dark hair tousled, wearing only that fine white linen shirt and silver waistcoat to cover his chest and those wide and muscled shoulders, with his throat revealed, black pantaloons fitting tautly across his thighs and the long length of his legs, he was quite literally, breathtaking. In fact, Genevieve could not recall having taken a breath since first looking across the bedchamber at him.

She drew one in deeply now. 'I am sorry if I have enquired into something you feel is too personal to discuss with a woman who is little more than a stranger to you—'

'Please be quiet, Genevieve.' His voice was soft, but all the more of a warning because of it, his eyes once again that glittering black onyx as he glared across the room at her. 'My reluctance to discuss with you my progress, or rather, lack of it, in regard to finding my parents' murderer, has nothing to do with how well I do or do not know you—and I know you very well, Genevieve. Intimately. Both inside and out. Do I make myself clear?' The darkness of his gaze was so compelling it was impossible for Genevieve to look away.

Her cheeks burned at memory of that 'intimacy'. 'Very.'

'Good.' Benedict nodded tersely. 'I do not choose to discuss the subject with you, or anyone else, because there is nothing to tell. No new evidence which has suddenly come to light. Nothing,' he added bleakly. 'My godfather investigated the matter thoroughly at the time and I have continued those enquiries since, and there is no new evidence of why they died or who killed them.'

Genevieve winced. 'I am sorry.'

'No more so than I.' He nodded grimly.

'Did you talk to the servants? They are much more astute than they are ever given credit for, you know—'

'Genevieve, much as I appreciate your efforts to divert my attention, it will not wash.' He raised dark and pointed brows. 'I am not a man easily diverted from my purpose. I will have the name of the man who hurt you and I will have it now.'

And his will, Genevieve knew, was as determined as her own. For different reasons, of course. Benedict was by nature strong and self-confident. Genevieve's own stubbornness, in refusing to give in to Benedict's demand, came from a continued need she felt to avoid

any sort of confrontation between him and
William Forster. Not because she feared Benedict would not emerge the victor in any fair
exchange between the two men—his rapier-
sharp words could be as lethal as his prow-
ess with both sword and pistol were reputed
to be!—but because she knew William Forster was not a man who played by any rules
but his own.

'Are you and Suffolk perhaps…better acquainted than previously stated?'

Genevieve looked at him blankly. 'You are
referring to Frederick St James, the Earl of
Suffolk?'

'Obviously, it was not him,' Benedict
drawled self-derisively, Genevieve's bewildered expression enough to tell him he had
been well off the mark with that particular
guess. He rose to his feet. 'You know, Genevieve, this would all be so much simpler if you
were to just give me the man's name.'

'I cannot.' She gave a determined shake of
her head.

Benedict looked at her through narrowed
lids; her red curls were tousled, with several
having escaped their pins to fall down the
slender column of her throat, and her face was

still deathly pale, despite the four hours' sleep she had enjoyed earlier.

Those same four hours when Benedict had lain beside her and watched her as she slept, appreciating how young and delicate she looked without her feisty spirit in evidence, or any of the fire flashing in those deep-blue eyes.

'You love the man still?' he guessed shrewdly.

Her eyes widened. 'Sorry?'

He grimaced. 'I can think of no other reason why a woman would choose to protect a past lover from the present one.'

Was Benedict her lover? He had certainly kissed her two evenings ago, touched her intimately and given her immeasurable pleasure, but did that really make him her lover? Benedict appeared to think so...

She gave a shake of her head. 'How could I possibly continue to love someone who has physically hurt me?'

Benedict's mouth twisted wryly. 'I have absolutely no idea. But I believe that some women do. Never having been in love myself, I do not understand the drive of that emotion, nor the workings of a woman's heart in regard to the type of man they might choose to bestow that emotion upon.' He shrugged.

Benedict was undoubtedly telling her not to mistake the desire he had shown her as being that emotion, either, as his concern for her now was no doubt stating that he would only ever contemplate being her lover.

Which was exactly as it should be. Unlike Sophia and Pandora, Genevieve had no intentions of ever falling in love, let alone marrying again.

'I am told, however,' Benedict continued scathingly, 'that there is a very thin line between love and hate—and obviously you have not crossed over that line as yet with regard to your former lover.' He arched a coldly derisory brow.

Genevieve became very still as she took in the full import of what Benedict was saying to her. He truly did believe that a previous lover had done this to her? That a man she loved, and who professed to love her in return, had done this to her after discovering she was now involved with Benedict and that she was remaining silent now in order to protect him?

The whole idea was ludicrous, ridiculous; women did not really behave so stupidly, did they, as to continue to love a man who treated them with such cruelty and contempt? Genevieve had certainly not felt anything approaching that emotion for Josiah Forster.

But was it not better, for all concerned, if Benedict believed her to be one of those women rather than for him to learn that it was her vicious and cruel stepson who had hurt her? The stepson who had also threatened to harm her again if she were to cause a scandal before his marriage to Charlotte Darby were to take place. 'Did you end the relationship or did he?' Benedict watched Genevieve closely as he asked the question.

She gave a slight shake of her head, the directness of her gaze not meeting his. 'I was the one to—to sever that particular relationship.'

'At least you had that much sense!'

The eyes she raised flashed deeply blue at his obvious scorn. 'It does not seem to have done me much good!'

Benedict's top lip curled with distaste. 'Possibly because, despite bringing your intimacies to an end, you have allowed him to remain in your life?'

'I—' She drew in a deep and steadying breath. 'Could we...talk of something else, Benedict?'

His mouth thinned with distaste. 'If that is what you wish.'

'It is.'

'Then we will do so. For the moment,' he added softly. 'As it happens, there is something else I wished to discuss with you… The reason I came to see you yesterday, and again today, was to ask if you would care to accompany me to Carlton House in two evenings' time.' He picked up his jacket from the bedside chair where he had placed it earlier. 'Obviously, I will understand if, in the circumstances, you were to choose to refuse the invitation.' He looked at her with challenging black eyes.

'Carlton House…?' Genevieve breathed excitedly.

Benedict nodded. 'The Prince Regent has invited myself, and a companion of my choice, to dine with him that evening. I should warn you—it will not be a dinner of manners or propriety.' He grimaced. 'I do not believe any of Prinny's dinners could ever be called that!'

Genevieve had no idea what to say to such an invitation. Or why Benedict had bothered to mention it when he so obviously believed her to still be in love with another man. The same man who had broken her wrist.

But Carlton House!

She had lived in the country for almost the

whole of her marriage to Josiah Forster, followed by another year of enforced mourning for him, and these past few weeks of the
Season, whilst enjoyable, had certainly not
included dinner with the Prince Regent at
Carlton House.

Of course the Prince was so very unpopular
now with the general public, his reputation as
being a prolific rake, and for throwing exces-
sively lavish parties, not in the least approved
of by the majority of the country after the
years of war against Napoleon and the hard-
ships which had ensued. For all except the
Prince Regent, apparently.

But she had heard such rumours of the Regent's dinner parties, such tales of excess and
licentiousness… 'And is this invitation still
open to me?'

Benedict gave a haughty inclination of his
head. 'If you are not too easily shocked, and
your arm is not paining you as much by then.'

Genevieve would make sure that it was not,
even if she had to refrain completely from ex-
erting herself or removing her arm from the
sling for the next two days! 'Then I believe I
should very much like to accompany you to
dinner at Carlton House. Thank you for inviting me,' she accepted quietly.

Benedict's expression was enigmatic as he looked up from straightening the cuffs of his shirt beneath his jacket. 'And if this evening out in public with me should reach the ears of your previous lover?'

Genevieve's gaze sharpened suspiciously, knowing that suspicion was warranted as she now saw the look of challenge on Benedict's harshly handsome face as he met that gaze. 'You are hoping that it will,' she realised slowly. 'Knowing of my yearning for fun and adventure, you have dangled thoughts of going to Carlton House as a lure to entice me, for the sole purpose of hoping that this other man will then reveal himself to you, if it is reported I have once again spent the evening in your company.'

'Your intelligence is only one of the many things I admire about you, Genevieve!' He gave an acknowledging inclination of his head. 'Although it is to be hoped that the novelty of a visit to Carlton House is not the only lure for spending the evening with me?'

'Do not try to now divert me with your teasing, Benedict.' She eyed him impatiently.

He smiled wryly. 'As I said, intelligence as well as beauty. And, yes, Genevieve, as you have so rightly guessed, there are more ways than one to find the answer I seek.'

She gave a slow shake of her head. 'You are—'

'Now, now, Genevieve, there shall be no name calling.' Benedict crossed the bedchamber in long strides before tapping her playfully on the tip of her nose. 'Accept, pet, that I am simply more devious than you and let that be an end to it, hmmm?'

Benedict was so very much more devious than Genevieve could ever have imagined. And he had obviously come to know her nature well these past few days. Because try as she might, much as it might indeed reach the ears of William Forster, Genevieve knew she could not forgo the opportunity, the delicious excitement, of going to Carlton House with Benedict and dining with the Prince Regent himself.

She gave him an admiring glance. 'What a wicked, wicked man you are, Benedict Lucas.'

He gave a hard and mocking smile. 'As many others before you have noted.'

Genevieve had no doubt that they had and that most, if not all of them, were women, because Benedict had behaved, and no doubt would again in future, very wickedly indeed towards the women in his life.

It was no doubt part of the attraction…

Only part, of course, because Benedict was a man of fascinating contradictions: The coldly aloof and yet sensually dangerous Lucifer, and the lazily charming and yet equally as dangerous Benedict.

In either case, Genevieve admitted to finding those contradictions as fascinating as so many other women had before her.

As such, she was very much afraid that William Forster could be as displeased as he liked. She would not relinquish the pleasure of being with Benedict *or* Lucifer. 'How should I dress for this dinner party at Carlton House?'

'For Prinny's taste? Better not to dress at all,' Benedict drawled. 'For my own…? Ravishingly so will do.'

Genevieve laughed excitedly. 'I cannot begin to tell you how much I am looking forward to this.'

She did not have to when Benedict could clearly see that pleasure in the glow of her eyes and the excited flush to her cheeks.

He only hoped that he was at her side, or within the vicinity, when his efforts to flush out the bastard who had dared to hurt her came to fruition…

* * *

'I am sure there is no need for you to feed me yourself in this noticeable way, Benedict. Everyone, including the Prince Regent, is watching us!' Genevieve gave him a self-conscious glare from beneath long dark lashes as he enticingly held up a forkful of capon only inches from her lips.

Benedict sat beside her at Prinny's own long and noisily crowded dinner table, with at least half-a-dozen other tables set about the room for the hundred or so guests squeezed in the dining room at Carlton House. As Benedict had warned her, it was a gathering of excesses, with several of the ladies and gentlemen openly indulging in intimacies which would be far better left to the privacy of the bedchamber.

Prinny himself, as Genevieve had just remarked, glanced down the table at them often. Benedict knew the other man well enough, and had spent enough time in his company, to realise that although Prinny might no longer be the slender and handsome man he had once been, he was nevertheless as charming and affable as he had ever been, and his eye for a beautiful woman remained as astute.

To Benedict's intense irritation, the warmth

of his Regent's greeting earlier had shown that Prinny obviously considered Genevieve, in a satin gown of pale lemon, to be a very beautiful woman. 'Let them look,' Benedict answered with hard dismissal as he continued to hold the fork towards her temptingly.

To say that Genevieve felt slightly intimidated, by both her surroundings and the strange collection of people dining at Carlton House, would be an understatement.

Carlton House itself was perhaps smaller than she had expected for being the home of England's Regent, but this room and the ones she and Benedict had passed through earlier this evening on their way to the dining room were all elegantly and magnificently furnished, even if their opulence did not suit Genevieve's more reserved tastes. This dining room was decorated with such an array of artwork, both on the walls and upon the tables in the form of exquisitely decorated cakes and fancies. The tables were set with blazing candles and fine crystal and tableware glittered brightly beneath the dozens of chandeliers lit above them. It was obvious that no expense had been spared, even for what could only be called one of Prince Regent's more intimate gatherings.

But it was the people seated at the tables who intimidated Genevieve the most, the numerous guests obviously a mix of both the *ton* and the somewhat lesser classes—the latter usually in regard to the ladies present. Indeed, the revealing gowns some of those ladies wore—in some cases they possessed no bodice to them at all, leaving the woman's breasts bare for all to see, and in others the gowns were all but transparent—were indicative that they were not ladies at all! Although many female members of the *ton* were also present, most in the company of young gentlemen who were certainly not their husbands.

It was, at one and the same time, both fascinating and shocking to see so many members of the *ton*, both male and female, whom Genevieve usually encountered only in the formality of society's drawing rooms and ballrooms, indulging in intimacies with ladies and gentlemen to whom they had no public connection.

As for the Prince Regent himself!

He had made a great show earlier, when Benedict had presented her to him, of lingering over the kissing of the back of her gloved hand, his eyes merrily glinting up at her in male appreciation as he did so. Corpulent and red-faced, and no longer a young man, he should not have been in the least attractive, yet there was an air about him still, of good humour and gaiety, that was so very appealing.

'Prinny himself advised I take care of you,' Benedict reminded drily.

He had indeed, and the concern the Prince Regent had shown for the lace shawl noticeably draped about Genevieve's injured arm had appeared to be heartfelt.

Even so... 'I do not think he meant for you to actually feed me,' Genevieve muttered awkwardly.

'It is far less...shocking than the things others are doing at his dinner table.' Benedict looked about them pointedly.

It was true that the amount of alcohol which had been drunk, together with the copious amounts of food, was obviously taking its toll. The laughter and conversation had grown to almost a roar, one gentleman further down the table having unbuttoned his pantaloons, apparently on the excuse of showing the lady at his side his 'war wound'. The lady seated on Benedict's right was having her thighs fondled by another gentleman who had crawled under the table, all apparently without that lady missing so much of a word of the conversation she was having with the man seated to her right.

As Prinny's dinner parties went, Benedict knew this was nowhere near as licentious as it would become later. Nevertheless, he deeply regretted bringing Genevieve to such a raucous dinner party as this one. For all that she liked to pretend she was a sophisticated and widowed duchess, her wide-eyed and fascinated expression as she observed the carryings on indicated otherwise.

'I should not have brought you here.' Benedict sat back with a scowl, his effort of sitting forwards and feeding Genevieve, and therefore using his body to shield her from some of the worst excesses on view, obviously serving little purpose when the couple opposite were engaged in—Lord knew what they were engaged in. 'I believe it is time we left.'

'Why, Benedict, I do believe you are discomforted by the behaviour of our dining companions?' Genevieve looked at him with laughing blue eyes.

His eyes narrowed. 'Do not look so mischievously satisfied that might be the case, Genevieve—or I too might disappear beneath the table and discomfort *you*!'

'Discomfort me…?' she repeated interestedly.

He drew his breath in with a hiss. 'I do not believe this…company to be entirely suitable for you.'

She widened innocent eyes. 'Surely we cannot leave now, with the meal still only half over? Would the Prince Regent not be offended?'

Benedict's scowl deepened. 'You are right, of course; we could not leave without bringing our departure to his notice when we make our necessary farewells, and he is sure to object.' He glanced about them impatiently, wondering if Prinny's entertainments were usually this scandalous—and knowing that they were. He had just never taken notice of it until in Genevieve's more innocent company.

Besides which, he had not managed as yet to speak with the gentleman Eric Cargill had asked him to contact this evening, and the real reason for his having accepted Prinny's invitation…

Nor was Benedict sure that he was going to be able to do so, not when it would necessitate leaving Genevieve alone whilst he talked to the other man. Several gentlemen—other than Prinny—had eyed her as if she were a tasty morsel they wished to gobble up and devour in a single bite. And if any man was going to take a bite out of Genevieve this evening, then Benedict had every intention of it being himself!

Indeed, this whole evening had become one of physical frustration and discomfort for Benedict, because he had been disturbed by Genevieve's presence at his side since the moment she had greeted him at her home earlier. She looked so beautiful in the lemon-satin gown, which made her skin appear as pale and translucent as the pearls drops once again adorning her hair. There was a glow of excitement in her eyes, making them sparkle and shine, the flush to her cheeks adding to that glow. As to the laughter that never seemed far from those delectable lips as he fed her mouthfuls of food…!

They were the same delectable lips Benedict now ached to feel about his aching and throbbing cock as it pressed more and more insistently for release against the front of his pantaloons.

None of which was helped by the improper antics of those sitting close to them!

'You seem troubled, Benedict?' Genevieve placed her hand lightly upon the rigidity of his muscled thigh as she turned to him, her expression becoming even more concerned as he gave a low groan. 'Is there anything I might do to relieve your discomfort?'

From any other woman, Benedict knew such a question would most certainly have carried a flirtatious innuendo, but from Genevieve it was no doubt exactly as it seemed: concern for the no doubt pained expression upon his face.

He drew in a deep breath. 'I do not believe anyone would object if we were to step outside on to the terrace for some air before the next course is served.' He threw his linen napkin abruptly down on the table before standing up—instantly giving Genevieve an eye-level view of the tented front of his tailored pantaloons.

She glanced up at him beneath heavy dark lashes. 'Are you sure that it is air you are in need of, Benedict?'

Perhaps he had been wrong, and there had been innuendo in her earlier remark, after all?

His jaw was now so tightly clenched he felt as if his teeth were in danger of snapping off at the roots. 'I believe a breath of fresh air will do to start with!'

She placed her folded napkin carefully upon

the table before standing up slowly. 'And to finish…?'

'That, my dear Genevieve, will depend entirely upon you!' Benedict took a firm hold of the elbow of her uninjured arm to escort her across the room and out through the French doors, which had been left open, no doubt in an effort to prevent the room from becoming too overheated with so many people crowded into it.

Obviously it had not worked in Benedict's case; he was overheated to the point of bursting by his need to make love to Genevieve again!

Chapter Eight

As they stepped outside, Genevieve was unsure as to which was her more predominant emotion: nervousness at being outside alone on the terrace with Benedict, or her need to laugh at his obvious discomfort—both with her having witnessed the scandalous behaviour of some of their dining companions and the unmistakable state of his own arousal. She firmly believed this to have been behind Benedict's driving need to escape the dining room, if only for a few minutes' respite. Indeed, his last comment to her would seem to confirm that it was…

'I trust you are not about to laugh, madam?'

Benedict's disgusted tone was Genevieve's undoing and she instantly burst into the laughter she had been fighting against since they both stood up from the table. 'I am so sorry, Benedict.' She finally sobered enough to look up at him in the bright glow given out by the hundreds of candles burning in the dining room behind them, only to burst out laughing again as she saw the look of haughty reproach on the harsh planes of his aristocratically handsome face as he looked down the long length of his nose at her.

'I trust you will forgive me if I find your apology less than sincere,' he murmured after several more minutes of her obvious amusement.

'But it was. Truly it was.' It took all her effort to hold back her humour for a third time. 'Some of our fellow guests *are* behaving extremely badly.'

His nostrils flared. 'If you were meaning to imply that it is viewing their antics which is to blame for my inappropriate condition—'

'I was not, Benedict.' She placed her hand on his tensed forearm as she looked up at him shyly through the sweep of her lashes. 'Really, I was not.'

He drew his breath in sharply. 'Genevieve—'

'Benedict?'

A nerve pulsed in his tightly clenched jaw.

'Do you have any idea how close I am to dragging you off somewhere and taking you right now, this minute, quickly and explosively, but hopefully also to both our satisfactions?'

Genevieve gave a slight squeak at his honesty. 'You would not dare, Benedict!' She moistened her lips with the tip of her tongue.

'Would I not?' Benedict gave a self-disgusted groan, closing his eyes before passing a hand across them.

'Would you…?'

He lowered his hand, but kept his lids closed over those jet-black eyes. 'At this moment I wish for nothing more than to be alone with you, preferably with a bed near at hand, so that I could do the job properly.'

'The "job", Benedict…?' Genevieve pressed her lips firmly together as laughter threatened once again.

Not at Benedict, but from the euphoria of knowing it was desire for her, Genevieve Forster, that had totally penetrated this handsome gentleman's defences, to the point that Lucifer's cold and legendary control was now balanced upon a knife's edge. That knowledge empowered her, tempted her, to learn more.

He gave a self-disgusted snort as he looked down at her once again. 'Do you have any idea how many ways, and in how many positions, I would enjoy making love to you at this moment?'

'No,' Genevieve answered honestly—how could she have, when she was completely innocent of how many different 'ways and positions' there were in which to make love? 'But it does sound…interesting?'

A nerve pulsed in that tightly clenched jaw. 'You are playing with fire again, Genevieve.'

Yes, she believed that she was. And it was all the more surprising, in view of the fact that Lord Benedict Lucas, Lucifer, was known as being a cold and unemotional gentleman by the majority of the *ton*. But Genevieve trusted him in a way she had never trusted any man. 'Would you prefer that I did not…?'

'No!' Benedict's nostrils flared. 'Perhaps no one will notice if we steal just a few more minutes of privacy!' He stepped forwards to draw her purposefully into his arms, careful to avoid her broken wrist as he did so, the long length of his arousal now pressed intimately against the warmth of Genevieve's thighs as he lowered his head and claimed her lips with his own.

She tasted of wine and honey, her lips soft and yielding beneath Benedict's as he drank his fill of them, not assuaging his desire for her in the slightest, but instead increasing it, to the point that he could feel the pulsing surge and swell of his cock. He gave a low groan in his throat as he felt Genevieve's fingers gently threading into the dark thickness of the hair at his nape, before she deepened the kiss by parting her lips and slanting them more accommodatingly beneath his.

It was, at one and the same time, both heaven and hell.

Heaven, because Benedict had been longing to kiss her again since the moment he had first arrived at her home earlier this evening and looked at her glowing beauty as she obviously anticipated the excitement of the evening ahead.

And hell, because the terrace of Carlton House really was not the place for Benedict to be able to make love to Genevieve as fully, and as thoroughly, as he might wish to do.

Might? There was no 'might' to him at all at this moment, Genevieve's vivacity and sensuality having broken through his defences, so completely and utterly, that it robbed him of any strength or willpower to resist her to the point that nothing else mattered at this moment, but the need to continue kissing her as he enjoyed the perfect fit of the softness of her breast in the palm of his hand.

Genevieve ceased to breathe as she felt the heat of Benedict's hand cupping her breast, squeezing, kneading her aroused flesh, before seeking out the swollen and engorged tip with the soft pad of his thumb, those slow and rhythmic caresses inciting an answering throb that centred between her thighs.

An aching need, which although utterly new to her since meeting Benedict, she already knew he could assuage, that he had already assuaged several times four days ago, with the merest touch of his fingers against that swollen nubbin nestled amongst the red-gold curls between her thighs.

'Sorry to keep you waiting— Ah! Excuse me for intruding. I had not realised! Well. I— you will both accept my apologies, it is to be hoped?'

Genevieve had pulled quickly away from Benedict at the first sound of another man's voice—a slightly accented, foreign voice?—on the terrace behind them, glad to have her back towards that gentleman so that he should not see the deep blush that now coloured her cheeks, or witness that Benedict's hand still cupped the swell of her breast.

Benedict gave a soft groan as he rested his forehead against hers. 'Sorry for ruining our evening, pet,' he murmured so that only she could hear.

Genevieve was equally as sorry to have their interlude together so rudely interrupted. 'The evening is not yet over, Benedict,' she returned equally as softly.

He squeezed his eyes closed briefly before opening them again. 'I am afraid it is over for the moment. I suggest you excuse yourself and go to the ladies' retiring room, whilst I remain here and deal with this unmannered buffoon.'

Genevieve chuckled softly. 'Please try to be gentle with him, Benedict!'

He arched one dark brow. 'Strangulation is out of the question, then?'

'I believe so. Especially so, considering where we are.' She nodded, her eyes once again glowing with laughter. 'Even the Prince Regent would not be able to condone murder taking place upon his own terrace!'

Benedict released her before straightening with obvious reluctance. 'I will rejoin you in the dining room in just a few minutes.'

'I shall look forward to it.' She gave him a last meaningful glance, before turning to bestow a haughty nod to the foreign gentleman who had interrupted them as she moved past him and returned to the dining room with a brisk swish of her skirts.

Benedict's eyes narrowed as he looked across at the man standing slightly in the shadows of the house. 'I believe you have some information for me, *monsieur*?'

'I hope I did not interrupt at a crucial moment—'

'You hope no such thing, Devereaux, otherwise you would not have interrupted at all,' Benedict rasped scathingly. 'Now say what you have to say and then be on your way.'

'Your...haste to return to your lady is—'

'There will be no conversation, either now or in the future, in regard to the lady who has just left us!' Benedict's anger was barely contained.

'She is very beautiful—'

'And absolutely none of your damned business!' Benedict's eyes glittered as hard and black as the jet they resembled. 'Do I make myself clear?'

'Of course.' The other man gave a mocking bow in acknowledgement.

'Well, get on with it, man.' Benedict might have to deal with these traitors to their own country, out of the need to protect his own, but he did not have to respect them for it.

And he was, as Devereux had just remarked, 'in some haste to return to his lady.'

'You have been very quiet these past few hours, Benedict...?'

He turned from where he had been staring broodingly out of the carriage window watching the dawn break, only late-night revellers like themselves returning home in their carriages, and the early morning bustle of traders starting to deliver their wares, travelling the otherwise deserted London streets.

Genevieve's remark, as to his distraction during the latter part of the night, was wholly merited. Benedict had indeed been broodingly silent since his conversation with Devereux.

Understandably so, when it seemed that even now Napoleon still plotted and planned for what surely must be an impossible escape from his incarceration on the remote island of St Helena. Nevertheless, as was always the case, Benedict would pass the information on to Eric Cargill as soon as was possible, so that his godfather might deal with it as he saw fit.

God, how Benedict was starting to hate this constant need for secrecy, this seemingly never-ending deluge of information of Napoleon's machinations for his escape, impossible as most seemed to be, but none of which could be ignored; England and its allies dared not risk allowing the Corsican to escape and run amok for a second time.

He smiled briefly at Genevieve as she continued to look up at him enquiringly. 'I have no idea how Prinny maintains the stamina for such jaded and lengthy entertainments; I find myself exhausted just from having attended!'

Genevieve gave a dreamy smile. 'It truly was just as exciting as I hoped it might be.'

Benedict's smile turned to one of indulgence as he saw the happiness shining in her eyes. 'Then I consider my own boredom with the evening to have been well worth it.'

Mischief glowed once again in Genevieve's expressive eyes. 'I am sure that you—and all the other gentlemen present—did not find the evening quite so tedious when the beautiful Countess of Montgomery decided she was far too hot and began to disrobe completely?'

'She does have rather lovely— Ouch! There was no need to pinch, Genevieve!' He winced as she delivered a painful pinch to his thigh.

Genevieve raised mocking brows. 'Then perhaps you should not remark on the merits of one lady's…attractions when in the company of another?'

'I do not see the harm as long as one does not touch?'

'Perhaps you should tell that to your pinched thigh?' She arched derisive brows.

Light-hearted teasing, as seemed to be the case more often than not whenever Benedict was with Genevieve, was something completely new to him in regard to a woman. His own humour usually ran to mockery or sarcasm, rather than playful bantering, and he found the experience, although slightly alien, to be as refreshing as Genevieve was herself.

'You are right.' He nodded, straight-faced. 'I am sure, when the countess bent down to remove her stockings, that I detected a bulge of unsightly flesh— Ouch! My thigh will be bruised as black and blue as your wrist before this night is over, Genevieve!' He clasped his aggrieved thigh once again just as the carriage came to a stop outside her home.

She turned to him. 'Do you really wish for the night to end quite yet, Benedict?'

He stilled. 'What do you mean…?'

Genevieve suddenly felt extremely shy. It truly had been a magical evening for her. Being introduced to the Prince Regent and basking in his flattering comments. Able to see all the opulence with which he surrounded himself. Observing the glittering array of his strange mix of dinner guests—and their excess of behaviour! Enjoying the bounteous dinner table of the Prince Regent, both visually and gastronomically.

But best of all had been spending the evening at Benedict's side, something Genevieve was finding she enjoyed more and more each time they met.

Not only did she know him to be too honourable a man to ever resort to the physical violence with which she had been treated these past seven years—Benedict was far too confident, both of himself and his attraction, to ever resort to such measures in order to dominate—but he was also entertaining and attentive, yet not suffocatingly so. A single glare from those coal-black eyes had been enough to quell even the most daring of advances made to her by some of the other gentlemen present this evening.

Benedict was also, in Genevieve's opinion, the most handsome gentleman in England. So much so she had felt proud just being at his side, his obvious choice of companion for the evening—much to the chagrin of many of the other female guests, as they gave Benedict admiring and covetous glances and Genevieve envious glares.

It had felt wonderfully exhilarating to know that she, Genevieve Forster, was the lady Lord Benedict Lucas had chosen to spend his evening with, the woman whom he so obviously desired.

As to the heat of the kisses they had shared outside on the terrace…! Genevieve quivered with delight just thinking about them, of how much she wished they had not been interrupted when they had. Although it would perhaps not have been seemly, despite the licentious behaviour of some of the other dinner guests, to have taken their lovemaking any further whilst at the home of their Regent!

Even so, Genevieve felt a little shy in regard to voicing her wish that they might continue that lovemaking now… 'I had thought perhaps you might come into the house and join me in a nightcap? There is something I had wished to discuss with you,' she added quickly as she saw him frown.

'Oh?'

'Yes.' She kept her lashes downcast over her eyes, so that Benedict should not observe the disappointment in them, which she felt in his

not having immediately accepted her suggestion for what it was—an invitation to continue
their lovemaking of earlier. 'It—something
you said to me two days ago, in regard to the
investigation into your parents' deaths, troubled me.'

'Why did you not mention this earlier tonight?'

She shrugged her shoulders beneath her
evening cloak. 'I—it is not a matter in need
of urgent discussion, just something I wished
to discuss with you more fully the next time
we found ourselves alone in private conversation.'

'I see.'

Did Benedict 'see', and was this delay in
answering her his way of indicating he had
no interest in resuming their lovemaking of
earlier this evening?

Genevieve had no experience upon which
she might draw in order to know the answer to
that particular question—betrothed and married before her very first Season had come to
an end had given her little opportunity to understand the workings of a true gentleman's
mind. Her brother, Colin, had been transparent to her from childhood, of course, but in

Genevieve's mind, Josiah and William Forster did not count in the least as being gentlemen!

Whatever the reasoning behind it, she found Benedict's less-than-enthusiastic response to her invitation to be less than flattering to her fragile ego. 'I will understand, of course, if you feel this is not the right time for such a conversation?'

Benedict was not convinced for a moment of that understanding, knew by the edge to Genevieve's tone that she was more than a little piqued that he had not readily accepted her invitation to accompany her inside, for a nightcap or anything else. Under normal circumstances he would have been happy to do so; this constant state of physical frustration was starting to wear a bit thin. But…

There was always a but, it seemed, whenever his actions involved the work he did secretly for the Crown. And, this evening, despite Genevieve's obvious enjoyment of it, had been another occasion when Benedict had needed to be in a certain place at a certain time, in order to receive vital information. A case of mutual needs being satisfied, he had reasoned with himself when he had asked Genevieve to accompany him this evening.

The problem now was what to do with that

information; Devereux had been most insistent it be passed on to the powers that be—in this case, Eric Cargill—at the earliest opportunity. And Benedict was very aware that he had already delayed relaying that information for several crucial hours, as he remained at the dinner party far longer than he needed, because he had been loath to bring Genevieve's enjoyment of the evening to a close.

The temptation to say to hell with it and delay passing along Deveraux's information for several more hours—hours he might spend making love to Genevieve!—was highly tempting. Even if Benedict knew he could not, in all conscience, act upon it... 'I have something else I need to do this morning, but I would be more than happy to return later in the day?'

'Of course.' Genevieve drew back into herself, her expression one of politeness now rather than the mischievous one Benedict had so enjoyed just a few minutes ago. 'I fear I will probably sleep away most of today anyway, following such a late night, so perhaps you might consider calling tomorrow, if you find you can spare the time?'

He winced. 'Genevieve—'

'I really should go in, Benedict.' Her smile

was as coldly dismissive as her tone. 'Thank you again for a wonderful evening. I have enjoyed it immensely.'

Benedict breathed out his frustration with her cool politeness. As if she were thanking a benevolent uncle for taking her on an outing; Benedict did not feel in the least benevolent at this moment, nor did he have any wish to be treated as Genevieve's uncle!

He reached out and laid a hand on Genevieve's as his groom opened the door to the carriage so that she might step down. 'I insist on calling upon you later this afternoon, Genevieve, if that is convenient?'

Her gaze remained distant. 'As you please.'

'Genevieve—'

'I really am very tired, Benedict.'

He wanted to say more, to say something—anything!—which might prevent them from parting in this distantly polite manner. But his oath of secrecy meant he could not tell her the truth of why he must leave her now, and none of the excuses that immediately sprang to mind, to explain his refusal of her invitation, sounded in the least convincing, even to him!

No, Benedict knew he had no choice but to part from Genevieve, knowing that she believed him to be less than eager to make love with her again. Nevertheless… 'I promise I will make it up to you later today.'

'I am sure, when I have already expressed my enjoyment of the evening, that there is nothing you need make up to me for, either later today or any other,' she cut in sharply, her eyes flashing deeply blue. 'Now I really am most fatigued, Benedict, and—and my arm is once again paining me a little, too.'

Damn it, Benedict had all but forgotten about Genevieve's broken wrist and bruised arm in his need to reassure her he was not refusing her invitation, merely delaying it! 'Of course.' He nodded tersely, stepping down from the carriage before her and dismissing the groom to the back of the coach as he turned and helped her down the carriage steps. 'You must call for Dr McNeill again if you feel it necessary.'

Genevieve kept her face averted from Benedict's in an effort not to let him see the tears of humiliation she was sure must, or very shortly would be, glistening in her eyes. 'I am sure that it is only a case of over-exertion and that I shall feel better after a few hours' rest. Goodnight, Benedict.' She gave him another cool nod. 'It really has been a most entertaining evening.'

He sighed heavily. 'Must we part at odds with each other, Genevieve?'

'Why, what on earth do you mean?' Years of hiding her true emotions from both her husband and her stepson—she had refused to give either of them the satisfaction of knowing if she was upset or hurting from anything they had said or done to her—now stood her in good stead as she gave a lightly dismissive laugh. 'Have I not just told you that I had a most entertaining evening?'

Benedict scowled darkly. 'Yes. But—'

'Do you doubt my sincerity?'

'Not in the least. It is only—'

'Really, Benedict, you are making no sense at all. And I had thought it was the ladies who were accused of being contrary!' she taunted.

His mouth tightened. 'Do not pretend to act the tease with me, Genevieve. You are angry with me because I have refused your invitation—'

'I am not in the least angry with you—'

'—and quite rightly so,' he continued determinedly. 'Damn it, I would spend the rest of the night and day with you if I could—'

'I do not believe I asked you to do so—'

'You implied it—'

'I am sure I did not, Benedict. Can it be that you are slightly foxed?' She eyed him disapprovingly.

'You know damn well I barely drank anything at all this evening!' he snapped his impatience.

'Then I can only assume that the rumours about you are correct, and that you really are just arrogance personified!' Genevieve glared up at him indignantly, even as a blush of that humiliation now warmed her cheeks. 'I invited you in for a nightcap as a pleasant way of ending our evening together and you have turned it around in your mind into being something else completely! You then have the gall to imagine I am piqued because of your refusal.' She gave a disgusted shake of her head. 'Goodnight, Benedict.' She tilted her chin disdainfully. 'I sincerely hope that the next time we meet you have remembered your manners!'

Benedict could only stand on the cobbled roadside and watch in frustration as Genevieve walked briskly away from him and entered her house, knowing that there was nothing he could say at this moment that would put matters right between the two of them.

Women came and went in his life—not as often as the *ton* imagined—with never a single moment of regret on Benedict's part when they 'went'.

It was unfortunate that Genevieve was angry with him—and he knew her well enough to know that she was very angry with him, no matter what she might claim to the contrary!—but he could no more allow himself to feel regrets over her than he had any of those other women who had passed so briefly through his life.

Benedict had set himself two missions in life: to work for the Crown and to continue to search for the person responsible for murdering his parents, no matter how long it took, and the complication of a woman such as Genevieve Forster was something he most assuredly did not need or want.

Damn it, he had already allowed himself to be distracted enough by her this evening that he had neglected his other duties by not reporting to Eric Cargill as soon as Deveraux had imparted his information.

If Genevieve wished to be angry with him, then she could damn well stay angry with him, and to hell with her!

Chapter Nine

❧❧❧

'His Grace, the Duke of Woollerton, Lady Amelia Darby, Countess of Ramsey, and Lady Charlotte Darby,' Jenkins announced two afternoons later as he showed three more visitors into Genevieve's gold salon.

Genevieve's already crowded gold salon. At least a dozen other members of the *ton* had already made visits this afternoon, two ladies and four gentleman still gathered there in conversation.

But none of those callers had been Benedict...

He had been noticeably absent both yesterday and today, despite having told her he would call upon her yesterday afternoon. Of course, their last conversation had not been conducive to them being able to exchange pleasantries in front of an audience, but even so Genevieve could not help her inner feelings of disappointment that Benedict had so obviously taken her at her word, and not bothered to call on her at all.

She would certainly have much rather received a visit from Benedict today, despite the humiliation she had suffered at their last conversation, than William Forster, the Duke of Woollerton, accompanied by his fiancée and future mother-in-law!

She had been expecting them, of course, William having sent round a note earlier, informing her of the intended visit. Not asking for her permission, of course, or if it was convenient, but merely stating it was his intention to call this afternoon with the idea of introducing his future bride, and her mother, to the woman who had been married to his father and was now the Dowager Duchess of Woollerton.

Genevieve had suffered a familiar trepidation earlier today when she had received William's note, instantly recognising the seal on the outside of the missive, and knowing that William must now have heard of her visit to Carlton House in the company of Lord Benedict Lucas, and was no doubt intending to berate her by letter before appearing himself to add more stringent—and physical—recriminations. The announcement of his true intention had taken her completely by surprise.

But Genevieve had not allowed herself to become complacent, knew she could not completely rule out William's visit as having two purposes, rather than just the one. Indeed, several of her visitors today had already asked as to her enjoyment of the evening she had spent at Carlton House, and so it would be naïve on Genevieve's part to assume that William had not heard of that evening out, too, as well as the name of her escort, and to expect the worst.

She suppressed those feelings of unease as she dealt with the necessary courtesies and introductions, before taking a closer look, as Charlotte and her mother conversed with one of the other gentlemen present, at the young woman who was shortly to become William's bride.

Genevieve's feelings of misgiving, when William had informed her of the betrothal several days ago, now seemed completely warranted as she found herself looking at a delicate wisp of a girl, fresh-faced and blonde-

haired and blue-eyed, young but certainly not
a beauty, and who did not look capable of saying boo to a goose, let alone standing up to
the bullying William Forster once he became
her husband!

'You appear to have hurt your arm, madam?'

Genevieve briefly cursed herself for allowing her attention to wander as she studied the
young Charlotte Darby, to a degree that, for
once, she had not taken note of William Forster's whereabouts until he now spoke softly
behind her.

She turned to face him, her eyes coldly contemptuous as she looked up into those pale
and triumphant ones. God, how she hated
this man! Hated, as well as despised him. 'As
you are only too well aware, it was not of my
own doing,' she bit out disdainfully. 'And the
doctor believes there is a bone broken in my
wrist.' Her arm was once again resting in the
lace shawl tied at her nape.

William raised a mocking brow. 'How unfortunate.'

Her mouth tightened at his obvious satisfaction. 'Indeed.'

'Perhaps you should take better care in future?' His eyes had chilled. 'Indeed, I believe

I advised as much when I called six days ago? A warning you do not seem to have heeded in the slightest,' he added hardly.

'You are no doubt referring to my having been to dinner at Carlton House?'

'I am referring to your choice of escort for that evening entertainment, madam!'

Genevieve refused to so much as blink in the face of William's obvious displeasure, aware as she was that she was the one facing into the salon, and that William's expression was the one now hidden from the other people enjoying refreshment and chatting amiably. 'As I informed you some days ago, I fully intend to behave in whatever manner I choose. As I also intend to choose my own escorts.'

His pugnacious jaw tightened. 'I expressly forbade you to go anywhere near Lucifer again until after my wedding to Charlotte has taken place!'

'You have no right to forbid me to do anything any more, William. Not that you ever did!' It was this man's bullying of her that had not only resulted in the broken bone in her wrist, but also caused her to irritate Benedict by turning him away from her door, for fear he might see that injury to her arm. 'Neither is this the time nor the place for such a conversation.'

'Would you rather I called back later today, so that we might continue this conversation in private?' His eyes glittered.

Genevieve looked at him coldly. 'I am sure I have made it more than obvious that I would not be in the least concerned if you were never to call upon me again,' she returned insultingly.

William eyed her scathingly. 'Perhaps if you learnt to behave yourself.'

'I am not a child, nor will I any longer be told by you or anyone else what I may or may not do, or with whom I may do it!' Her cheeks were flushed with temper.

He eyed her consideringly. 'Your…friendship with Lucifer appears to have given you the courage you previously lacked,' he finally drawled. 'Let us hope, for your own sake, that this friendship soon comes to an end.'

Her cheeks felt warm. 'I do not consider that my friendship with Lord Benedict Lucas as being any of your business!'

Contemptuous amusement suddenly glittered in those already pale grey eyes. 'Grown bored with you already, has he?' William guessed shrewdly. 'Thrown you over for some other, more obliging woman?'

Genevieve had absolutely no idea how Benedict felt towards her now, although his noticeable absence these past two days would seem to imply that he had indeed grown tired of both her and their tenuous friendship. 'If that is the case, then it is not because of anything you have said or done to me.'

'What does that matter, as long as it is over?' William chuckled unpleasantly.

'You—'

'Lord Benedict Lucas, your Grace.'

Genevieve turned sharply at Jenkins's announcement, just in time to watch as Benedict strode confidently into the suddenly silent room, instantly making her heart rate increase at she took in how dark and broodingly handsome he looked in his usual completely black attire and snowy white linen.

The darkness of Benedict's gaze moved lazily over the other members of the *ton* now openly gaping at him, until it alighted on her and stopped, before then moving on again to narrow on the scowling and obviously displeased gentleman standing at Genevieve's side.

'Lucifer!' William hissed under cover of the

return of the murmured conversation in the room, as Genevieve's other guests obviously became aware that they were staring impolitely at this new—and unexpected—arrival in their midst.

Genevieve's gaze gleamed with triumph as she turned to look briefly up at William. 'So it is,' she murmured with warm satisfaction. 'If you will excuse me? I really must go and greet my new guest.'

'Do not make the mistake of thinking you have heard the last of this, Genevieve,' William warned softly.

Her eyes flashed. 'I advise that *you* do not make the mistake of thinking I will allow myself to be cowed by any more of your threats!' She walked away without so much as a backward glance, her attention now focused completely on the pleasure of seeing Benedict again.

He was here.

It was all that mattered…

Benedict's feeling of impatience—already irrationally high after two days of deliberately staying away from Genevieve, a totally futile gesture, when he had done nothing but think about her instead—had deepened the instant he entered Genevieve's salon and saw all of her other visitors already gathered there.

The darkness of his mood lifted slightly, however, at the look of genuine welcome upon Genevieve's face as she now crossed the room towards him, her pale cream gown a perfect foil for her red curls and ivory complexion, as was the gold-and-cream décor of this elegantly furnished salon.

To Benedict's eyes, Genevieve's face seemed paler than usual, however. Because her arm was still paining her? Or because of the gentleman she had been in conversation with when he entered the room?

Benedict's narrowed gaze shifted back to that gentleman. William Forster, the Duke of Woollerton—and Genevieve's stepson from her marriage to Josiah Forster. Which seemed slightly farcical, considering that the florid and overweight William Forster was noticeably several years her senior. Benedict did not know the other man well, but the little he did know he did not particularly like, and if Woollerton was the reason behind Genevieve's pallor, then that dislike was likely to increase.

'I am so pleased to see you again, Benedict.'

Benedict turned his attention from William Forster as Genevieve greeted him warmly once she reached his side, his expression softening as he looked down into the obvious welcome in her deep-blue eyes. 'And I you,' he returned gruffly, continuing to hold her gaze as he raised her hand to his lips.

She smiled up at him shyly. 'In truth, I was unsure as to whether or not I would ever see you again.'

Benedict drew his breath in sharply as he was once again overwhelmed by her honesty. 'I assure you, there was never any doubt of it being so,' he murmured huskily as he maintained his hold upon her hand.

Her eyes brightened as she continued to gaze up at him. 'I cannot tell you how pleased I am to hear it.'

She did not have to when that pleasure shone in the depth of her blue eyes. 'Damn it, why were we not alone when you said that!' Benedict rasped gruffly. 'I hate such social inanities as this with a passion!' He scowled darkly at the other guests, totally startling the Countess of Ramsey, as she had chanced to cast them a sideways glance before quickly looking away again, two bright spots of embarrassed colour now in her cheeks.

Genevieve laughed softly. 'That remark was

not at all complimentary to my own charms, Benedict!'

He smiled ruefully. 'And after you advised me to bring my manners with me the next time we met!'

Her laughter faded. 'I fear we were at cross-purposes the last time we spoke together, Benedict.'

He gave a shake of his head. 'I believe I am completely to blame for that. For which you have my heartfelt apologies.' He looked down at her intently. 'You look pale, Genevieve—is your arm still paining you?'

'Not at all,' she assured warmly. 'In fact, when the doctor called this morning he assured me that I am healing well, and may even dispense with this silly sling about my arm for several hours a day, when I am either sitting or lying down.'

Benedict raised dark brows. 'That sounds… interesting.'

'Benedict!' Genevieve looked about them self-consciously as the warmth coloured her cheeks.

He chuckled huskily. 'But you blush so very prettily, Genevieve.'

She cast him a reproving glance, an effect totally ruined by the mischievous laughter gleaming in her eyes. 'I believe you must let go of my hand now, Benedict,' she advised softly as she turned to look at her other guests and realised they were still being closely observed, despite the efforts being undertaken not to reveal that observation.

'Must I?'

She nodded. 'I believe people are staring at us.'

'Let them.'

'I would be glad to, I assure you, but I believe we are only giving my other guests reason to gossip.' She cast down long lashes against her cheeks.

Benedict scowled at those other guests as he reluctantly released Genevieve's hand, his gaze settling on Woollerton. 'Your stepson looks as if he has recently swallowed something sour!' The other man looked positively dyspeptic as he glowered across the room at the two of them. 'A second visit in one week, Genevieve; I thought you said that the two of you were not on such socially amiable terms?'

'We are not.' Genevieve's mouth had tightened. 'I believe he merely felt obliged to introduce Lady Charlotte and her mother to me.'

Benedict did not in the least care for the way in which Woollerton was looking down his nose at Genevieve, as if she were an unpleasant insect he wished to crush beneath the heel of one of his highly polished boots. 'Is he intending to invite you to the wedding, after all?'

'I suppose he will have to, if only for appearances' sake.' Genevieve gave a pained frown at the realisation. Bad enough that she'd had to suffer William calling upon her again this afternoon without the possibility of having to keep up this socially polite farce for hours upon end at his wedding next month. 'Perhaps you would care to escort me there, if that should be the case—please, forget I said that.' She gave a self-conscious shake of her head as her gaze now avoided meeting his. 'There is no guarantee that the two of us will even still be talking to each other by next month,' she dismissed lightly.

'We will see each other at Dante and your friend Sophia's wedding next month at least,' Benedict reminded her.

'Of course, yes.'

'And I believe, despite our having witnessed their marriage last week, that Rupert and Pandora are now intending to have a big society wedding later in the summer, too.'

'Really?' Genevieve's eyes lit up with pleasure.

'It would appear so,' Benedict confirmed. 'Having declared his deep love for your friend Pandora, and she for him, Rupert now seems to wish it to be publicly known he is well and truly leg-shackled!'

Genevieve could not have been happier for her two closest friends and sincerely wished them both every happiness with all her heart, the same heart which had minutes ago sunk just at the thought of no longer having Benedict in her life, even as a friend. It was a friendship, she had realised during this past two days of silence from him, upon which she had all too quickly come to depend…

Which was most unwise on her part.

She already knew that Benedict was a man who rebuffed all emotions, apart from the friendships he had with Devil Stirling and Dante Carfax, and that those particular friendships had been forged during their years together in the army. Certainly no woman had ever held Benedict's sexual interest for long, and none of those women had ever retained his friendship once that physical interest came to an end.

Besides which, Genevieve had vowed to herself, when Josiah died and she was finally free to do as she pleased, never to become dependent upon any man again, for anything. Her independence, emotionally as well as financial, was now as necessary to her as the air she breathed—the first free-and-easy air Genevieve had been able to draw for more years than she cared to think about.

She gave Benedict a bright but insincere smile. 'I am very pleased for all of them. Now, if you will excuse me? I fear I have neglected my other guests for quite long enough.'

'Of course.' Benedict had absolutely no idea what thoughts had been running through Genevieve's head these past few minutes, but whatever they had been they did not seem to have been pleasant ones. 'I believe that I shall go and renew my acquaintance with Woollerton.'

Her eyes widened at the suggestion. 'I had thought—you gave me the impression, when last we spoke of him, that you were no fonder of him than I?'

'I am not,' Benedict assured her drily. 'But someone should talk to him, don't you think?' It was noticeable, to Benedict at least, that not even Woollerton's fiancée seemed particularly eager to seek out the other man's company. 'One cannot help but feel sorry for the nervous little rabbit who is to become his wife!'

To Benedict's eyes Lady Charlotte Darby did indeed resemble a scared rabbit, with her pale colouring and wide, ingenuous eyes.

'That is unkind, Benedict.' Geneveive shot him a reproving glance.

'The real unkindness is surely in Ramsey having agreed to his only daughter marrying one such as Woollerton?'

'Possibly.' Genevieve could not help but inwardly agree wholeheartedly with this statement, to a degree that she was still uncertain as to what to do about it, having now had chance to see how very young and delicate Charlotte Darby actually was. Far too much so for her to suffer having such a brute as William Forster as her husband. But for her to interfere, by talking to the Earl of Ramsey of her concerns for his daughter, would result in William's fury. With the result that she might suffer more than just a broken bone in her wrist. 'Viewed with pragmatism, it is surely a good marriage on both sides? He is a duke, she is the daughter of an earl.'

'But?'

Genevieve frowned. 'I cannot help but agree with you that it was not a kindness on Ramsey's part to have accepted William's suit on behalf of his only daughter.'

'Unless it is a love match—no,' Benedict instantly dismissed such an idea. 'Woollerton has neither the looks nor character to incite such passions in one so young and obviously romantically inclined as Charlotte Darby.'

'"Obviously"…?'

He nodded ruefully. 'The chit has been giving *me* cow-eyed glances these past few minutes.'

'Understandably so.' Genevieve chuckled softly. 'You are Lucifer, one of—if not *the*—most handsome and sought-after gentlemen of the *ton*,' she added teasingly as Benedict raised dark and questioning brows.

'Ye gods,' he muttered disgustedly. 'If that is true—'

'Oh, I assure you that it is!'

'—then let me assure you that my own tastes do not run to young ladies barely out of the schoolroom!'

Genevieve looked at him beneath the sweep of her long lashes. 'Then what do they "run to"?'

He arched his dark brows. 'At this moment? A beautiful and widowed duchess.'

A blush brightened the pallor of Genevieve's cheeks. 'I am gratified to hear it.'

Benedict's expression tightened. 'Enough,

dare I hope, to hasten the departure of your other guests with all possible speed?'

She laughed again softly. 'Oh, I believe I might just mention in the next few minutes that my arm is starting to ache and that the doctor has advised I need to rest when that happens.'

'"Resting" is not quite what I had in mind for the remainder of the afternoon and evening,' Benedict growled.

Genevieve's blush deepened. 'I really must go and talk to my guests now—before you have a chance to say anything even more shocking!'

Benedict made no effort to join Woollerton for several minutes after Genevieve had crossed the room to engage the Countess of Ramsey in polite conversation. Instead he simply stood and watched her as she talked easily and charmingly with the older woman, feeling more at ease with himself than he had for the past two days.

Two days, when he readily admitted he had sorely missed their bantering together. As he had felt the loss of Genevieve herself.

Those same two days when Benedict had once again found his thoughts turning far too often to those frustrating memories of their lovemaking, both at Vauxhall Gardens and Carlton House. Both of them occasions when they had come very close—but not close enough for his liking!—to consummating that lovemaking.

'I am not sure that I altogether care for the way in which you are looking at my stepmother, Lucas.'

Benedict's shoulders tensed, his eyes narrowing as he slowly turned to look at William Forster, the Duke of Woollerton, the other man scowling at him, his round face florid in his vexation. 'I do not recall asking for your approval?' he bit out with a chilling softness the other man would have known to be wary of if he had known Benedict better. If he had known Lucifer better...

'I am Genevieve's closest male relative,' the other man reminded him pompously.

'And a poor example of it you are, too, if her broken wrist is any example of the guardianship you have shown her these past weeks!' Benedict eyed the younger man coldly.

The duke's pale grey eyes narrowed suspiciously. 'And what do you know of Genevieve's broken wrist?'

Benedict shrugged. 'Only that she did not,

as she claims, do it by catching the sleeve of her robe upon a door handle.'

'Indeed?' Woollerton gave a mocking smile. 'Then, no doubt, if you are not the one responsible—'

'I most certainly am not and I would advise that you not suggest such a possibility in my hearing again!' The chill warning of Benedict's tone would have silenced any man possessed of even the slightest sense of self-preservation.

Unfortunately, William Forster was far too full of his own self-importance to heed that warning. 'Then I can only assume that one of her other lovers must have been a little too... rough with her during their love play?'

The fact that it had been Benedict's thinking, too, did not detract from the insult just levelled to both himself and Genevieve; Woollerton was implying both that Benedict was a fool, if he believed himself to be Genevieve's only lover, and that Genevieve was nothing more than a trollop because of the existence of those other lovers. It was also designed, Benedict had no doubt, to put the doubt of suspicion into his own mind in regard to Genevieve's fidelity to their own supposed relationship.

And had it succeeded in doing that?

A part of Benedict knew that he and Genevieve should not even have a relationship, not when he had only approached her initially with thoughts of using her as a shield for his real activities during his necessary ventures into society!

Something which they seemed to have moved beyond almost from that very first carriage ride together…

As for whether Woollerton's arrow had met its target…?

If it had, then Benedict had no intention of revealing as much to the other man.

Genevieve felt nothing but relief when she saw the last of her callers finally depart an hour or so later—William, his fiancée, and future mother-in-law had all thankfully departed shortly after the end of his conversation with Benedict.

A Benedict who, thankfully, still lingered in the salon awaiting her return…

It had been something of a strain to maintain her social façade as gracious hostess once she had seen William Forster approach Benedict and the two men had fallen into quiet but intense conversation together. And her unease had not been in the least assuaged by the stiffness of the manner in which those two gentlemen had finally parted some minutes later, William to move across the room to stand silently at the side of his fiancée, Benedict striking a brooding pose by one of the windows, the coldness of his expression not encouraging any present to so much as think of approaching him with the idea of engaging him in conversation.

Leading Genevieve to fear, whatever William's remarks to Benedict might have been, they would not have been in the least complimentary to her...

Chapter Ten

Benedict kept his gaze hooded when Genevieve returned alone to the salon some few minutes later, her guests having now all departed—no doubt some of them discussing his own arrival and continued presence in Genevieve's home!

Gossip was, and ever would be, something Benedict deeply abhorred—possibly because of some of the ridiculous, and scandalous tales, which had followed the unusual death of both his parents—but he doubted Genevieve would feel the same disregard he did...

She was only newly arrived back into society, after her years spent in the country, and much as Benedict had disliked intensely having William Forster question him in regard to his own friendship with Genevieve, it was an indication, at least, of the gossip which was already circulating amongst the *ton* regarding the two of them.

As he was only too aware, Genevieve could be quite determined in her quest for fun and adventure, sometimes without thought for her own reputation. Indeed, it was one of the reasons he had felt he had no choice but to offer to escort her to Vauxhall Gardens; left to her own devices, Genevieve was more likely than not to call on the services of a bounder like Suffolk, and so embroil herself in a scandalous tangle which could result in her total exclusion from society.

But Benedict knew it was not the only reason he had escorted her to Vauxhall Gardens...

Nor was it the reason he was here again today, after telling himself it would be far better, for both of them, if he were to stay well away from the temptation Genevieve Forster constantly presented to him whenever the two of them were together.

Because he wanted her, to such a degree that Benedict found he could think of little else. To the point that he really felt he had no choice—if he ever wanted to sleep at night again!—with regard to seeing her again today.

Worst of all, he acknowledged that his desire for Genevieve was becoming a weakness. And it was a weakness that his enemies could—and surely would—exploit to the full, if they were to realise it existed; indeed, Devereux had clearly given the impression that he already suspected as much at Carlton House. Ergo, the weakness had to be dealt with and then dismissed.

Genevieve had to be dismissed.

Not so easily done when she now crossed the room with her usual graceful elegance, having removed the lace shawl from about her arm whilst out of the room, so that she was now able to hold out both her hands to lightly clasp his. 'It really is so good to have you here again, Benedict.'

He closed his eyes briefly to shut out the effect of the warmth shining in the blue of her eyes. This woman knew no subtlety, played none of the games which other women seemed to so enjoy, but instead blurted out exactly how she felt. About everything, it seemed. And it was as disconcerting as it was refreshing.

Benedict gave a smile as he opened his

eyes. 'I believe, when last we spoke, you had mentioned there was something you wished to discuss with me, in regard to my parents' deaths?'

She looked disappointed. 'And is that your only reason for returning?'

Incorrigible baggage! 'You must know that it is not.' Benedict found himself smiling, the first time he had found reason to do so in days. Not that he was a man usually known for his humorous demeanour. No, that appeared to have come about only when he was in Genevieve's company, otherwise he was known as being somewhat surly of nature. 'But it would seem a place for us to begin...?'

Her laughing eyes looked up challengingly into his. 'To begin what?'

Benedict drew his breath in sharply even as a frown appeared between his eyes. 'Genevieve—'

'I am sorry, Benedict.' She gave a shake of her head. 'I am just so happy—pleased—to see you, to be with you, again.'

He carefully pulled his hands free of hers before answering. 'As usual, your candour does nothing whatsoever to aid a gentleman's self-control!'

Genevieve eyed him teasingly. 'Perhaps

that is because, in your case, I have discovered I have no wish for it to do so?'

'Is it only in my case—forget I said that.' Benedict gave a self-disgusted shake of his head. 'No doubt Woollerton would enjoy knowing that his remarks earlier have had their desired effect!' he added harshly.

All the laughter left Genevieve's expressive blue eyes, the smile fading from her lips. 'And what remarks might they have been?' The lightness of her tone was in complete contradiction to the sharpness of her gaze.

'Nothing of any consequence,' Benedict dismissed impatiently as he moved away abruptly and placed his hands behind his back, annoyed with both himself and Forster for making him sound as if he were a jealous schoolboy in regard to any other men who might currently be in Genevieve's life. 'But you say Dr McNeill is more than satisfied with your progress?'

'Yes.' Genevieve had no interest in discussing the progress, or otherwise, of her injured wrist, knowing by the remoteness of Benedict's expression that she had been right to be filled with apprehension earlier when she saw William Forster deliberately engage him in conversation. 'Benedict, William is—'

'I have no wish to discuss William Forster with you, now or at any other time. The man is a complete bore—'

'But he is a vindictive bore,' Genevieve put in softly. 'And he obviously said something earlier which has…disturbed you.'

'Not in the least,' Benedict dismissed tersely as he stepped impatiently towards her. 'And as you seem no more interested in engaging in light conversation than I, perhaps we should just go straight upstairs to your bedchamber?'

'Benedict!' She took a shocked step back.

He gave a seductive smile as he came to a halt inches in front of her. 'You do not enjoy having your own directness of conversation returned?'

Genevieve had absolutely no problem with Benedict being as direct as she was herself, it was the tone in which he made those comments which now bothered her. Unemotionally. Practically. Disrespectfully…

And Genevieve had no doubts exactly whom she had to thank for the latter! 'William's conversation obviously contained its usual lack of niceties in regard to myself?'

Benedict shrugged his broadness of shoulders. 'As I said, the man is a complete bore.'

Genevieve looked down at her hands as she clasped them together in front of her. 'Perhaps you are right and we should talk of something else.' She forced a smile as she looked at the vase of roses on the low coffee table in front of the chaise. 'I received these beautiful roses from the Prince Regent on the morning following our dinner at Carlton House.'

Benedict's brows rose. He had noticed the vase of fifty or so yellow roses earlier—it was difficult to miss seeing them when they sat in pride of place in the centre of the room! From Prinny. He should have guessed that the Prince Regent would not pass up an opportunity to pay his respects to a young and beautiful widow. Benedict supposed he should feel grateful Prinny had at least had the good sense not to send Genevieve red roses!

'Very nice,' he dismissed drily.

'Four-dozen yellow roses.' Genevieve nodded. 'I did not mistake them for anything more than the politeness they are, of course,' she said softly. 'But I appreciate his having sent them, just the same,' she added as she gazed at them with telling wistfulness.

A gentle reminder, perhaps, that Benedict, unlike so many of her admirers, had not sent her any flowers during their own short acquaintance? Even though he had told her he would not.

Damn it, he never sent flowers to a woman he was bedding, so why would he have sent flowers to Genevieve, whom he was not?

As yet, at least…

He gave an impatient shake of his head. 'I have already told you, if you are expecting to receive flowers from me, Genevieve, bearing insincere messages, then I am afraid you will be disappointed.'

She arched delicate brows. 'Did I say that I thought you lacking in some way?'

His mouth firmed. 'The implication was there.'

'No, Benedict, it was not,' she spoke softly. 'And, unless I am mistaken, we are well on the way to having yet another disagreement. By your own design, perhaps?'

He stiffened. 'Exactly what do you mean by that?'

Genevieve sighed, knowing she was not imagining Benedict's confrontational manner and demeanour. Some of which she had no doubt she owed to William Forster's conversation with Benedict earlier. As for the rest…? She felt sure that was of Benedict's own doing.

Because he did not wish to be here with her at all? Did not wish it, and resented it?

She smiled sadly. 'I have much appreciated and enjoyed our friendship, Benedict, but if you do not wish to continue with it, I will quite understand.'

He began to pace the room. 'You make no sense, woman—'

'I make every sense, Benedict.' Her smile once again became wistful. 'You do not act, or speak, as if you wish to be in my company. Much as I am pleased to have seen you again, I am now giving you leave to go, with the assurance of there being no bad feelings between the two of us. On my part, at least.'

'On my part, either,' he bit out between clenched teeth.

'There.' She gave a gentle nod. 'We are agreed, you will leave now, and even though we shall not be alone together like this again, we shall remain on good terms with each other, if only from a distance.'

Benedict gave a terse shake of his head. 'I have absolutely no idea what that means!'

Genevieve gave an exasperated sigh, wishing that Benedict would depart if that was what he wished to do, before she could no longer maintain this air of quiet dignity. Before she gave in to the emotions simmering beneath her calm demeanour. Rage at William Forster, for one. Disappointment in Benedict, for another.

William, she knew, was vicious by nature, in word as well as deed, and enjoyed nothing more than hurting her. But Benedict—Benedict should know better than to listen to the opinions of a man he did not even like. Especially in regard to a woman he claimed he did like. A woman, he had shown on more than one occasion, he also desired.

She sighed. 'I believe it means that, when we meet again at the wedding of our mutual friends, we shall be polite to each other, if nothing else—'

'I am not feeling very polite at this moment!' Benedict's eyes gleamed as black as jet as he glowered down at her.

She gave a rueful shake of her head. 'I am only too aware of that. But perhaps in time—'

'Time! Genevieve, I have spent the past two days battling my desire for you, to absolutely no avail!'

She blinked up at him. 'You have?'

'I have,' he confirmed grimly. 'And I do not expect that doing so for another two days—

two weeks even!—will have any greater effect!'

Benedict had stayed away from her because he was trying to deny the desire he felt for her?

Genevieve looked up at him searchingly, at last knowing the reason for the lines of strain beside those beautiful black eyes and sensually sculptured mouth, the nerve pulsing in his tightly clenched jaw and the tension in his shoulders, arms and thighs.

Her expression softened. 'If you genuinely feel that way—'

'I do.'

'Then why are we arguing?'

Why indeed?

But Benedict knew exactly why he had battled against his desire for this woman. Against Genevieve herself. Because, although he might try to deny that, too, he knew that she touched that part of him he had thought long buried. Ten years buried. In the same crypt where his parents' bodies lay lifeless and still.

Genevieve reached inside him to the Benedict who had once seen the world with the same wonder and pleasure as she now did. The Benedict who had basked in his parents' adoration of him, as well as the adoration of every young and beautiful woman he met. The Benedict who had been young and happy, and without the cynicism or ruthlessness which were both now such a part of him.

That was why he fought against this desire he felt for Genevieve. Why he fought against and mocked the wonder and enjoyment she seemed to find in everything and everyone. Well…almost everyone—the one exception was William Forster and their dislike of each other was undoubtedly mutual.

Because Forster genuinely disliked Genevieve? Or could the other man's dislike have more to do with the fact that his father had remarried again so late in his life, to a young woman who was not only beautiful, but also of childbearing age, and in doing so had threatened William as being sole heir to the Woollerton fortune, if not the titles?

Whatever his reasons, Forster's dislike of Genevieve had very little to do with Benedict's own contradictory feelings towards her, inasmuch as he wanted to push her away at the same time as he wished to have her so close to him that he had no idea where he stopped and she began!

He gave a self-derisive smile. 'I have absolutely no idea,' he admitted heavily.

Genevieve did not believe Benedict for a moment, had watched the emotions he had been unable to hide as they flickered across his usually unreadable face. Anger. Frustration. Resignation. Not the usual emotions one associated with a lover, she felt sure, but he at last seemed to be at peace with himself when he reached that state of resignation.

She held out her hand to him. 'Then shall we, as you suggested earlier, go upstairs to my bedchamber?'

'Even though I was extremely boorish, and something of an idiot in the way I suggested it?'

Genevieve smiled ruefully. 'Even then.'

Benedict's fingers were firm about her own as he at last took her hand and the two of them left the salon together, to walk through the deserted silence of the entrance hall and ascend the stairs to her bedchamber.

Not laughing together, or filled with excitement as they rushed impatiently up the stairs, as Genevieve had envisaged in both her daytime imaginings, and her night-time dreams, about this particular man. Instead they moved slowly, neither of them making a sound, as if to do so might bring an end to even the tenuous and tense peace that now existed between the two of them.

Which indeed it might when Genevieve's nervousness increased with each step they took, her heart pounding rapidly in her chest, a fine sheen of perspiration on her brow, even breathing becoming difficult as they walked down the hallway leading to her bedchamber.

Because she was not just nervous in regard to what was about to happen—she was terrified! For fear that this time with Benedict might turn out to be just as much of an ordeal as her wedding night had been. And if it should be, if she disappointed Benedict because of what Josiah had done to her—

No, no, *no*!

She must not think about Josiah. Must not allow even the briefest of memories of him, of the horror of her wedding night, to intrude upon this time with Benedict, a man she had come to trust this past week.

She could not allow the past to affect her future, knew now that not all men could be as monstrous as her husband had been, that Benedict certainly was not a monster. She had known only pleasure in his arms, in his touch and his caresses, and there was no reason to suppose she would not do so again.

Dear God, please do not let me fail in this, Genevieve prayed inwardly as the rapid pounding of her heart, to her at least, grew even louder. *I will be good. I will be kind. I will not ask—expect—anything else from You. Just please, please let me have this one time at least, with Benedict, that I may look back on with pleasure rather than pain...*

'Can you be having second thoughts...?'

She turned to look at Benedict once they had entered her sunlit bedchamber and he had closed the door behind him, his expression as unreadable as she hoped her own was as he looked at her beneath hooded lids, and knowing that he must have sensed her trepidation, if not her fear. 'Why on earth should you think that?' She infused a lightness to her tone which she was far from feeling, the sun shining brightly in the windows adding to her nervousness.

It had been late evening when Benedict had made love to her at Vauxhall Gardens, with only the golden glow of the lanterns overhead to see by; what if Benedict did not like her naked body in the daylight? If he saw some blemish there that he found unattractive and unsightly?

'Possibly because,' Benedict answered

her ruefully, 'you are now looking at me as if you expect me to rip the clothes from your body and ravish you where you stand— Genevieve...?' His tone sharpened as he saw the way her eyes had widened with apprehension. 'I trust you know me well enough to realise that I would never behave in such a loutish fashion towards a lady?'

'Of course.' Genevieve forced the tension to ease from her body as she smiled up at him, knowing that it was too late for her to be concerned as to whether or not Benedict would still like her body in the daylight. Far too late... 'I was merely fearful for my new gown,' she dismissed softly. 'It is very pretty and only arrived from the dressmaker this morning, and I should not like to lose it quite so soon!'

Benedict smiled indulgently. 'In that case, I suggest you allow me to remove it, and put it to one side, before we progress any further?'

She moistened the dry stiffness of her lips before answering him. 'I believe I should like that.' She turned her back obligingly.

Benedict knew he would 'more than like it', that he had been anticipating, aching, for this moment since he arrived at the house almost two hours ago!

Even so, he was surprised to note that his hands were actually shaking slightly as he moved to stand behind Genevieve and began to slowly unfasten the buttons down the length of her spine, pushing the material aside to reveal that she wore a gossamer-thin white camisole beneath the gown, which did little to conceal the creamy delicacy of her pearly skin, thin ribbon straps crossing over the slenderness of her shoulders.

'Benedict...?' Genevieve voiced her uncertainty as Benedict paused, arrested by the vulnerability of her nape as she bowed her head slightly forwards.

He stepped close behind her, warmed by the heat of her body as he bent his head slightly to touch his lips against that delicate vulnerability. She tasted of a heady combination of flowers and honey. 'You are so beautiful, Genevieve...' His hands rested on the slenderness of her hips and he pulled her back against him as his lips now travelled the length of her throat.

Genevieve quivered as a multitude of sensations swept through her; relief that Benedict did not find her unsightly so far, hot and cold shivers running up and down the length of her spine at the feel of his lips against her heated flesh, causing her skin to tingle, the fine hairs on her arms to rise and a dampness to her palms as she fought her rising trepidation.

Her breath caught as Benedict slipped one of the ribbon straps of her camisole from her shoulder before she felt those warm and sensuous lips against her bared flesh, groaning low in her throat, her head falling back against his shoulder as his hands moved slowly up her abdomen, igniting a fire wherever he touched, before those same hands cupped beneath her breasts. 'Benedict...!' Her groan became a keening cry as he ran the soft pad of his thumbs across the aching tips, infusing her with a heat that travelled quickly down to between her thighs.

Just looking down at those golden-skinned hands as they cupped and kneaded her breasts, thumb and finger gently squeezing the engorged and rosy tips visible through the thin material of her camisole, made her ache with longing, with a need for the same overwhelming pleasure Benedict had shown her she was capable of feeling.

'Benedict.' She straightened her spine to move slightly forwards and away from Benedict before slowly turning to face him. 'You are wearing far too many clothes,' she explained huskily at the question she could see in the jet of his eyes. 'May I…?' She reached up with the clear intention of removing his jacket.

'Gods, yes!' A nerve pulsed in Benedict's tightly clenched jaw as he stood perfectly still in order to allow Genevieve to remove his jacket before unbuttoning his waistcoat, his hands clenching at his sides as she removed that before unfastening his neckcloth and disposing of that, too. He was able to feel the slight trembling of her fingers against his flesh as she unbuttoned his shirt before touching, caressing, the heated flesh beneath, his chest softly rising and falling as he found it difficult to breathe. 'Take it off, Genevieve, please!' Benedict longed to feel those caressing fingers against his bared chest.

Her gaze held his as she pulled the shirt from the waistband of his pantaloons, bending forwards slightly to place her lips against his hot and burning skin as she pulled the material slowly upwards, her little pink tongue a rasping caress against his sensitised flesh.

Benedict pulled the shirt up impatiently over his head before discarding it completely, his breathing becoming laboured as he felt the rasp of that little moist tongue against his nipple, licking, at his now pebble-hard little nubbin. 'Will you let down your hair for me, love?' Several curling red-gold tendrils had already escaped the confines of their pins and now lay silkily against her nape, inducing a longing in Benedict to entangle his fingers in that silky softness as she continued to pleasure him with her lips and tongue.

Her eyes were a deep and hypnotic blue as she raised her head to look at him. 'You may do it for me if you wish, Benedict...' she invited softly. 'There are but three pins at my crown,' she added helpfully before returning to her sensual ministrations of his muscle-defined chest, her fingers a light caress against the heated skin of his back as she turned the attention of her tongue and teeth to his other nipple.

'Dear Lord...!' Benedict groaned low in his throat as he felt the nip of those little white teeth against his roused flesh, causing his cock to surge eagerly both up and forwards beneath his pantaloons and his fingers to fumble slightly as they sought the three pins that secured Genevieve's hair.

She glanced up at him beneath long lashes. 'Am I hurting you? Do you wish me to stop?' There was no teasing or tormenting in her tone, only that trepidation he could see in her eyes.

'Gods, no!' Benedict breathed harshly again as his hand cupped the back of her head to tug her close again. 'I do not want you to ever stop, Genevieve!' His fingers found the last of the pins securing her hair as he once again felt the soft rasp of her tongue against him, allowing those soft red-gold curls to cascade down on to her shoulders before falling halfway down the length of her slender spine. 'Magnificent…!' he breathed hoarsely as he at last tangled a long length of those silky curls about his fingers. 'I have never seen such beautiful hair as yours,' he assured gruffly as he looked down at her in wonder.

Genevieve's lips curved against him as she smiled her pleasure at his compliment, her earlier feelings of nervousness beginning to ease. If not completely…

She knew there was still so much more to lovemaking than she had so far shared with Benedict. So very much more. And she so hoped, fervently prayed, that she would not lose her nerve before that should happen—

'Genevieve…?'

She was very aware that another shuddering quiver had swept through her before she could call a halt to her panicked thoughts, no doubt alerting Benedict to her predicament, although she hoped not the reason for it. She smiled tentatively as she looked up at him. 'I am a little cold. Perhaps we should finish undressing quickly and get beneath the bed-covers?'

'If that is what you wish…' A frown creased Benedict's brow at Genevieve calling this sudden and unexpected halt to their lovemaking. She did not feel cold to his touch, in fact the opposite; her skin was ablaze with heat, her cheeks flushed, a slight feverishness to the blue of her eyes.

'I believe it is.' She stepped back and away from him before walking over to the bedside, her back still turned towards him as she slid the remaining strap of her camisole quickly down her arm before allowing the garment to fall to the carpeted floor, giving Benedict a brief glimpse of the delicate arch of her naked spine and the firm curve of her bottom before she slid quickly beneath the bedcovers and that nakedness was completely hidden from him as she pulled those covers up to her chin.

Almost as if Genevieve were shy of revealing her nakedness in front of him…

Benedict shook his head at his own fanciful thoughts. Of course Genevieve was not shy, she had been married for six years and a widow for one—a year during which he very much doubted she had spent all of her nights, or her days, completely alone in her bedchamber. No, Genevieve must, as she claimed, just be slightly chilled.

And he knew the way in which he intended to warm her. How they would warm each other…

Chapter Eleven

Genevieve clutched the bedcovers beneath her chin, watching Benedict as he slowly sat down on the end of the bed to remove his boots before standing up again to face her, the darkness of his gaze holding hers as he slowly removed the rest of clothes. Hose. Pantaloons. Drawers…

Her breath caught in her throat as he straightened after removing the latter, the darkness of his hair rakishly tousled, his naked flesh that same golden hue all over as he was bathed in the warmth of the sunlight shining in through the windows of her bedchamber. The width of his shoulders. His muscled chest covered with its light dusting of dark hair. The flatness of his abdomen. Down the long length of his legs, and even his long and elegant feet.

Her gaze moved up slowly from those feet to his ankles, his calves, his knees, thighs, and finally to his—

Genevieve stopped breathing altogether as she finally looked at the long length of Benedict's arousal, long and proud as it jutted upwards from the thick thatch of silky dark curls, and so wide she doubted she would be able to span it with her fingers.

She was allowing herself to think too much! Benedict had been kind and considerate during their lovemaking to date. There was no reason to suppose that would ever change.

'Genevieve…?'

'Yes…?' She looked at Benedict now with wide and startled eyes, swallowing hard as she saw the questioning look on his harshly handsome face.

Benedict gave a frown. 'You seem…nervous. As if you were unsure of me? Of this?'

The lightness of her laugh was supposed to sound dismissive, but even to her own ears it sounded strained. 'You are being fanciful, Benedict. Come. Join me…' She threw back the bedcovers beside her enticingly, at the same time as she kept the ones on her side of the bed pulled tightly over her own nakedness, watching now as Benedict strolled slowly round to the other side of the bed, the darkness of his gaze never leaving hers.

As Genevieve's gaze remained firmly fixed on his; she could not, dared not, look at the evidence of his arousal for a second time, knew that her control over her nerves was now stretched to such a point of breaking that it might snap altogether if she did so.

She could do this. She *must* do this, if she were ever to find any shred of normality in her personal life.

Normality…

What did she know of normality between a man and a woman? Married at eighteen, to a monster of a man who had raped her on their wedding night, and allowed—no, encouraged!—his own son to beat her during the miserable six years that had followed, whenever Josiah considered she had committed the merest infringement of his rules in regard to what he expected of her behaviour.

Just being in Benedict's company this past two weeks had shown Genevieve that was not the normal behaviour of a gentleman towards a lady, even one newly met, let alone the woman to whom you were married. As for their lovemaking! Benedict had thought only of Genevieve, of her pleasure, during their times of intimacy together.

As, she hoped, he would do so again today.

'Are you going to release your death grip on the bedsheets and allow me to look at you, pet?'

She smiled tentatively as Benedict lay down on the bed beside her before turning on his side to look at her teasingly, having made no effort to pull the bedcovers up over his own nakedness, that nakedness so much more— more immediate, now that she could feel the actual heat of his body only inches away from her own. 'It is only that it is the middle of the afternoon, and that I am feeling…a little shy.'

'You have no reason to be.' One of Benedict's hands moved to cup the side of her face. 'You are very beautiful, Genevieve,' he assured gruffly, his breath a warm caress against her throat as he lowered his head to kiss her there, his lips a silky caress against her flesh. 'Every part of you that I have been privileged to see is deliciously feminine and desirable.'

She thankfully felt some of her icy fear melt under the warmth of Benedict's approval.

'Perhaps we should not talk further but just—just—'

'Just…?' Benedict prompted lightly as his lips now travelled the length of her creamy throat down to the hollows beneath.

'Cease teasing and kiss me, Benedict!'

Benedict enjoyed teasing this beautiful and unexpectedly shy woman, found that shyness entirely adorable after the years of bedding women who were usually as experienced and cynical as he in regard to their own physical gratification. Genevieve, in contrast, held an air of mystery for him, the feeling of caressing and making love to and with a woman who held hidden depths of passion not yet explored.

Which was indeed fanciful of him when Genevieve had been married for six years…

Nevertheless, Benedict could feel the tension in her as he took Genevieve fully into his arms to claim her lips with his own, deepening, lengthening that kiss as his own desire for her soared higher at the first touch of those full and sensuous lips beneath his own.

As usually happened when Benedict kissed her, Genevieve's misgivings began to dissipate. The dark hair on his head feeling soft and silky to the touch as her fingers became entangled in its long length, her breasts crushed against the hardness of his chest, the softness of hair there a pleasurable abrasion against her sensitised breasts. The heat and overwhelming feelings of desire and trust she had for this man once again taking precedence over everything else as she parted her lips to allow for the thrusting possession of his tongue into the heat of her mouth.

One of his hands, those warm and sensual hands, roamed freely across her naked curves—her back, the arch of her spine, the globes of her bottom—before moving up to cup her breast, squeezing, kneading that soft orb before rolling the nipple between finger and thumb. Genevieve was at once engulfed in that now-familiar heated pleasure that coursed through her hotly, warming and dampening between her restlessly parted thighs and causing the tiny nubbin there to throb and ache.

An ache Benedict immediately satisfied as his hand travelled down the curve of her waist and hips before moving surely between her thighs, caressing, stroking that heat to a fire that blazed out of control almost at his first touch. That *did* blaze out of control as he continued to caress her whilst at the same time one long finger penetrated her sheath and began to thrust into that moist heat.

The pleasure that ripped through Genevieve was almost painful in its intensity, Benedict continuing to thrust and caress her as her inner muscles convulsed in a lengthy and pleasurable climax.

'You are beautiful, Genevieve!' Benedict wrenched his mouth from hers to move down her body and suckle deeply, strongly, on her engorged nipple, prolonging her pleasure, her eyes squeezed tightly shut as her hips bucked and surged instinctively. 'So very beautiful...!' Benedict lifted his lips from her breast, moving down the bed as he kissed his way slowly over the dip of her abdomen, the curve of her hip, before settling between her parted thighs, lowering his head and gently claiming that most sensitive spot with the slow rasp of his tongue.

'Benedict...!'

'Shh, love,' he soothed as he looked up to see that Genevieve had shot up into a sitting position and now looked down at him with alarm.

'But—but— That is—I have never— Is it quite correct for you to—to—?'

'Nothing is forbidden between lovers, Genevieve,' he assured soothingly even as he felt a surge of satisfaction in hearing that no other man had ever kissed Genevieve with such intimacy.

What an old stick in the mud old Josiah Forster must have been not to have introduced Genevieve, his young and beautiful wife, to this particular sensual delight. As for her other lovers…! Genevieve had obviously not chosen well there, either, if they had never loved her in this highly satisfying fashion.

'Nothing, love.' He held her gaze with his as he once again rasped his tongue across her sensitive and swollen nubbin and heard her gasp even as her cheeks flushed a becoming pink. 'No part of you is forbidden to me, as no part of me is forbidden to you. You may touch and caress any part of me that you choose. As I will touch you…' He allowed the tips of his fingers to graze her swollen folds before moving lower still, caressing, stroking, and able to feel Genevieve's response to those caresses as she shuddered and trembled with renewed arousal. 'You are beautiful here too, Genevieve. Utterly. Erotically. Beautiful.' He lowered his head again.

Genevieve's head felt back against the pillows as she relaxed into the ecstasy of those caresses. She had never known such intimacy as this existed. That such pleasure as this existed. She felt both cherished and completely claimed at the same time, as that pleasure once again spiralled and rose out of all control.

She moved restlessly into those exploring lips and fingers, wanting, needing—oh God, *hungering* for more of the pleasure Benedict had already given her. That he gave her again as Genevieve once again became lost to those waves of heat and fire, and her body convulsed and shook in a long and tortuous release that left her breathless.

'Will you touch me now, pet?'

She finally lifted heavy lids to find Benedict gazing down at her with a look of indulgence and satisfaction as he lay beside her. 'If you wish me to…?'

He arched a teasing brow. 'As desperately as I need to draw my next breath.'

Her earlier embarrassment at her own nakedness was forgotten as she moved up on to her knees beside him. 'That seems only fair, when you—you have twice made love to me now and I have as yet had no opportunity to—to touch you.'

Benedict's smile widened even as he lay back against the pillows, arms behind his head as Genevieve moved to kneel between his splayed legs, her breasts firm and uptilting, and tipped by those rosy nipples. 'You may touch wherever the fancy takes you, love,' he invited again gruffly.

She moistened her lips with the tip of her tongue. 'And you will like it?'

'Anywhere and everywhere,' he repeated softly.

Benedict very quickly had reason to regret that largesse as, after her initial hesitation, Genevieve took him completely at his word, with one of her hands immediately cupped beneath his sac as her tiny fingers encircled and caressed the heaviness of his erection before he felt the soft and moist rasp of her tongue along its length before encircling and stroking against the swollen and bulbous ridge above.

Benedict drew his breath in sharply even as his fingers clenched into the pillows beneath his head, able to feel the heated surge of moisture that escaped his control as it pulsed down the length of his shaft before instantly being lapped up by the rasping heat of Genevieve's tongue as her hand continued to cup the tightness of his sac. Her fingers were a light caress along the length of his pulsing shaft as she repeated that caress with her tongue again and again, emitting a low and satisfied purr deep in her throat.

'You have to stop now, love!' Benedict reached down to grasp her wrists, unable to stand a moment more of this pleasurable torture, knowing that if Genevieve did not stop now that he would release himself into the heated cavern of her mouth.

'You did not like it, after all...?' She frowned her uncertainty.

His smile was self-derisive. 'I just need to be inside you now, Genevieve.' He sat up to lower her on to the bed beside him. 'I want to feel you around me, taking me, when I find my own pleasure.' His voice had lowered gruffly just thinking about finally being inside Genevieve. 'Open up for me, love,' he encouraged teasingly as she kept her knees firmly together despite his gentleness.

Genevieve could not move!

Those earlier fears, those feelings of panic, had now returned with a vengeance, totally erasing the wondrous pleasure she had so recently found in being caressed by and caressing Benedict. Only that panic and fear now remained, stiffening her limbs to ice, numbing her brain, just at the thought of the painful invasion she knew was about to come.

It did no good telling herself that Benedict was not Josiah. That Benedict had never hurt her, but only given her pleasure. The memory—the pain and humiliation of her wedding night—was too predominant still in her mind. Too raw, too much a part of her, for Genevieve to be able to accept what was about to happen.

Benedict stilled as he looked down and saw the fear in the darkness of Genevieve's eyes as she gazed up at him with wide-eyed apprehension, her cheeks sudden pale. Fear? Was it possible that Genevieve did fear him after all? But why? What had he done that could have so alarmed her about their lovemaking just now, that she should look at him in this way?

He gave a puzzled shake of his head. 'Genevieve…?'

She moistened the stiffness of her lips before speaking. 'I— Do not be concerned about me, Benedict. I know—I accept that you must now do what needs to be done.'

Benedict barely breathed. 'And what is that exactly…?'

She gave a slight shake of her head. 'I realise—understand, that you need to—that you must now put your—your hardness inside me to achieve your own pleasure—'

'I neither need nor must do anything, Genevieve,' he cut in softly. 'I ache to make love to you, yes, but it is not something I would ever wish to do without your full consent, without knowing of your own enjoyment of whatever we choose to do together.' He gave a pained frown. 'In truth, I believe I am somewhat insulted that you might imagine I would ever do such a thing.'

Something was not right here. Benedict had no idea what that something was as yet, but he would be a fool if he did not realise that Genevieve was not that woman seeking 'fun and excitement' in her life, or that teasing woman of earlier today, nor the responsive lover of just a few short minutes ago; she was now a woman with fear, terror, in her eyes!

She blinked. 'It was not my intention to ever insult you.'

He gave a pained frown. 'And yet I find I am insulted.'

Her throat moved convulsively. 'And angry.'

Yes, Benedict was angry. But at whom he was as yet unsure…

One thing was for certain, it was not Genevieve.

Nor, he found, could he even think of making love to a woman who looked as terrified as she now did. A fact his rapidly softening cock appeared to have recognised well before he had!

Benedict fell down on to the bed beside Genevieve, his arm thrown across his eyes as he lay there drawing deep and steadying breaths into his lungs, trying to make sense of what had just occurred. Genevieve had seemed happy just now, even eager, to enjoy their lovemaking. Admittedly neither her husband, nor any of her previous lovers, appeared to have shared any of the more intimate delights of lovemaking with her, but Benedict had found a certain satisfaction in being the first man to experience Genevieve's responses to having his mouth upon her.

Where had it all gone wrong? One minute he had been talking of the anticipated delight of being inside her, and the next she had been talking of 'accepting what he must do' to her. As if—

Benedict removed his arm from over his eyes to slowly turn and look at her. 'Genevieve…?'

She had pulled the covers back up to her chin, her face appearing all tear-wet blue eyes as she continued to watch him apprehensively. 'I am sorry if I have d-disappointed you.' Her bottom lip trembled precariously. 'I kn-knew from the f-first that I am n-not what you are—

are used to. I had h-hoped—I—I so much
w-wanted not to d-disappoint you—'

'Why do you keep using that word, "disap-
point"?' The hand Benedict had raised to cup
her cheek stilled in mid-air as she flinched
away from him instinctively. 'I was not going
to strike you, Genevieve.' He moved up on
to his elbow to look down at her searchingly.
'Did your husband beat you?'

'Not after that first night. He was not
able—' She gave a fierce shake of her head
as the tears began to fall down her cheeks. 'I
do not wish to talk about that, Benedict.'

'But—'

'I will not talk about this any more, Benedict,' she insisted fiercely as she scrabbled to
the side of the bed, taking the sheet to cover
her as she stood up to reach for her robe where
it lay draped across the chair. 'I would ask that
you leave now.' She kept her back towards him
as she dropped the sheet to pull on the robe
and tie it tightly about the slenderness of her
waist before releasing the fiery cascade of her
curls from beneath the collar and then thrusting her hands into the pockets.

Leave? Now? When Genevieve had not answered a single one of Benedict's questions to
his satisfaction? 'I do not think so,' he told her

firmly even as he swung his own legs to the side of the bed to pull on his shirt and pantaloons before standing up.

Genevieve turned just in time to see Benedict fastening his pantaloons before he straightened and looking so—so fiercely male, so intensely beautiful, that her heart skipped a beat just looking at him. She had wanted this so much, had wanted Benedict so much, and instead she had only discovered that she was irrevocably damaged by the past. By *her* past. A past which had nothing to do with Benedict.

Her hands bunched into fists in the pockets of her robe. 'You should go now, Benedict,' she repeated softly. 'And never come back.'

'Explain to me what just happened, Genevieve. Talk to me, damn it!' He ran a hand through the already tousled darkness of his hair, his eyes as black and as unfathomable as a night sky.

She gave a sharp shake of her head. 'I cannot.'

'You must!' he groaned as he crossed the room in long strides to stand only inches in front of her, not touching her, but overwhelming her by his close proximity none the less. 'What did Woollerton do to you?' he demanded harshly.

Her face became even paler. 'William...?'

Benedict had meant the father, Josiah Forster, the previous Duke of Woollerton and Genevieve's husband. But... 'Father or son. What did they do to you?'

Once again her tongue moved nervously across her lips. 'Josiah was my husband.'

'I am well aware of what he was.'

'Then you must also know that the law provides little protection for a wife in any marriage!' Her eyes flashed in anger at his persistence. 'That she is nothing more than another piece of property, a possession, and subject to her husband's whims and fancies.'

A pulse beat rapidly in Benedict's tightly clenched jaw. 'Which in Josiah Forster's case were...?'

Genevieve gave a firm and determined shake of her head. 'I swore I would never talk of it to anyone.'

'Swore to whom?'

'Myself!' She glared defensively up at Benedict now.

Benedict stared down at her with an equal amount of frustration, knowing by the almost desperate look in Genevieve's eyes that she was not being difficult or unnecessarily stubborn, but that the details of her marriage to

Josiah Forster really were too painful for her to remember, let alone talk about.

His eyes narrowed. 'You said that your husband did not hurt you "after that first night"… You are referring to your wedding night?'

Her gaze skittered away from meeting his as she worried her top lip between her tiny white teeth. 'I doubt any woman recalls losing their virginity with any degree of pleasure.'

'I do not believe it should ever be so painful that a woman cannot bear to talk about it—'

'And what would you know about it, Benedict?' Genevieve rounded on him fiercely. 'What does any man *care* to know about it as long as he may take his own pleasure?'

'I would care!'

Her breasts quickly rose and fell as she breathed her agitation. 'Women are nothing but a receptacle for a man's pleasure. A convenient and warm hole for him to—'

'That is enough, Genevieve!' Benedict rasped harshly at her deliberate crudeness. 'Did I behave towards you like that today? At Vauxhall Gardens? Have I ever, in any way, treated you with less than the care and gentleness you deserve?'

Her cheeks flushed hotly. 'You—'

'Did I take my pleasure just now?' he continued softly. 'When you showed hesitation, spoke of your uncertainty, did I continue to make love to you as if you had not voiced those concerns? As if what you wanted was of no matter to me?'

Genevieve could no longer meet the fierceness of his dark gaze. 'You know you did not.'

'And so?'

'Can you not see that it does not make any difference?' The heat of her tears began to fall unchecked down her cheeks now. 'I believed, after our time together at Vauxhall Gardens, that it would be different with you. That, because I have come to trust you, I would be different with you. That I would be able to—able to—' She broke off as the tears fell so heavily she could no longer speak coherently. 'Please go, Benedict,' she pleaded. 'Please!'

Instead of hearing his footsteps departing, she felt the warmth of his arms engulf her as he drew her tenderly against his chest and held her to him gently. 'I cannot, Genevieve. Not until you have told me what the bastard did to you!'

If anything she sobbed harder, deeper, the slenderness of her body trembling as she glared up at him. 'My husband raped me on our wedding night! But first he beat me. Then he threw me on to the bed, ripped my night-gown from my body before he ripped into me. There. Is that what you wished to know, Benedict? What you wished to hear?'

Chapter Twelve

Was that what Benedict wished to hear…?

Did Genevieve really believe that he wished to hear of any man, any husband, beating his wife—beating Genevieve!—and then raping her on their wedding night? On any night?

Benedict was so angered at hearing of it now, seven years after the event, that if Josiah Forster were not already dead then he would have taken great pleasure in killing the other man himself!

As it was he still felt like seeking out the man's grave and running a sword through the bastard's coffin, just to make sure he was definitely dead.

Which might help to appease some of his

own angry frustration, but was not of the least comfort to Genevieve…

'Or perhaps, as he was my legal husband, his to do with as he wished, you do not consider it rape?' she murmured heavily at Benedict's silence. 'Or believe, as Josiah did, that he had every right to beat and abuse me as he wished once I was his wife.'

'No, Genevieve, I do not believe that for a moment.' Benedict kept his raging anger towards Josiah Forster under firm control as he answered her softly, knowing that Genevieve needed that gentleness now, that she was so distressed by talking of these past events that she was likely to misinterpret his anger as being directed towards her.

And how could Genevieve possibly imagine that he might be angry with her? She had been but eighteen years old when she had married Josiah Forster, a man almost forty years her senior, and moreover one who had already buried one wife; knowing what he did now, Benedict could not help but wonder if the previous Duchess of Woollerton had not chosen to die out of self-defence, as her only means of escaping the clutches of her brutal husband!

'Let's sit down over there, love, and talk quietly together,' he suggested gently as he gathered Genevieve up into his arms before lowering his lean length into the bedroom chair beside the window. 'Lean against me, love,' he encouraged as she held herself stiffly in his arms. Benedict waited until some of the tension had eased from her body, her head resting against his shoulder, before speaking again. 'I want—I should like it very much, Genevieve, if you were able to tell me everything about your marriage,' he spoke soothingly.

'Everything?' She sounded doubtful.

'If it will not distress you too much to do so.'

Would it distress her too much, Genevieve wondered, or would the relief of sharing with someone those horrible years of being Josiah's wife, perhaps help to ease some of the aching burden she had carried in her heart for so long?

It was difficult for her to think at all when she was cradled within the comfort and strength of Benedict's arms. When she knew, by the gentleness he now showed towards her, that whatever she told Benedict of the past, he would listen without comment or judgement.

She had known instinctively from the first that Benedict was not a man who would ever use brute strength against a woman to attain his own ends, least of all in the bedchamber; she did not believe she would have learnt to trust Benedict if she had thought that would ever be the case!

Even so, she was not sure she could relive those memories of her wedding night, or those bleak and unhappy years that had followed...

'Please, Genevieve,' Benedict spoke gruffly, persuasively. 'I do not ask this of you lightly, or with any intention of causing you further pain—God forbid I should ever do that!' he added grimly. 'It is only so that I will know in future how—how not to hurt you again.'

Genevieve looked up at him uncertainly. 'In future?'

Having decided before coming here that he would spend only this one afternoon in Genevieve's bed, before walking away from her never to return, Benedict surprised himself by now talking to her of the future...

But how could he ask her to talk to him of the past, listen to everything Genevieve had suffered at her husband's hands and then just walk away from her? He could not. Knew that to do so would hurt Genevieve even further and deeply wound the chrysalis of the self-composed and confident woman she was striving so hard to be, and in ways he did not even care to think about.

No, despite what he might have decided before coming here today, he would not walk away from Genevieve now.

'Grateful as I am for your concern, Benedict, I do not need or require your pity.'

'That is as well—because you do not have it,' he rasped forcefully.

'No?'

'Most certainly not!' Benedict assured firmly.

And she did not, he realised with dismay, knowing that his reasoning just now had been at fault. The truth was he wished to spend more time with Genevieve, to be her lover, to share with her the depth and warmth of lovemaking rather than the memories she now had of it, and for as long as it pleased her to do so.

'Genevieve, I do not pity you,' he repeated huskily. 'I admire and respect you for the graciously beautiful woman you are, despite all that you have suffered.' He placed his hand gently against her cheek as he guided her head back down on to his shoulder. 'Now talk to me, love, and I promise I will listen without comment,' he assured.

A promise Benedict very quickly discov-

ered he should not have made as Genevieve
told him of her brother's debts that had caused
her to marry Josiah Forster, of those painful
years of being his wife, haltingly at first, and
then more quickly, more fiercely, as her own
inner outrage at her treatment took over her
narrative.

A rage that Benedict very quickly under-
stood—and more than equalled!—as he listened to the way in which Josiah Forster had
tricked Genevieve into marrying him by
promising to pay off her brother's gambling
debts, and then refused to honour that debt
before the ink was even dry on the marriage
certificate. A refusal which had later resulted
in the suicide of Genevieve's brother, the last
of her close family, and so leaving her completely alone and defenceless against Josiah
Forster and his equally repulsive son, William.

Her wedding night had been even more horrific than Benedict could ever have imagined.
Beaten by her husband, raped by him, Genevieve had then had to endure having that husband suffer a fit whilst committing that rape,
resulting in his collapsing upon her as a dead
and unmovable weight, and causing her further humiliation as she had to cry out for the
help of the servants and her stepson, William,

to aid in her husband's removal, both from her body and her bed.

'He remained paralysed down one side of his body for the rest of his life,' Genevieve added huskily. 'Unable to walk or talk properly, to so much as eat without the food dribbling down his chin and soiling his clothing. Disabilities for which he held me completely accountable.'

'You?' Benedict repeated disbelievingly.

She gave a shaky sigh. 'He said I was the devil's spawn. That it was the temptation of my—my beauty, my body, which had led him to commit the sin of lust and as a consequence for him to be punished for that sin by being paralysed, so preventing him from ever being tempted again.'

'He—but—' Benedict stared down at her. 'Your marriage was never— The two of you never again—'

'No.' Her lashes remained downcast. 'Oh, he tried, several times, but he—I—'

'You do not need to tell me any more on that subject, Genevieve,' Benedict cut in quickly, completely sickened by imagining in what way Josiah Forster might have 'tried, several times' to take Genevieve's body again. And furious at the other man's cruelty to a young

girl, his own bride, whose only sin was to be
beautiful and desirable.

She shuddered in his arms. 'I see no reason not to tell you all now that I have begun.'

Genevieve had only begun to tell him of
her husband's cruelties to her?

Benedict was unsure if his own stomach
could take listening to any more!

Which was unbelievably cowardly of him;
he was only hearing of these events second-
hand, but Genevieve had lived through them.
That she was now the woman she was, beautiful, vivacious, kind, able to see the excitement
and promise of the life before her, seemed to
him to be nothing short of a miracle.

Benedict had lost both of his parents ten
years ago to an unknown murderer, seen
things during his years in the army he would
never forget, lost friends in battle and to long
lingering deaths after, and been emotionally
scarred by all of them. Genevieve's suffering
had been equal to, if not worse than his own,
and yet here she was, beautiful, generous of
nature and eagerly seeking out the goodness
in people, the excitement life still had to offer
her. Oh, Benedict had no doubt that Genevieve's inner scars were etched as deeply as
his own, but they did not prevent her from liv-

ing, from enjoying all the freedoms she now had in her life.

His admiration for her grew, and then grew again.

So he remained silent as Genevieve continued to talk softly, telling him of those occasions when her husband had attempted to bed her again and failed, his body no longer capable of attaining an erection no matter what the inducement, after which she would receive yet another beating.

'But how, if your husband was paralysed, did he manage to beat— Oh, my God! William Forster?' Benedict prompted sharply.

'Yes.' Genevieve gave a shiver of revulsion.

William Forster had! 'What possible reason could he have had to agree to carry out his father's bidding?'

She gave another shudder. 'I believe— I know that he was—displeased when his father married again. Most especially to a woman who was several years younger than he was himself.' Genevieve grimaced. 'No doubt, after five years of widowhood, he had not thought of his father ever marrying again. He despised me utterly from the moment we first met, accused me of marrying his father merely for his fortune. He was right, of course.' She sighed. 'Except I did not want any of that money for myself.'

No, she had wanted it so that her brother would be able pay off his gambling debts. The brother who had taken his own life...

Benedict gave a terse shake of his head. 'And is William Forster also responsible for the broken bone you recently suffered in your wrist?' He spoke softly, so as not to reveal the burn of anger churning so strongly inside him.

She stiffened. 'Benedict—'

'Please answer me, Genevieve!' A nerve pulsed so strongly in Benedict's tightly clenched jaw it was almost painful.

'Yes.'

'The bastard!' Benedict could no longer hold in that anger. 'Why? What did you do—or should I say, what did his warped and twisted mind believe you had done, to deserve having your wrist snapped like a twig?'

Her lashes lowered. 'He...disapproved of my choice of lover.'

Benedict scowled darkly. 'Me?'

'Yes.'

'And he broke your wrist because of it?' he prompted incredulously.

Her breath caught in her throat. 'Not only that, he demanded that I not see you again, that I not bring so much as a whiff of scandal to the Forster name, until after his marriage to Charlotte Darby has taken place.'

'And yet still you defied him by going to Vauxhall Gardens with me, and later attending the dinner at Carlton House?'

'I decided that I could not—cannot—let him continue to rule my life in that way. The result of my defiance was to have him come here this afternoon and threaten me with more physical violence if I defied him again. You must not do anything to retaliate, Benedict!' Genevieve protested as she saw how his mouth had thinned with displeasure. 'William was brought up by a sadistic bully—'

'And he is now a sadistic bully himself!'

'Yes.' She sighed. 'Which is why I have decided I cannot just sit idly by and watch him take that young and fragile creature as his wife.'

'It is your intention to intercede by talking to Ramsey?' Benedict frowned darkly.

'I believe I shall have to, yes.' Genevieve gave a shrug of her slender shoulders. 'To do anything else would be a cruelty to Charlotte Darby.'

'And what of your own well-being?' Benedict rasped grimly. 'You must know that

Forster will not just sit idly by either if you interfere in his marriage arrangements.'

Yes, of course Genevieve knew that, just as surely as she accepted she had to talk to the Earl of Ramsey in regard to the man he intended taking as his son-in-law; she really did not have a choice when just the thought of the fragile Charlotte Darby as William's wife was enough to send a shiver down the length of Genevieve's spine.

Her smile more resembled a grimace. 'No doubt I will survive another beating as I have survived all the others.'

'I forbid you to—' Benedict drew in a deep, controlling breath. 'Genevieve, I *ask* that you leave this matter to me?' he corrected stiffly.

Genevieve gave a shake of her head. 'I could not possibly involve you any further.'

He looked down the length of his nose at her. 'I am your lover, Genevieve, and as such I have the right to offer you my protection. From all who would dare to harm you.'

Genevieve looked up at him quizzically. The two of them had been intimate several times and she had now confided all to Benedict with regard to her marriage and William Forster, but that did not make them lovers.

In truth, after today Genevieve had no idea if she would ever succeed in taking a lover!

She enjoyed Benedict's company more than she could say and she trusted him as she had trusted no other man, and obviously she responded to his caresses, but even he, with all of his expertise in lovemaking, had not managed to pierce those inner barriers which prevented her from knowing true physical intimacy, from moving past the memories of that ripping, tearing pain she had suffered on her wedding night.

She gave a sad shake of her head as she released herself from Benedict's arms before rising shakily to her feet, needing to put some distance between the two of them, to remove herself from the succour and comfort Benedict's arms now offered to her. 'I may be totally ignorant in regard to—to physical matters, Benedict, but even I know enough to realise that you have not—you have not become my lover.'

He looked up at her through narrowed lids for long, searching seconds, an expression of disbelief on his face. 'I am your first lover since your husband?' he finally murmured softly.

'He was not my lover, either!' Her eyes flashed deeply blue.

'Forgive me, I worded that badly.' Benedict grimaced. 'What I meant to ask was—no other man has made love to you since the end of your marriage?'

Her gaze avoided meeting his. 'Or before, or during.'

Or before or during... 'I am your first lover...?' Benedict murmured in hushed disbelief.

'We have not—'

'Genevieve, I have touched you intimately, given you pleasure, as you have touched me and given me pleasure in return,' he pointed out gently. 'That I have not joined with you does not mean we have not made love together. Now, please answer me, am I your first lover since—?'

'Since my fiasco of a wedding night?' she finished flatly. 'Yes, you would have become so.'

Benedict drew in a sharp breath at the enormity of her admission. At the knowledge that Genevieve had chosen him, above all other men, to be her lover. That she had trusted him enough, believed in him enough, to entrust her physical well-being into his care alone. It was as humbling as it was onerous.

'Obviously it did not happen,' she continued with brisk dismissal. 'Which is the reason I now assure you that you have no obligation to me, or—or to other events taking place in my life.'

'I disagree.'

Genevieve's expression became pained. 'Benedict, I cannot ask you to become involved in this situation with William.'

'You did not ask, I stated it as being my intention.'

She nodded distractedly. 'And in my turn I am asking you not to attempt to interfere in this. You will only succeed in bringing William's wrath to your own door.'

'And you believe I should be intimidated by the possibility?' He eyed her mockingly.

Genevieve sighed. 'No, I believe you would enjoy nothing more than the excuse to beat William within an inch of his life.'

'I should.' He gave a grim and arrogant inclination of his dark head in acknowledgement of that fact.

'And I appreciate your offer. I truly do. Know it is inborn in you to protect those you consider less able than you to take care of themselves. But—'

'I could never think of you as being less able than I, Genevieve.' He gave a pained frown at the suggestion. 'Than anyone,' he added grimly. 'You are, I believe, the strongest, most courageous woman I have ever known.'

'How can you possibly say that?' she groaned self-disgustedly. 'When for six years I allowed myself to be abused, not only by my husband, but also by his son?'

Benedict stood up abruptly. 'And what else should you have done?' he bit out harshly. 'The important thing is that you survived. Not only survived, but now flourish.' He took a step towards her, only to halt again as she instinctively took a step back. 'I will not harm you, Genevieve. I will never harm you. Nor will I allow anyone else to do so. Which is why William Forster must be dealt with, so that he can no longer continue to bully and hurt you, or anyone else, in this cruel way.'

Genevieve eyed him warily. 'Dealt with…?'

Benedict gave a terse inclination of his head. 'I will start by suggesting he remove himself permanently from London and all polite society.'

'And if that fails…?'

His eyes narrowed grimly. 'Then it will be my pleasure to ensure that he does so.'

'How?'

His mouth thinned with hard, uncompromising humour. 'I believe I will find a way.'

'Not without bringing a scandal down upon your own head and mine.'

'It will be achieved without involving you in any way,' Benedict assured grimly.

Genevieve gave a shake of her head. 'I do not see how, when William's only sin has been to beat his father's wife on that father's instructions—'

'And for that alone he will be thoroughly thrashed himself before he is allowed to depart for ever to his country estates!' Benedict bit out harshly.

'Whilst I appreciate your concern, Benedict, I do not believe—do not dare to believe…' she gave a helpless shake of her head '…that even you will succeed in permanently ridding me of William's threats.'

He gave another humourless smile. 'Then you do not know me as well as I had hoped that you might.'

She looked at Benedict searchingly, easily noting the grimness of purpose in his expression and the hard and angry glitter of his eyes. 'I know you well enough to realise that you are not at all the cold and remote gentleman that you allow the *ton* to believe you to be.'

His expression softened. 'Then I ask that you also have a little faith in both me and my ability to protect you.'

Tears welled up in her expressive eyes. 'I could not bear it if—if you were to come to harm because of me.'

Benedict shook his head. 'I shall come to no harm, I assure you, Genevieve. I do not consider men like Forster, either father or son, to be men at all. They are worms. Lower than worms, when they choose to bully and abuse a woman as you have been bullied and abused.' His eyes gleamed darkly. 'The father is beyond my reach, but William Forster, at least, shall pay, and pay dearly, for his sins against you.'

He sounded so confident, so sure of himself, that Genevieve could do no other than believe him. Believe in him. If any man could rid her of William's oppressive presence in her life, then she now believed that man to be Benedict.

She gave a shake of her head. 'If you succeed, then how shall I ever repay you?'

Benedict eyed her ruefully. 'A lesser man would be insulted that you might ever consider I should require repayment.'

Her eyes widened. 'Oh, I meant you no insult, Benedict—' She broke off as he began to chuckle softly. 'I fail to see anything in the least funny about this situation, Benedict.'

Nor, in truth, did Benedict. But these past few minutes had been harrowing ones for Genevieve, as she relived the pain and fear she had suffered this past seven years. Seven years…! Damn it— No, he must not allow his anger to get the better of him now; that he intended saving until he was able to see and deal with William Forster as he deserved to be dealt with. And the sooner the better, as far as Benedict was concerned.

He reached out to take both Genevieve's hands in his before lifting one of those hands to his lips. 'Before you ask,' he murmured indulgently as he saw the question in her expressive blue eyes, 'I am saluting the bravery of a fellow soldier.'

She gave a puzzled shake of her head. 'I do not understand…'

'If we had a dozen as brave as you during our battle against the Corsican then I have no doubts that war would have been over years earlier than it was!' Benedict assured ruefully.

A delicate blush coloured her otherwise pale cheeks. 'It is not brave merely to have survived the battle.'

Benedict touched the warmth of her cheek. 'It is the way in which you have survived, Genevieve!' He looked down at her admiringly. 'There is no bitterness inside you. No drive for revenge against the people who harmed you.' He gave a disbelieving shake of his head that this should be the case.

Genevieve knew, as surely as if Benedict had spoken the words out loud, that he referred now to the bitterness and drive for revenge he still felt against whoever had murdered his parents all those years ago. That same bitterness and need for revenge which had driven Benedict, moulded his character, for these past ten years.

'Such destructive emotions only damage those who feel them,' she chided gently.

He gave a heavy sigh. 'And yet I find it impossible not to feel those emotions when I know that a murderer still walks free whilst my parents are both dead.'

Genevieve gave a pained frown. 'I do not mean to interfere, Benedict, but—you said that your godfather carried out the initial investigation?'

'Yes.'

'And do you know if he questioned all of the servants?'

'I am sure that he will have done so. Yes, I know that he did.' Benedict nodded grimly. 'As I recall, there were two of them that I was unable to question when I carried out my own investigation some months later.'

'And why was that?'

'They had moved on to another household.' He shrugged. 'And who can blame them? Two people had been murdered in their present household.'

'You are sure they went to another household?'

'Genevieve, what are you implying?'

'I know, from personal experience, that the household servants are usually privy to much more than we give them credit for.' She grimaced. 'For example, whenever I had been locked in my bedchamber, cook would help my maid to bring me food and water to drink.'

'When were you locked away in your bedchamber—?'

'Please do not let us become distracted from this conversation again, Benedict—'

'I will know who locked you away in your bedchamber!' A nerve pulsed in Benedict's jaw. 'No, do not bother answering; I can see by your expression exactly who is to blame for that!' His eyes glittered darkly as he envisaged all of the things he would do to William Forster when he saw him next.

Which he intended to be very soon indeed...

Chapter Thirteen

'I do not wish to make a fuss, but—I am afraid you are crushing my fingers, Benedict!'

Benedict brought his tormented thoughts under control as he focused on Genevieve, realising as he did so that he was indeed crushing her tiny fingers in his much larger ones. His eyes widened in horror as he immediately released her to mutter, 'Your poor wrist!' He inspected it for further damage.

'It is unharmed, Benedict,' she assured softly. 'But I do think that you should look further into where those two servants went after they left your employ.'

'You believe they may have seen something they should not?' Benedict frowned.

'I believe it is worth investigating further,'

Genevieve answered cautiously. 'If only so that you might ask if they have remembered anything of import since—since leaving.'

His expression softened as he looked down and saw Genevieve's anxiety of expression. 'Do not look so troubled, Genevieve,' he murmured ruefully. 'I assure you, I am grateful for any help you may give me in this matter.'

'There may be no reason for your gratitude.' She sighed. 'I may be completely wrong about these two servants.'

'And you may not.' Benedict smiled at her. 'And as a reward for your caring—'

'Of course I care, Benedict!' Her cheeks became warm as she realised what she had said. 'I cannot imagine how awful it must have been for you these past ten years,' she added. 'To have lost your parents so tragically, and then not to know who had killed them...'

'—as a reward for your caring,' Benedict repeated firmly, 'I intend to indulge you in something else you would consider "fun and adventure".'

Her eyes widened. 'You do?'

'I do.' He nodded. 'God help me!'

She chuckled. 'There is something I should like so very much...'

'Yes...?' Benedict answered warily as he

saw the return of that familiar reckless gleam in her eyes.

She smiled eagerly. 'I would so like to go for a ride in the park in your carriage tomorrow afternoon!'

He frowned slightly. 'I never ride my carriage in the park.'

'Which is exactly the reason I should like to accompany you the first time that you do so!' Genevieve grinned her satisfaction.

'Minx!' Benedict gave a rueful shake of his head. 'In that case, we will make the arrangements for the outing when I join you for dinner this evening.'

Her smile faltered slightly. 'You intend dining here, with me, this evening?'

'It is what lovers do, is it not?'

Genevieve's gaze lowered from meeting Benedict's as she felt the warmth of colour in her cheeks. 'I believe this afternoon has shown that I—I am not capable of taking a lover—'

'All this afternoon has shown is that you are a very warm and responsive woman.'

'But—' She looked up shyly beneath her long lashes as Benedict placed his fingers against her lips in order to silence her.

'You are a very warm and responsive woman, Genevieve,' he repeated firmly. 'And it will be my pleasure at some time in the future—and I hope, your own—to enable you to see that physical pleasure is not meant to be painful.' His jaw hardened.

The colour deepened in Genevieve's cheeks at discussing such a delicate subject. Which was slightly ridiculous, after all she had already confided in Benedict this afternoon!

It still disappointed her that she had reacted in the way that she had earlier. She had so wanted—hoped—that she would feel differently with Benedict. And up to a point she had, having once again enjoyed his caresses until she climaxed. It was only thoughts of penetration which had sent her into a panic.

She gave a slow shake of her head. 'I am not sure that any amount of patience on your part, in—in this regard, will make the slightest difference to my own…aversion to—to such a depth of intimacy.'

Benedict tapped her playfully on the tip of her nose. 'But you will allow me the privilege of trying?'

She swallowed hard. 'Only if I can be completely sure that you do not offer out of pity?'

'Does this feel like pity to you, Genevieve?' Benedict's gaze held hers as he slowly guided her hand to the front of his pantaloons, allowing her to feel the once again hardness of his pulsing arousal.

Her cheeks felt fevered. 'You desire me still, after all—after all I have told you?'

'Why should I not?' His brows lowered to a glower. 'You had no choice in the matter— how could you have, when you were completely at the mercy of the two Forster men!'

'Benedict, you will not—I could not bear it if you came to any harm on my behalf,' she amended as she knew by Benedict's harsh expression that he would not be persuaded out of his decision to pay William Forster a visit.

'And risk being unable to join you later this evening?' he teased huskily.

Her cheeks warmed at the seductive note she detected in his tone. 'In that case, I will organise a delicious dinner for us both. Would eight-thirty suit?'

He nodded distractedly. 'Admirably. And now I should like to kiss you goodbye until later, if that is agreeable to you?'

Genevieve's heart leapt, her breasts tingling, just at thoughts of being kissed again by Benedict. And surely, if she liked and enjoyed Benedict's kisses so much, then all was not lost to her after all? Maybe even, with time, she might be able to—

'You seem to be taking an unflattering amount of time deciding, pet?' Benedict teased gruffly, hoping he was not pushing Genevieve too far too quickly. It was not his intention to do so, but neither did he feel they should take a single step backwards in their relationship—to do so would only lead to Genevieve becoming even more nervous and shy in regard to physical intimacy.

The glow of anticipation in Genevieve's eyes was neither nervous nor shy. 'On condition that you do not kiss me any less passionately than you have done before today.'

'I would not dream of doing so,' Benedict murmured huskily, his arms moving assuredly about her waist and pulling her against him even as his head lowered and his lips claimed hers.

It was a different sort of kiss, though, he very quickly realised. More intense, sweeter, as he tasted and sipped from those full and delectable lips and Genevieve curled her luscious curves against his much harder ones, her arms up about his shoulders as she returned the heat of those kisses.

'Enough for now, love.' Benedict finally broke the kiss with a groan, his arousal throbbing even more painfully against the welcoming softness of her thighs. 'We will continue this when I return later this evening,' he promised gruffly.

But before then, Benedict had two visits to make.

Firstly, to Eric Cargill, to ask that gentleman to see if he could locate the two servants who had left his parents' employ soon after the shooting; Eric, besides being a spymaster for the Crown and so having the means at his disposal to make such enquiries, was also one of his parents' oldest friends, hence his having been chosen as one of Benedict's godfathers. The older man's interest, in finding the person responsible for their deaths, was as intense as Benedict's own.

Secondly—and this was the visit Benedict anticipated the most!—he would call upon William Forster at his London home, and make it known to the other man that he was now conversant with events of both the past and present in regard to Genevieve, and that in the circumstances he would not welcome— in fact, it might be detrimental to William's own health—if he were to find the other man anywhere within Genevieve's vicinity in the future.

A challenge Benedict sincerely hoped that

the other man would take him up on——he would enjoy nothing more than, as Genevieve had already stated, 'the excuse to beat William Forster within an inch of his life'!

'You need to see my opponent to realise the triviality of my own injuries!' Benedict assured with satisfaction as Genevieve's eyes widened in concern later that evening as she obviously spotted the bruise upon his cheek the moment the butler showed him into her gold salon.

'Thank you, Jenkins.' She waited until her butler had departed before turning back to Benedict. 'And do I really need to take a guess as to whom that "opponent" might have been?'

'As a woman of intelligence, I rather think not,' Benedict drawled as he stepped further into the room, eyes dark with appreciation as he took in Genevieve's appearance in a deep-blue silk gown the exact same colour as her eyes. 'You are looking very beautiful this evening, love.'

It was impossible for Genevieve to hold back the flush of pleasure that warmed her cheeks. Just as it was impossible for her not to be affected, in turn, by Benedict's dark good looks, the darkness of his hair lightly tousled, that bruise he now sported upon his cheek only adding to that air of danger he carried so easily.

She gave a rueful shake of her head. 'If you are hoping to divert my attention with flattery—'

'The truth can never be called flattery, Genevieve,' he assured her softly.

'You *are* attempting to divert me.' She eyed him reprovingly.

He laughed softly. 'But only by telling the truth.'

'Then do me the service of answering me as truthfully in regard to your meeting with William Forster!'

'Tenacious as well as beautiful,' Benedict murmured appreciatively.

Genevieve reached up to gently touch the livid discolouration upon his cheek. 'Your poor face,' she murmured with compassion. 'Did the brute dare to hit you?' Her expression darkened with displeasure.

Benedict continued to grin his satisfaction. 'Only after I had hit him. And he did not touch me with his fist, but the heel of his boot, as he toppled over with all the grace and trumpeting of a bull elephant!'

'Now that you mention it, he does rather

resemble one!' Benedict had described the scene so well that Genevieve could not help but smile at the vision which had appeared so vividly in her mind. 'Even so...' she sobered with a frown '...you promised me that you would not allow yourself to come to any harm when you met with William.'

'I seem to recall my precise words were that I would not allow anything to prevent me from joining you here for dinner this evening,' Benedict reminded her softly as he reached out to clasp both her gloved hands in his own. 'And now that I have, I believe I would prefer to eat you up rather than any meal your cook may have prepared for us...'

'Benedict...!'

'Yes, love?' He lowered his head to nuzzle his lips against the bare skin between her shoulders and throat.

'I—is this what lovers do, too?'

'I believe so...' he murmured distractedly.

'I—but you— Surely you are so much more conversant in these things than—than I...?' Genevieve's heart was pounding loudly in her chest, her pulse racing to the point that she could barely think, let alone answer him coherently.

'Am I?'

'Well, are you not?' She gave an inelegant squeak as the warmth of his lips grazed the tops of her breasts left bare above the low neckline of her gown.

He shrugged elegant shoulders as his lips continued to blaze a trail of fire across the swell of her breasts. 'I do not recall being so, no.'

'Benedict…!'

His eyes were dark as onyx as he lifted his head slightly, his lips now only inches from her own. 'It is not gentlemanly to discuss previous…relationships, pet. Not that there have been any in my own life which could be called such,' he added softly as Genevieve's frown deepened. 'Very few women have captured my interest for as long as you have, love.'

'But we have only been acquainted for two weeks.'

He gave an acknowledging inclination of his head. 'And that is twelve, or perhaps thirteen days longer than any other woman has succeeded in holding my interest.'

Genevieve looked up at him searchingly, unsure whether or not Benedict was teasing her. The directness of his dark gaze implied he was not. 'I had thought—I believed—'

'Yes, love?' Benedict looked down at her with dark and mocking eyes.

Genevieve's frown became pained. 'I believe there is something else which I must tell you, Benedict, if we are to proceed any further…'

He arched dark brows. 'Oh?'

'Yes. I—I would hate for you to learn of this by any other means.'

He stepped back slightly, his own expression guarded. 'Proceed, Genevieve.'

She moistened the plumpness of her lips with the tip of her tongue before continuing. 'The truth is, that several weeks ago, the night of Sophia Rowlands's ball, as it happens, I—I made a deliberately outrageous statement to my two dearest friends, declaring that if we had any sense at all, now that our year of mourning was over, we should all take a lover or two before this dreary Season came to an end.' She gave a sad shake of her head. 'At the time I had believed that I would be able to—I had thought I might succeed— No matter.' She grimaced. 'You arrived at the ball with Devil Stirling at the very time I made my announcement and I impulsively stated that either of you fine gentlemen would make one of us a splendid lover.'

Benedict had listened to Genevieve's confession with ever-increasing amusement. Would this woman ever cease to surprise him? 'And you now wish to confess that you are disappointed Devil preferred your friend Pandora?'

'Not at all!' She gave him an impatient frown. 'Indeed, I find him even more fearful than I do you!'

His brows rose. 'Fearful, pet...?'

'Top-lofty and arrogant.'

'And you do not now consider me to be either of those things?'

'On the contrary, I *know* that you are both of those things,' she assured airily. 'It is just that, having come to know you better, I tend to forget to feel nervous of you the moment you kiss me.'

'I am glad to hear it,' Benedict drawled.

'Yes. Well.' Her cheeks were once again aflame with embarrassment. 'I had not realised at the time I made that statement that you did not take mistresses and that any interest you might show me would place you in a position where you would be made the subject of gossip and speculation,' she continued earnestly. 'Otherwise I should not have—should not have—'

'Allowed me to pursue you?'

'Exactly!'

Benedict held back his laughter with effort. 'In that case, I believe I have a confession of my own to make.'

Her eyes widened guilelessly. 'You do?'

'Hmmm.' He nodded. 'Do you remember, on the day of Devil and Pandora's wedding, when I asked you if you would care to come for a ride with me in my carriage?'

'I recall it very well,' she answered cautiously.

'Well, I am afraid that the ride I was suggesting was not one where you sat on your side of the carriage and I sat on mine!'

She stared at him blankly for several minutes, before her eyes widened, her cheeks reddened and she gave a shocked gasp. 'Benedict!'

He chuckled softly. 'I also confess to not giving a single thought to the gossip of the *ton* either then or since. There, are we done with confessions for now, pet, or do we need to delay our dinner a while longer?' He held out his arm pointedly.

'I think it best that we do not!' Genevieve placed her gloved hand upon that arm.

* * *

It was not until much later, when Genevieve, at Benedict's insistence, remained seated opposite him at the small dinner table enjoying a cup of coffee as he indulged in a brandy and cigar after Jenkins had served them a delicious dinner, that she realised he had once again succeeded in diverting her attention, this time from his meeting earlier with William Forster.

Having spent the past two hours or so looking across the candlelit dining table at Benedict, answering his conversation more and more distractedly as her complete physical awareness of him deepened—the darkness of his hair was rakishly tousled, the blackness of his gaze hooded as he returned her gaze often, those patrician features appearing harshly etched in the candlelight—Genevieve confessed to having found it difficult to concentrate on anything else but the physical splendour of the gentleman with whom she was currently enjoying an intimate dinner.

It was shockingly improper, of course, for a young widow to dine alone in her home with any gentleman, but she doubted that Benedict was any more eager than she was to have that knowledge made public; he was, despite what she had said earlier, the arrogantly elusive Lord Benedict Lucas as well as the disreputable Lucifer.

Although Genevieve confessed to finding herself thinking of him less and less as Lucifer, and more and more as Benedict—the gentleman who excited her more than she could ever have imagined and who had today leapt so ably to her defence—she did not believe the face he chose to present to the *ton*, that of the bored and arrogant Lucifer, would ever have cared to stir himself enough to bother leaping to any lady's defence!

'What are you thinking of now, pet?' Benedict eyed her through the haze of the smoke given off from his cigar, having been aware of her shy glances in his direction through dinner, as well as noting the flush of arousal that had now spread from her cheeks down to the swell of her breasts, and the return of that reckless light to the deep blue of her eyes.

An awareness that he had felt just as deeply as their dinner had progressed and he attempted to keep up a light conversation. So much so that he was unable to stand up at this moment without revealing the throbbing state of his own arousal!

Those deep-blue eyes now avoided meeting his. 'You did not finish telling me earlier of the conclusion of your visit to William Forster.'

'Possibly because I am grown bored by the subject—do not look so stricken, pet!' Benedict instantly regretted his impatience as he saw the way Genevieve's cheeks had paled at his harsh dismissal. 'It was not my intention to hurt you, Genevieve—'

'Please ignore me, Benedict, I am merely being silly.' She blinked back the tears swimming in those deep-blue eyes as she looked across at him. 'I should have realised how bored you have become by all this talk of my disreputable family.'

'Forster was never your family, disreputable or otherwise,' he assured her firmly, wanting to stand up and go to her, but knowing that his physical arousal was now such that he very much doubted they would be able to finish this conversation if he were to do so. 'Nor is it now his intention to become a member of the Earl of Ramsey's family next month,' he added with satisfaction.

Genevieve gasped. 'William has agreed to end his engagement to Charlotte Darby?'

The hardness of Benedict's smile lacked all humour. 'That would never do, Genevieve;

the lady must always be the one to end the betrothal if she is to maintain her place in the marriage mart.' He grimaced at thoughts of the social strictures society placed upon them all. 'No, what Forster has agreed to do is give Charlotte Darby every reason to break the engagement.'

'How…?'

'I have left the details of that arrangement to Forster. My only condition was that it be accomplished as soon as is possible and that he then as quickly remove himself, and remain removed, from all polite society.' Benedict's expression hardened as his thoughts lingered on the unpleasantness of his conversation with William Forster earlier this evening.

His meeting with Eric Cargill having been quickly completed, the earl showing he was as eager as Benedict to reopen the investigation into the death of Benedict's parents, Benedict had then wasted no time in calling upon the Duke of Woollerton.

The other man had at first refused to receive him, something which Benedict had taken exception to, to the point that he had pushed his way inside the house and sought that gentleman out in his study. Nor had he spared a moment's interest in hearing his indignant blustering at this infringement of good manners, dismissing Forster's butler himself before coldly informing the other man of the exact reason he was there.

The insults and scorn Forster had then proceeded to rain down upon Genevieve's innocent head were not for repeating to anyone, let alone to Genevieve herself, and had earned William Forster a hefty right hook to the chin for his trouble!

Once the other man recovered enough to be able to talk through his swollen lips and bruised jaw, it had quickly become obvious that Forster did indeed feel deep resentment towards Genevieve for having married his father, a man old enough to be her own father, and that his main reason for that resentment was the huge financial settlement he knew Genevieve was to receive upon his father's death—too late to be of any help to Genevieve's hapless brother, but timely enough to allow Genevieve to set up her own household and rejoin the society she had been forced to leave so abruptly seven years ago.

The Forster fortune was not, it seemed, as healthy as it had once been, the previous Duke of Woollerton having squandered much of that fortune, first on the extravagant life he had

chosen to lead in London for so many years,
and latterly on the doctors he constantly had
brought to his country estate with a view to
finding a cure for his affliction. It seemed that
Genevieve's widow settlement had been the
final straw that broke that particular camel's
back, necessitating Forster now needing to
find himself a wife in possession of her own
fortune, a role Charlotte Darby suited admirably.

Benedict's chilling promise to expose the
other man to the Earl of Ramsey for the vicious and violent bully that he was had succeeded in persuading Forster into deciding
Charlotte Darby would not make him a suitable wife, after all.

None of which Genevieve needed to know
in any detail, but most especially those vi-
ciously insulting remarks Forster had made
in regard to her personally...

Benedict stubbed out his cigar before rising slowly to his feet. 'I believe it is enough
that he will not be bothering you again, Genevieve. Especially as the two of us now have
a more pressing matter to attend to.'

Genevieve's eyes widened as Benedict
walked slowly, and with lethally elegant in-

tent, about the table until he stood at her side, the evidence of that 'more pressing matter' unmistakable even to her innocent gaze.

Chapter Fourteen

And instantly brought about a return of Genevieve's previous feelings of nervousness!

What if Benedict were to attempt to make love to her and she failed him once again?

Benedict's statement of earlier, in regard to the women he had known previously, confirmed that he was a gentleman who was accustomed to much more worldly women than she, women who did not need to be coaxed and petted in order to share their bed with him. The type of woman, in fact, that Genevieve now sincerely doubted she could ever be.

'You are giving far too much thought to the matter, Genevieve, instead of allowing your actions to speak for themselves,' Benedict

murmured softly as he took both her hands
in his and pulled her effortlessly to her feet so
that she now stood in front of him. 'And this
evening it is you who will decide what those
actions shall be. You approve of that idea?'
he prompted huskily as her eyes instantly lit
up with interest.

Her little pink tongue moved in a moist
sweep across the fullness of her lips before
she answered him. 'If it means I may touch
you intimately, as I did earlier today…?'

Benedict's breath caught in his throat at
thoughts of having Genevieve's hands and
lips upon him once again. 'If that is what you
would like?'

'Oh, yes.' Her eyes glowed in anticipation.
'I believe I should enjoy that very much.'

Benedict's breath stilled altogether. 'Then
that is what we shall do.' He released her
hands before moving to the door and turning
the key in the lock.

Genevieve eyed him uncertainly. 'What are
you doing?'

'All evening, as we ate our dinner together,
I have imagined you with your hair down,
posing naked and tempting upon the *chaise*
over there in front of the window.' He moved

back towards her with those purposeful and predatory strides.

Genevieve's cheeks warmed at the knowledge that Benedict's thoughts had been as distracted as her own. 'You wish me to undress now, in the dining room...?'

'We shall undress each other, Genevieve,' he assured her huskily, the intensity of those black eyes fixed upon her parted lips. 'You have dismissed Jenkins for the night, but I still think it best to lock the door for the sake of your modesty, so that there is absolutely no risk of anyone walking in and finding us together.'

Genevieve very much doubted that Jenkins, if he should return and discover the door was locked, would dare to knock for entry—but that would not prevent him from drawing his own conclusions as to the reason his mistress and Lord Benedict Lucas were alone together on the other side of that locked door!

Instead of filling her with dismay, Genevieve found herself titillated by the thoughts of her household staff knowing—or, at least, guessing—that she and Benedict were being intimate together.

As Benedict had no doubts intended she should.

She looked up at him admiringly as she removed the pins from her hair and allowed those red-gold tresses to fall loosely about her shoulders. 'I believe you to be an extremely wicked gentleman.'

He gazed at her hair admiringly. 'One does one's best to oblige.'

Genevieve chuckled softly. 'And are you now going to "oblige" me even further by undressing…?'

'Oh, no, love, in that it is you who will oblige me, by removing my clothes.' He smiled down at her rakishly.

Genevieve felt that now-familiar warmth enter her cheeks at thoughts of removing Benedict's clothes, one by one. Something she found both unacceptable and exciting to contemplate. To be given the freedom, the invitation, to undress Benedict, to slowly reveal the splendid nakedness of his muscled body, to her avid gaze and caressing hands, seemed impossible for her to do at the same time as she found it thrilling beyond belief.

She looked up at him shyly from beneath the fullness of her long lashes. 'I trust you will make the necessary…allowances for my lack of finesse in such matters?' She began to slowly unfasten the buttons upon his waistcoat.

A nerve pulsed in his tightly clenched jaw. 'I believe I shall be too busy enjoying the experience to concern myself with how it is done!'

Benedict did not look as if he were enjoying himself as Genevieve removed first his jacket and then his waistcoat, an expression of strained tension etched into the harshness of his features as she then removed his neckcloth before unbuttoning the collar of his shirt, her fingers lingering caressingly on the silky dark hair revealed by his unbuttoned collar, his breath drawn in sharply as her fingertips skimmed the hardness of his nipples.

'You seemed to enjoy this earlier… Are you—can it be that you are as…sensitive here as I am?' she prompted curiously.

'If a single caress to your breasts succeeds in making your cock pulse and your balls tighten in pleasure to the point of pain, then, yes, I believe I am,' he bit out tautly.

Such frankness of speech should have shocked her, Genevieve knew, and yet once again she found herself excited, her breasts tightening beneath the bodice of her gown, a warm dampness gathering between her heated thighs. 'I am sure, if I were in possession of a cock or balls, that its pulsing and their tightening would equal my own depths of pleasure when you caress my breasts, yes.'

Benedict stared down at her blankly for several long seconds, before he closed his eyes briefly, and then opened again as he gave a sharp bark of laughter. 'You were not meant to repeat my words, love,' he finally sobered enough to reprove drily.

'Then perhaps you should not have spoken so frankly in my presence?'

He gave a self-derisive shake of his head. 'I believe I shall know better not to do so another time!'

She eyed him beneath lowered lashes. 'And do you also enjoy it when I place my lips against you, and lick and suckle in the same way you do to me?'

Benedict groaned low in answer, that groan deepening as Genevieve suited her actions to her words, first pushing his shirt aside as she first kissed his nipples, before licking them with the moist rasp of her tongue and then lightly suckling. 'I have created a monster!'

Again she gave him a sidelong glance from beneath the heavy weight of her lashes. 'And you wish you had not…?'

'God, no!' he assured fervently as his fingers became entangled in those loose red-gold curls.

What Genevieve lacked in experience Benedict very quickly learnt that she more than made up for with instinct, as she removed his shirt completely before running her hands in slow exploration over and across his chest, and then moving to stand behind him to do the same with the tensed muscles of his back, the lace of her gloves adding to the pleasure of those caresses.

Benedict's jaw now felt as if it were permanently locked and his hands clenched into fists at his sides, as he fought to maintain control. Fought to control the need he had to take Genevieve in his arms and strip her naked before laying her on the *chaise* and making love to her, as he had imagined doing for most of the evening.

Except he could not. This, whatever transpired between himself and Genevieve this evening, had to come from her, as she took them both to the level of intimacy she found acceptable.

Benedict only hoped he did not suffer a seizure—much like the one her husband had suffered on their wedding night!—before that happened!

Standing completely naked before a woman who remained completely clothed in her evening gown and gloves was yet another new experience for Benedict. One he found exciting. And he had never given particular thought to his own body before now, to its attractions or otherwise, but as Genevieve ran her hands slowly, tortuously, in a light caress over the flatness of his abdomen, the leanness of his hips and down the long length of his muscled legs, before starting an equally as intimate exploration of his back and buttocks, he found himself tensing for her reaction.

He had not received any complaints from women before as to the way he looked, but, as he knew only too well, Genevieve was unlike any other woman he had ever known.

Finally Benedict could stand that tension no longer. 'Do you like what you see, love?'

Genevieve allowed her hands to once again trail lightly down the length of Benedict's bared spine before slowly moving round to face him. 'You must know that I do,' she chided huskily. 'You are everything I have ever imagined a man should be. Wickedly handsome of face.' She smiled at him. 'Wide and powerful across the shoulders.' Her gaze lowered as her fingers trailed lightly across that bared flesh. 'Muscled about the chest.' Her fingers moved lower. 'Slender of waist and—and thighs.' She hesitated, moving lower still.

'Take off your gloves, love, and touch me there as you did earlier,' Benedict bit out between gritted teeth.

Her cheeks were ablaze with colour as she slid her gloves slowly down her arms before removing them completely, her hands trembling slightly as she reached out tentatively to touch the pulsing length of Benedict's arousal, her caresses becoming bolder as she heard his sharply indrawn breath. 'Are all gentlemen as long and thick around as you?'

'Ye gods…!' He gave a strangled groan.

'Is that a yes or a no?' Her fingers curled about that steel encased in velvet.

'It is—I believe I might be slightly larger than the average,' Benedict managed to gasp between gritted teeth as Genevieve ran the soft pad of her thumb across the moisture that leaked from the slit at the top of that engorged tip just at the feel of her soft flesh encircling him.

'You are certainly much larger and longer than—' She broke off to draw her bottom lip sharply between her teeth, her hands also ceasing their caresses before dropping away completely. 'I apologise.' She gave him a stricken look. 'It was very wrong of me to talk of—to—'

'All is allowed between us, Genevieve. All and everything,' he reminded her tautly as he took a light grasp of her hand and replaced her fingers about him.

Her fascinated gaze also returned to that long and throbbing length. 'I had no idea until today that a man could be so beautiful here...'

Benedict bit back another groan as she gave a swipe of her lips with the moist tip of her little pink tongue. Genevieve was both the most innocent and sensually exciting woman he had ever known; that very innocence, the honesty of her comments, excited him as the caresses and attentions of a more experienced women never had or ever could.

'No, love.' Benedict lightly grasped her arm to prevent her from moving on to her knees in front of him, knowing that his own knees would surely buckle completely if he were to still be standing on his feet when she placed those warm and delectable lips about him. 'Allow me to be the one to drape myself decorously on the *chaise* before your explorations become any more...intimate!'

Genevieve could not help but admire the fluidity and elegance of movement of Benedict's naked body as they crossed to the *chaise*, his muscles as lithe as a cat's—and just as predatory!—beneath the silkiness of his tanned flesh.

She should still be feeling shy, embarrassed by their intimacy in the bright candlelight, and with the curtains not even drawn across the windows against nosy neighbours or passers-by. And yet somehow she no longer felt that way as Benedict lay his lean length upon the *chaise* before drawing her down to sit beside him, the blaze of candlelight, and the daring of those undrawn curtains, only seeming to add to Genevieve's own state of arousal.

Perhaps she was every bit as wanton, after all, as she had tried to give the appearance of being on the night of Sophia's ball, when she had first made the suggestion regarding the three young widows taking lovers?

Whatever the reason, Genevieve now felt no hesitation as she once again curled her fingers about Benedict's jutting arousal before lowering her head, her hair falling silkily across Benedict's thighs as she took him into the heat of her mouth.

Benedict drew in another sharp breath as

the heat of Genevieve's mouth surrounded him, pleasure coursing through him as he watched her head bob slowly up and down as she sucked and licked, her teeth a gentle and yet arousing scrape along his length, her tongue stroking across and around his bulbous tip, lingering to lathe that sensitive spot just beneath the bulbous head as she obviously felt and heard Benedict's groaned reaction to that intensely pleasurable caress.

She was an unrelenting siren. A witch. She seemed to know instinctively which caresses gave him the most pleasure, those caresses making him harder and more swollen, and driving him ever closer to release.

Benedict gave another groan as Genevieve hummed her own satisfaction as she tasted and lapped up the dribbles of moisture that had already escaped his control, the blood roaring through his veins, his vision blurring as he felt his release burning inside him to be set free. 'You have to stop now, love!' He reached down to gently grasp her arms and lift her up and away from him—only to groan anew as he saw the sultry arousal so evident in Genevieve's face; her eyes heavy and deeply blue, her cheeks flushed, her lips—oh God, those lips!—so swollen, and wet and glistening from her ministrations to him.

She pouted those swollen lips. 'But you said you like it?'

Benedict gave a choked laugh. 'Very much. Too much,' he added as she would have made another protest.

Her expression became quizzical. 'How can you possibly like it "too much"?'

He gave a restless shake of his head. 'Because if you do not stop I am seriously in danger of—of releasing whilst still in your mouth!'

'You said that everything and everything was allowed between us?'

'I did, yes.' A statement he was now having serious reservations about having made to one who was proving as adventurous as Genevieve. 'Genevieve, do you understand about ejaculation? The release of a man's seed?'

'I am not a complete ninnyhead, Benedict,' she assured him indignantly, although her cheeks coloured prettily. 'It is the release of a man's seed inside a woman which produces babies. But,' she continued before Benedict could answer her, 'you are not inside me, so there is no danger of that happening.'

'No danger of pregnancy, no…' Benedict acknowledged weakly.

'Then what is there the danger of?'

'Gods, Genevieve, when a man—when he reaches his climax he—well, he—' He gave an impatient shake of his head. 'How to explain this…? Have you ever seen pictures, possibly in books, of a volcano erupting?'

Her eyes widened. 'You are likening the release of a man's seed to the erupting of a volcano?'

At this moment, Benedict was dearly wishing that he had never started this conversation! 'It is similar in its lack of…control, yes,' he acknowledged through gritted teeth. 'And if I were to be inside your mouth when it happened, then—then— Damn it, Genevieve, can you not imagine my seed pumping copiously into your mouth, choking you?'

'It would not choke or drown me were I to swallow when it erupted—'

Benedict pushed up and away from her at the erotic image her words portrayed, standing up to pace the room—and very aware that pacing lacked its usual authority when he was completely naked, his arousal jutting long and thick as it bobbed up and down in front of him! 'Women—ladies do not *swal-*

low a man's—they do not—Genevieve, a lady does not swallow a man's seed.'

'Why not?'

'I—they just don't!'

'Then what else do they do with it?'

'They do not do anything "with it".' Benedict glared his frustration. 'From all that I have heard, most ladies of society would be—scandalised, at the very least, if their husbands were to ask them to perform such an act of intimacy.'

'Why?'

He frowned darkly. 'I believe they consider it— It is not something a lady is supposed to enjoy.'

Genevieve sat back against the *chaise* to look up at him. 'I enjoy it very much, so does that mean I am not a lady, after all?'

This conversation was, as was usual when he discussed such things with Genevieve, getting far beyond Benedict's control. 'You are more of a lady, more of a woman, than any other I have known.'

Her eyes lit up with pleasure. 'That is good.' She nodded. 'But do the gentlemen of the *ton* not enjoy this intimacy?'

Benedict gave another hard laugh. 'So much so, I believe, that any of them would get down on his knees and kiss the feet of the woman who offered to service him in the way you are suggesting completing me!'

She looked thoughtful. 'Could that be why many of them go to the beds of whores within months of being married?'

'Genevieve…!'

'Benedict.' She held his gaze steadily. 'How am I to understand, to know how to please my lover, in all ways, if you do not explain such things to me?'

Benedict scowled darkly even as his hands clenched at his sides. 'And is that what this is all about, my tutoring you in the ways and desires of men, so that you might know best how to pleasure your next lover?'

Genevieve had been referring to Benedict himself when she talked of her lover, of how she might learn how to please him, and had not given so much as a thought as to there ever being a 'next lover'. Because she did not want another lover. Only Benedict.

Which was not only silly of her, but dangerous, too. Benedict had never given any indication, any hint that he intended their relationship to continue beyond the few weeks it might take him to become bored, with both her company and with teaching her how best to enjoy her own body and that of the gentleman she was with.

Which was not to say she could not enjoy those few short and pleasurable—and memorable!—weeks with him to the full…

She stood up, the steadiness of her gaze holding his as she crossed the room to where Benedict stood tensely. 'It is not polite to talk of other lovers, for either of us, when it is the two of us who are here together now.' Her hands once again moved, caressing across his shoulders and chest. 'Will you not return to the *chaise*, so that I might continue—Benedict…?' She looked up at him with hurt eyes as he flinched away from her and began to pull his shirt on over his head. 'You are leaving?'

Benedict's eyes glittered darkly. 'It may have escaped your notice, but I am no longer in any danger of "erupting" anywhere!'

Her gaze moved down to where the heaviness of his shaft was no longer rampant and straining for release but had become considerably deflated. Still impressive to behold, to be sure, but obviously no longer eager for play. 'I am sure that if we were to return to the *chaise*—'

'I am no longer in the mood!' He sat down

on the *chaise* to pull on his pantaloons over that rapidly deflating erection, followed by his boots, with such violence he was in danger of damaging the fine leather.

Genevieve had no idea what to do, what to say, to ease the tension now so palpable between them. 'Perhaps conversation was not such a good idea at that point in the proceedings?' she attempted to tease.

Only to receive a fierce black scowl for her trouble as Benedict stood up to continue dressing with less than his usual elegance; his shirt still hung outside his pantaloons, neither his waist or superfine were refastened, and his neckcloth was ignored altogether as it lay forlorn and alone upon the rug in front of the unlit fireplace where Benedict had discarded it earlier.

Genevieve gave a pained wince. 'I—Benedict, I am sorry if I have done or said anything to—to offend you.'

His nostrils flared. 'I am not in the least offended, the mood has passed, that is all.'

And he so obviously did not wish for it to return at this moment… 'If you would rather not take me for a ride in your carriage in the park tomorrow afternoon—'

His expression was one of remote haughti-

ness. 'I have said that I will take you and so
I will.'

'I do not recall if I said so earlier... I am
more grateful than I can say that you have succeeded in ridding me of William from my life
once and for all.'

'I believe I have already received a demonstration of the depth of that gratitude.' His
mouth twisted derisively as he gave a pointed
glance in the direction of the *chaise*.

Her eyes widened and her face paled. 'You
believe that I—' She moistened the dryness of
her lips. 'That was unfair, Benedict. Not only
unfair, but unkind, too.'

Yes, Benedict was aware he was currently
being both of those things. Because he could
not seem to stop himself. And he had no idea
why he was behaving in this objectionable
way.

He and Genevieve had developed a friendship of sorts these past two weeks. And they
now had an understanding; she was nervous
and fearful of physical intimacy because of
her experience in her marriage and he had
decided to be the one to help her through that
fear, to introduce Genevieve slowly and gently to the finer points of intimacy, which at

the same time allowed him to enjoy her just as intimately.

But he had not made that offer, Benedict now realised, with the intention that Genevieve might go on to practise her obviously increasing enjoyment of that intimacy with another, as yet faceless, lover in the future. 'It is late, Genevieve, and well past time I take my leave.' He bent abruptly to collect up his neckcloth from where it lay on the fireside rug. 'I will call for you here at three o'clock tomorrow afternoon, if that suits?'

Genevieve gave a pained frown. 'If you are sure you still wish to take me?'

His expression darkened. 'What I wish—! Never mind what I wish.' He scowled dismissively. 'It would perhaps be as well, if Woollerton is still in town tomorrow, if he were to hear of our outing together in the park as further proof of my continued protection of you.'

Genevieve had no idea what had gone amiss with this evening—an evening when Benedict's mood had seemed light and carefree when he first arrived, indulgent as she made love to him, only to have now turned dark and unpredictable.

Perhaps he was becoming bored with her already? With her incessant questions in regard to lovemaking? Most especially when those questions occurred at an inappropriate time. 'They do say that practise makes perfect, Benedict, and I have no doubts I shall do better tomorrow,' she promised warmly.

He looked at her blankly. 'Do what better tomorrow?'

'Did you not say you offered, the afternoon of Devil and Pandora's wedding, to take me for a ride in your carriage?'

Much as Benedict tried, he found he could not maintain the air of haughtiness he had assumed, as a shield to the confusion of his thoughts, in the face of the impish smile that accompanied Genevieve's improper suggestion. 'In my carriage in the park, Genevieve, in broad daylight, with the rest of the *ton* posing in their own carriages?' He arched a disbelieving brow.

'No one will see if I am kneeling beneath the level of the window,' she assured audaciously. 'And I have always wanted to see a volcano erupt.'

Benedict groaned. 'I *have* created a monster!'

Her smile widened as she obviously sensed that the blackness of his mood had passed.

Quite how or why it had Benedict was unsure, except to know that Genevieve had the ability to lift or darken his mood seemingly without trying.

Just as he did not wish to delve too deeply as yet into the why his mood had turned so black in the first place... 'I believe I should like to be the one kneeling tomorrow, my head beneath your skirts, witnessing your own volcano erupting, several times and with increasing force.'

Genevieve's cheeks became flushed, whether with embarrassment, or anticipation, Benedict was unsure. 'People would surely notice if only the Dowager Duchess of Woollerton were visibly seated in Lord Benedict Lucas's carriage.'

He arched a brow. 'I suppose, if you think it necessary, I might briefly come up for air between those eruptions and give our audience a wave or a bow?'

Genevieve burst out laughing at the image he projected, relieved beyond measure that whatever blackness had overtaken Benedict now seemed to have dissipated. 'I am sure, as you are only too well aware, that would only succeed in making matters worse!'

'If I am to die from lack of oxygen, then I

am sure I can think of no other place I would rather be!'

'I am sure this conversation is not in the least proper, Benedict.'

'Not in the least.' He still grinned as he took her into his arms. 'But it is more fun than I have had in an age.' He sobered as he looked down at her with serious intensity. '*You* are more fun than I have known for more years than I care to think about.'

'The same is true of me with regard to you,' she said slowly. 'Strange, is it not?'

It was not a question which required an answer. Nor did Benedict have one. At this point in time he only knew that it was thoughts of Genevieve sharing her laughter and her *joie de vivre*, as well as her body, with another man, which had brought on his earlier blackness of mood. 'Give me a kiss goodnight, pet,' he encouraged gruffly as he lowered his head and gently captured her parted lips with his own.

'Do you really have to go just yet?' Genevieve looked up at him wistfully once that lengthy kiss came to an end. 'It is not even midnight—'

'And the Dowager Duchess of Woollerton is still recovering from having a bone broken in her wrist,' he reminded gravely, and instantly wished he had not as he saw the shadows return to those beautiful and candid blue eyes. 'I promise he shall not trouble you again, Genevieve,' he assured her firmly, his arms tightening about the slenderness of her waist as he felt the trembling of her body against his. 'He is under threat of public exposure for his crimes if he should ever so much as come near you again.' Benedict pressed his cheek gently on top of her red-gold curls as she lay her head trustingly against his shoulder.

'His crimes…?'

'His father may have been your legal husband, Genevieve, but that legality did not give the whole family licence to beat you for the slightest reason, or lock you in your bedchamber when the mood took them,' Benedict bit out grimly. 'And I have left Woollerton in no doubts that I will take great pleasure in publicly ruining him if in future he so much as enters a room you are in.'

She gave a soft sigh. 'I feel so safe when you hold me in your arms like this.'

'Safe?' He looked down at her teasingly. 'When I am like to throw caution to the wind and make love to you at any given moment?'

Genevieve had not been referring to that sort of safety, and Benedict knew she had not, but had chosen to ignore it by teasing her. She followed his lead and did the same. 'As I am like to throw that same caution to the wind and make love to you!'

Benedict chuckled wryly. 'It is what makes our friendship so interesting.'

Their friendship.

Yes, Genevieve acknowledged, she and Benedict had become friends as well as lovers. A friendship she could only hope would continue once they ceased to be lovers. To contemplate anything else, that of no longer having Benedict in her life, was completely unacceptable to her.

She stepped back out of his arms to tuck her hand companionably into the crook of his arm. 'As I have dismissed Jenkins for the night I will walk with you to the door.'

'And kiss me goodnight on the doorstep?'

She laughed huskily as she waited for him to unlock the dining-room door before the two of them strolled out into the hallway, three candles alight in candelabra beside the door to light their way. 'You should not start things you do not intend finishing, Benedict.'

Benedict knew he was likely to 'finish' all too quickly where this particular woman was concerned! Which was why he needed to part from her now, so that he might have time alone to sit and contemplate the reason for those uncharacteristic feelings of possessiveness he had suffered earlier when talking of Genevieve taking any other lover but him.

'I was only teasing you, Benedict,' Genevieve chided lightly once she had opened the front door and the brightness of the moon silhouetted them as they stood close together in the doorway.

'Or possibly challenging me into staying the night...?'

'Perhaps,' she conceded softly.

Benedict smiled down at her as his hands gently cupped either side of her face. 'I assure you, I am only being the gentleman by leaving now; today has already been...emotional enough for you. But ask me to stay with you another night, love, and I am sure my answer will be different.'

Her eyes shone brightly in the moonlight. 'Oh, I do so hope so!'

He laughed huskily. 'You are a shameless—' Benedict broke off his own teasing comment as he heard a familiar sound, which he quickly realised should never be heard in a quiet residential London street at midnight! 'Get back, Genevieve!' he had time to instruct fiercely as he thrust her behind him and just a second later felt the painful ripping of his flesh and knew no more.

Genevieve had no idea what was happening as she heard a sharp crack followed by a soft whistling noise as Benedict stepped forwards and pushed her roughly behind him, before he gave a slight grunt, his back arched and then he began to crumple lifelessly on to the step in front of her.

It was only when she fell down on to her knees beside him and was able to see the stain of red rapidly soaking through his waistcoat that she realised that sharp crack and whistling noise had been the sound of a bullet being fired and then fast approaching its target.

Which was when she began to scream…

Chapter Fifteen

'Cook has prepared a delicious chicken broth and a milk pudding for your dinner, your Grace.' Jenkins placed the tray down upon the small table beside the chair where Genevieve sat in quiet contemplation.

She gave the butler a sad and wistful smile. 'Thank Cook for me, Jenkins, but I am afraid I am not hungry.'

'It has been days, your Grace… You really should try to eat something.' The elderly man looked down at her concernedly as she gave another shake of her head.

It had been days, Genevieve acknowledged. Far too many days. And nights. Days and nights when she had sat at Benedict's bedside, willing him to fight the fever that had beset him within hours of the doctor removing the bullet from his side, and then another day and another night once that fever had broken, willing him to awaken and look at her again with those beautiful black and fathomless eyes.

She glanced at Benedict now as he lay so still against the pillows, his face pale and gaunt against the white bedsheets; she had instructed he be carried to her own bedchamber the night he had been shot and the servants had come running in answer to her screams, pushing down her own hysteria long enough to issue instructions for one of the servants to go for the doctor and another to bring towels and bandages up to her bedchamber so that she might staunch the bleeding until the doctor arrived.

At which time she had insisted on assisting the doctor herself in removing the bullet that had penetrated Benedict's left side and helping to apply the bandage to his wound once the doctor had stitched it, grateful that Benedict was unconscious throughout and could not feel the pain or see the copious amount of blood he had lost. The bullet, miraculously, had not succeeded in piercing any of his vital organs.

And all the time she had worked, so silently

and efficiently at the doctor's side, it had been with the knowledge that someone had shot Benedict and that if the bullet had entered his body several inches higher than it had, they would have succeeded in killing him, whether or not he had been the intended target.

Which Genevieve was not sure he had been...

He had been shot outside her home, on her doorstep, and if he had not pushed her aside, Genevieve would as like as not have been the target rather than Benedict...

In the anxious days and nights that followed Genevieve had wondered if they had not succeeded in killing Benedict, anyway.

She had remained constantly at his side, allowing no one else to tend him and only the doctor and Jenkins allowed into the sickroom as Benedict fought the fever that had taken him into a state of delirium, his mutterings incomprehensible, his body burning hot, his nightshirt and bedlinens needing to be changed often as they became sweat-dampened.

She had sent word to his two closest friends of his condition, of course, but with the added proviso that Benedict could not receive visitors as yet and she would contact them both immediately the moment that he was conscious. They in turn had sent word of the shooting to Benedict's godfather, the Earl of Dartmouth, that gentleman having called personally himself yesterday, anxious to see his godson and reassure himself as to his well-being. Genevieve had gently but firmly refused that gentleman entry, too, but again with the added assurance she would send word as soon as Benedict was well enough to receive visitors. Until Benedict had awakened from his fever, and the two of them were able to speak together, to decide who could have fired the gun, Genevieve had no intention of allowing anyone but herself to be anywhere near him.

She gave the butler another apologetic smile. 'Please return the tray to the kitchen with my apologies to Cook, Jenkins.' In truth, the smell of the chicken broth was starting to make her feel nauseous.

'Cook will not be pleased, your Grace, and you really should keep up your strength if you are to continue to nurse his lordship so diligently.'

'I—'

'Eat the damned broth and pudding, Genevieve, and stop giving Jenkins a hard time,' Benedict instructed weakly.

'Benedict!' she gave a startled but relieved cry as she stood up to bend over him solicitously, tears filling her eyes as he looked up at her with shadowed but completely lucid black eyes. 'Oh, my dear!' She clasped one of his hands tightly to her breasts as those tears began to fall hotly down her cheeks.

Benedict felt as weak as a newborn kitten as he gazed up at Genevieve, but not so much so that he could not see that her face seemed much thinner than he remembered and there were dark shadows beneath her cornflower-blue eyes. 'What has happened here…?'

'You were shot six evenings ago,' she supplied huskily.

Damn it, yes, Benedict remembered now. Remembered hearing the distinct and unmistakable click of a gun being fired in the still of the night. The whistle of the bullet as it sped quickly towards them. His instinctive protection of Genevieve as he'd stepped forwards to push her behind him. And then the searing hot pain as the bullet ripped into his flesh. The same flesh which still throbbed painfully in his side…

He licked the dryness of his lips. 'Do you have some water I might drink?'

'Of course.' Genevieve seemed relieved to

be able to do something for him as she released his hand in order to turn her attention to pouring some water from the pitcher into a glass.

He lay in Genevieve's own bed, Benedict recognised with a frown. He had obviously spent the past six nights and days in Genevieve's bedchamber, in her bed, which begged the question of where had she slept? From the looks of her—the pallor of her face, those dark shadows beneath her eyes, the untidiness of her hair and the crumpled blue-silk gown she still wore—she had not slept, or eaten, or so much as changed her clothes for those past six days and nights. Which went a long way to explaining Jenkins's familiarity in his concern over his mistress's own health.

'Thank you.' Benedict lay back weakly against the pillows once he had taken several sips of the cool and refreshing water. 'Do you think Cook has another bowl of that broth and pudding to spare?' He glanced hopefully at Jenkins as the butler hovered anxiously at Genevieve's back.

'The doctor instructed that you were only to drink water if—when you awakened,' Genevieve cautioned worriedly.

'If' he awakened, Benedict noted with a

grimace. There had been some danger that he might not, then? 'Luckily the doctor is not here to see whether or not his instructions are being carried out—I need to eat something, Genevieve,' he spoke firmly as she would have interrupted him. 'Before I fade away from lack of nourishment,' he added disgustedly, aware that his own body had lost as much weight in the last six days as Genevieve's appeared to have done. 'We can sit and eat together.'

'A capital idea, your Grace.' The butler nodded his approval.

Genevieve gave a rueful shake of her head. 'You are awake two minutes and already you have my household staff eating out of the palm of your hand!'

Benedict grinned unrepentantly. 'I believe Jenkins merely sees the benefit of my suggestion.'

'I do indeed, my lord.'

'Very well,' she conceded irritably at the insistence of the two men. 'I shall see to giving you this cooling bowl of broth whilst Jenkins returns to the kitchen for another.'

'I think not,' Benedict drawled derisively. 'I see through your ruse, Genevieve; I shall be given this bowl of broth and then you will refuse to eat the second one.' He glanced at the butler. 'I am sure I can wait to eat until Jenkins returns in a minute or two?'

'I shall be but one minute, my lord,' the butler promised.

'And, Jenkins...' Genevieve halted him as he reached the door. 'Could you send word to the doctor, the Duke of Stratton, and the Earls of Sherborne and Dartmouth, as to his lordship's recovery?'

'Immediately, your Grace.' Jenkins hurried from the bedchamber.

Genevieve sat down heavily in the chair beside the bed once she and Benedict were alone, her face deathly pale as her hand once again moved to grip his tightly. 'I believed I—we might have lost you!'

Benedict smiled bleakly. 'Obviously I am made of much sterner stuff than was thought.'

'You have been so very ill, Benedict.' Her eyes were huge and dark with the memories of that illness. 'You developed an infection, which led to a fever, and—' She gave a helpless shake of her head. 'The doctor has called every morning and evening, but even he was not sure until yesterday whether or not you would survive.'

'What happened yesterday?' Much as he wished it were otherwise, Benedict felt at a

distinct disadvantage in his weakened state—
even his normally sharp thought processes
were not completely under his command.

'The fever finally broke.' She sighed her
relief. 'Although still you did not awaken…'
Genevieve frowned her consternation.

'And you have nursed me all this time yourself?'

'Of course.' She nodded firmly. 'Until we
know what—or should I say who?—did this,
then I dare not entrust your welfare to anyone else.'

Which was the reason she looked so exhausted, Benedict realised with a frown, and
why she was still wearing the blue gown in
which she had dined with him six evenings
ago. 'William Forster, do you think?'

Genevieve had thought of little else but who
could have done this to Benedict during the
long hours she had remained at his side, bathing his face and body with cold cloths when he
became too hot, lying beside him on the bed to
add her warmth to his whenever he was racked
with the cold shivers that followed. Over and
over again she had gone over that question in
her own mind.

William did seem to be the obvious culprit,
of course. The shot in the dark, from a face-

less assailant, would fit in perfectly with what she knew to be his cowardly nature.

And yet somehow, for some inexplicable reason, Genevieve still found difficulty in believing him to be the one responsible for having shot Benedict.

There was something, some fact which Genevieve could not grasp, but which she knew was significant, which had nagged and gnawed at the edges of her mind for all of these days and nights. Until Genevieve had become so befuddled by exhaustion and lack of sleep that she had not been able to think at all, but had instead concentrated what little energy she had on caring for Benedict's needs.

She felt too weary still to give the question the attention it deserved. 'Perhaps,' she finally dismissed doubtfully. 'As you no doubt realise, I have informed your friends Devil and Dante of your condition, and they in turn have contacted your godfather, Lord Cargill. Perhaps now that you are awake, and they may visit you, one of them may be able to make the necessary enquiries?'

'No doubt,' Benedict answered distractedly. 'I—ah, Jenkins.' He turned to the butler as he returned with a second laden tray, which he now placed on the bedside table beside the jug of water. 'When you return downstairs, could you possibly see to water being heated and then brought up so that her Grace might bathe once she has eaten her fill?'

Genevieve was suddenly self-consciously aware of the picture she must present to Benedict; her hair was falling in untidy wisps about her shoulders where it had escaped its pins, her gown not only crumpled, but also stained with Benedict's blood. She had not so much as glanced in a mirror these past six days, but no doubt her face was white with strain and lack of sleep, and also gaunt from lack of food she had refused to eat.

She put up a self-conscious hand to her bedraggled hair. 'Yes, please do that, Jenkins.' She waited until the butler had left before turning to Benedict. 'I must look a mess.'

'To me you have never looked more beautiful,' Benedict assured her gruffly.

Genevieve instantly frowned. 'Has your fever returned?' She moved to place a hand against his brow, but found it only mildly warm.

'Not a bit of it.' Benedict smiled ruefully as he realised that Genevieve thought his compliment was due to his once again being delirious with the fever, and wishing he had the strength to get up from the bed and take Genevieve into his arms as he reassured her of how beautiful she was to him. An ethereal and beautiful angel.

He remembered nothing of the past six days and nights, but it was obvious from Genevieve's appearance, and the butler's concern for her, that she had not left his side during all of that time. Nursing him. Bathing him. Caring for him.

That knowledge did very little for his self-esteem, of course, but it showed Genevieve's mettle. If Benedict had needed to be shown. Which he did not.

He gave her hand a squeeze. 'You should not have let me remain here, Genevieve.'

'And where else should you have gone?' She frowned.

'Your reputation—'

'To the devil with my reputation!' Her eyes snapped with temper. 'You have been too ill to be moved anywhere, nor would I have allowed it. Besides, no one knows of your presence here but your two friends, your godfather and my own household servants. And I do not believe that any one of them would breathe a word of it to anyone else.'

'Perhaps not,' Benedict conceded slowly. 'But—'

'Perhaps we should wait until you are feeling better before you commence once again lecturing me as to the wisdom or otherwise of my actions?' Genevieve reasoned drily. 'For now I shall see to feeding you the broth and pudding.'

'I am perfectly capable of feeding myself—' He broke off with a groan as the pain lanced through his side as he attempted to sit up, causing him to sink back weakly on to the pillows.

'Are you…?' She arched a pointed brow as she moved forwards to place a napkin across his chest before turning to pick up the bowl of broth.

Attempting to sit up had shown Benedict that he wore nothing on his chest but a bandage swathed about his lower torso, and the feel of the bedsheets now against his bare thighs and legs told him that he wore nothing beneath those sheets either. 'I trust you have not taken advantage of me as I slept, Genevieve?' He arched one mocking brow.

'I see that your sense of humour is as dry and wicked as it ever was.' She eyed him in exasperation.

'Did you ever doubt that it would be?'

'I hoped not,' she assured huskily. 'And the reason you are without a nightshirt is because it became too difficult to continually change them as the fever raged.'

'Did you change them your—? Hmm,' Benedict groaned his approval as Genevieve took advantage of his open mouth to spoon in the broth; after days of taking no sustenance at all it tasted as rich and nourishing as ambrosia! 'I was only going to enquire as to whether you were the one who undress—umph.' Another spoonful of the broth appeared in his mouth. 'You will soon run out of broth and pudding—then what shall you do to silence me?' He eyed her teasingly.

In truth, Genevieve was so relieved to have Benedict returned to her—wicked humour or otherwise—that it was difficult for her to stop herself from grinning. As it was, she smiled down at him mischievously. 'I thought I might take my bath before the fire over there and bedevil you in that way?'

Benedict gave a low groan. 'You are like to give me another fever!'

She chuckled softly. 'Then no doubt, if you are feeling strong enough, I shall find some way in which to ease it.'

Benedict eyed her speculatively. 'I will make sure that I am!'

Genevieve made no answer as her smile became enigmatic. These days and nights of sitting beside Benedict, unsure if he would ever wake up again and look at her with those beautiful and sensual dark eyes, had succeeded in showing Genevieve the depth of feelings she had for him.

She was in love with him.

Deeply.

Irrevocably.

And with the realisation of that love Genevieve's past had simply melted away, those nightmare years of being Josiah's wife no longer of any relevance, to a degree that all she wished for now was to have Benedict returned to her so that she might be with him, in every way, for as often and long as he wished her to remain with him.

Nothing else mattered to her now. Not the past. Certainly not the future. Here and now was all that mattered. With Benedict…

'I was unsure as to whether you were being serious…' Benedict could not take his eyes off Genevieve as she began to remove her clothes in readiness for climbing into the bathtub where a footman had placed it in front of the fire, before Jenkins returned to supervise several maids as they poured in the steaming hot water in readiness for Genevieve's bath.

Maids who had sent Benedict curious and sideways glances as he lay in their mistress's bed, before Jenkins had ushered them from the bedchamber and closed the door firmly behind them.

At which time Genevieve had risen gracefully to her feet, letting down her hair and stepping out of her slippers, before she began to unbutton and remove her gown.

She wore only her chemise now as she glanced across at him between thick dark lashes, her hair a silky red-gold curtain about the slenderness of her shoulders. 'You would rather I bathed elsewhere?'

'Not in the least.' Benedict eased himself up slightly and made himself comfortable against the half-dozen or so pillows piled behind him, the broth and pudding having surprisingly gone a long way to restoring much of his strength. Certainly enough that he was thoroughly enjoying watching Genevieve prepare for her bath!

She gave a gracious inclination of her head. 'In that case I shall continue to undress…'

That Benedict found it difficult to breathe, as Genevieve slipped the straps of her chemise down her arms before allowing it to fall on to the carpet at her feet, owed very little to his injury and all to the fact that she was now completely naked apart from delicate white stockings held in place with silky white garters adorned with tiny blue bows.

Her red-gold hair cascaded in wild abandon about her shoulders and the firmness of her uptilting breasts, tipped by rosy-red nipples that pouted invitingly through those silky tresses. Her waist was slender, hips softly curvaceous, red-gold curls at their apex.

Benedict's breathing became even more laboured as she perched facing him on the edge of the stool before the dressing table, allowing him glimpses of her most intimate part as she raised first one leg and then the other as she slowly removed her garters and stockings before once again standing up.

The next hour proved to be equally as tortuous for Benedict—and arousing!—as Genevieve's breasts swayed temptingly as she stepped slowly into the bathtub before sitting down facing him, the water lapping against those berry-red nipples as she slowly washed her hair before lathering each and every inch of her body with perfumed soap. Her shoulders and arms, her breasts, first one leg and then the other, as she lathered the soap along their length before she stood up to turn her attention to between her silky thighs.

'I believe I am in danger of suffering a relapse!' Benedict groaned, his cock hard and aching as he watched her soapy fingers sweep down and then dip into those delicate folds.

Genevieve's eyes were deeply blue and sultry as she stood in the bathtub, looking across at him between the darkness of her lashes. 'Shall I call for the doctor?'

'I believe the attentions of my nurse might be more beneficial to my present ailment,' he assured gruffly.

'Indeed…?' She arched her brows as she stepped out of the tub to wrap the dampness of her hair in a towel before picking up another to begin dabbing delicately at the moisture coating her breasts.

'Genevieve…!' The evidence of the fierceness of Benedict's erection now tented the bedclothes.

Still she made no move to come to him. 'I am not sure you are well enough as yet for those sort of attentions.' She turned away from him slightly as she continued to dry her arms, revealing the slender slope of her back and the delicate curve of her bottom.

A bottom Benedict longed to sink his teeth into!

The teeth he now gritted. 'I believe, if I may remain on my back, that I am more than well enough!' He threw off the weight of the bedcovers, his cock so engorged and hard it now throbbed more painfully than the wound in his side.

'That sounds…interesting.' She removed the towel from about the dampness of her hair before dropping both towels on the carpet and slowly walking towards him, Aphrodite incarnate as her sultry gaze fixed upon his pulsing arousal, her breasts high and nipples pouting invitingly, those silky red curls still damp between her thighs as she climbed on to the bed before moving to straddle his thighs with her own. 'Mmm, very interesting,' she murmured huskily as her fingers caressed the pulsing length of him before she slowly lowered her head so that Benedict might draw her down even further as he finally captured her lips with his own.

Genevieve had believed she might never be kissed by Benedict again, might never be with him like this again, and channelled all of that worry and fear into the intensity of the kiss they now shared, the depth of the desire she felt to be one with him. A desire Benedict more than shared if the throb of his erection nudging insistently between her thighs was any indication.

She briefly raised her mouth from his to look down at him searchingly. 'You are sure this will not hurt you?' The darkness of his gaze looked feverish and the harsh planes of his cheeks were flushed.

'I was never more sure of anything in my life,' he assured her gruffly, forcefully, even as his hands on her hips raised her in readiness over his straining erection.

Genevieve's gaze deliberately held his as she reached down between them, her fingers encircling that silken hardness as she guided him between her moist and swollen lips, her groan one of pleasure as she felt that hardness gliding smoothly into her, one slow inch at a time, filling her, stretching her with an intensity of pleasure she had never imagined existed.

'I am not hurting you…?' Benedict looked up at her concernedly.

She laughed exultantly. 'Not in the least!'

To prove the truth of her words she deliberately thrust her hips down, taking all of him inside her, his shaft so long and so thick that it claimed her so completely and felt as if he touched her womb. 'It feels wonderful, Benedict,' she assured breathlessly. 'It is still not causing you discomfort…?' She hesitated as she looked down at him anxiously, sure that she would die if he were to say yes and they had to stop.

'Not in the least,' he echoed her own words even as his hands moved to grasp her hips once again and he began to guide her up the length of his shaft before slowly easing her down again, setting a rhythm that was pleasurable to them both.

And causing Genevieve to gasp anew at the intensity of that pleasure. 'It feels so wonderful, Benedict! So gloriously wonderful!' Her back arched as she began to move faster, harder into the rhythm of those thrusts, the pleasure between her thighs, the heat, becoming deeper, higher, with each pulsing thrust of Benedict's shaft. 'I—Benedict, I—' She broke off to let out a keening cry as Benedict latched on to one of her roused nipples as her breasts bobbed in front of him, suckling her deeply into the warmth of his mouth, and sending her over the edge of that pleasure in a release so deep and intense Genevieve thought she might faint from the ecstasy that now so completely overwhelmed her.

'Again!' Benedict groaned harshly just minutes later, nothing else mattering, existing, as he thrust deeply up and into Genevieve as his own release became imminent amidst the continued clenching and unclenching of her inner muscles. 'God…!' he cried out as that release claimed him with a fierceness he had never experienced before, pumping hotly, deeply inside her as her second climax prolonged and deepened their pleasure to the point that Benedict believed she might be an angel after all, that he must have died and gone to heaven…

Chapter Sixteen

'I am sorry for disturbing you, your Grace.' Jenkins sounded slightly put out himself some ten or fifteen minutes later as he spoke to them from the hallway outside the closed and locked door to Genevieve's bedchamber. 'But his lordship's godfather, the Earl of Dartmouth, is here and is most insistent upon seeing him.'

'Damn it to hell!' Benedict muttered as Genevieve began to stir in his arms as she lay snuggled next to his uninjured side.

'Just a moment, Jenkins!' she called out huskily as she glanced up at Benedict teasingly. 'Lord Cargill only wishes to assure himself of your well-being, I am sure.'

Benedict scowled. 'Then he should have

waited until morning and called at a decent time. Unless, of course,' he added slowly, 'he has urgent news regarding the whereabouts of the two servants from my parents' estate.'

Genevieve's eyes widened. 'You spoke with Lord Cargill on the subject?'

'Six days ago, before I visited William Forster,' Benedict answered, still distractedly.

'I realise that Lord Cargill is your godfather, but I had not realised your friendship was such a close one that you confided such personal matters to him.' She looked at him expectantly.

'He is so much more than that, love.' Benedict gave a rueful grimace. 'But until I have spoken to Lord Cargill, and received his permission, I am afraid I am unable confide any more of that situation to you.'

'That all sounds very mysterious…'

He made a face. 'Tedious, as it happens, love, very tedious. But, nevertheless, it is not just my secret to tell.'

'Then I will ask no more on the subject,' she assured briskly.

'Would you mind very much, love, if Jenkins were to bring my godfather up here?' Benedict gave a self-derisive grimace as he attempted to sit up and failed. 'I am afraid our lovemaking has fatigued me more than I had thought.'

'Of course you must speak to him here.' Genevieve threw back the bedcovers before standing up to collect and pull on her robe. 'I will instruct Jenkins to bring him up to you immediately and then go through to my adjoining dressing room.'

Benedict gave her a lazy smile. 'Have I remarked recently on what a beautiful woman you are?'

Genevieve chuckled softly as she bent to brush her lips lightly against his. 'You may have mentioned it once or twice this evening.'

'Only once or twice?' He gave a shake of his head. 'Then I shall tell you so again, or more preferably show you, as soon as Dartmouth has departed,' he promised huskily.

Genevieve touched his cheek lightly. 'I believe you may already have exerted yourself enough for one evening, Benedict.'

He reached up to clasp her hand in his, the darkness of his gaze compelling as he looked up at her. 'We have much to talk about, to discuss, Genevieve, and I promise we will do so as soon as my godfather has gone.'

'I believe I should like that,' she assured him.

'As shall I.' He nodded.

Genevieve straightened slowly. 'I will be in the next room if you should need me.'

Benedict released her hand reluctantly. 'The sooner I have spoken to Dartmouth then the sooner the two of us may talk together. And, Genevieve...?' He halted her as she crossed to the door leading out into the hallway. 'Thank you,' he added huskily.

Her brows rose. 'For what?'

'My life, for one thing.'

She gave a shake of her head. 'Any one of your friends would have done the same as I.'

He eyed her quizzically. 'And is that what you are, Genevieve, my friend?'

'Amongst other things,' she said softly.

Benedict nodded. 'And it is those "other things" I wish to discuss with you as soon as we can be alone again.'

Genevieve's breath caught in her throat and her heart gave a leap in her chest at the warmth of emotion she saw in the darkness of Benedict's eyes. At the same time as an inner voice warned her not to read too much into Benedict's words or his expression; he was newly recovered from a fever resulting from the bullet wound in his side and the two of them had just made love together—was it any wonder that he was feeling somewhat emotional?

Her gaze dropped from meeting his in case he should see the love she felt for him shining there. 'Perhaps we should wait for any further conversation until you are feeling better?'

His eyes narrowed. 'What does that mean?'

'Exactly as it sounds.' She shrugged the slenderness of her shoulders. 'I am sure that your health will now improve by leaps and bounds, but until it does we should perhaps also refrain from any further...exertion.'

Benedict scowled darkly. 'I do not at all like the sound of that.'

She smiled ruefully. 'You are a gentleman far too fond of having his own way!'

He nodded tersely. 'Something I have every intention of reminding you of the moment Dartmouth has departed.'

Genevieve was still smiling slightly as she unlocked the door and gave the apologetic Jenkins his instructions in regard to Lord Cargill, the smile only fading from her lips once she had gone through to the adjoining dressing room and closed the door behind her.

She loved and was in love with Benedict so much that she could not now imagine her life without him in it. Without the wonder of the lovemaking they had so recently shared. And which she longed to share with him again. And again.

But she did not want Benedict to mistake the gratitude he now felt towards her for anything other than what it was, could not bear it if he were to imagine it was more than that, only to realise in a matter of days, or possibly weeks, that he was bored with her and by her, and wished to end the relationship.

She wanted him to be fully recovered before the two of them spoke so intimately again...

'I am hoping you have information in regard to the two servants who left my parents' estate.' Benedict spoke tersely to his godfather in his impatience to be alone again with Genevieve, chafing at even this brief interruption to their intimacy for whatever reason. Which, considering his parents' death had been the driving force behind his every action this past ten years, was telling indeed...

Eric Cargill smiled wryly as he eyed Benedict from the doorway of the bedchamber. 'Could I not just have been anxious to see for myself that you are recovering?'

Benedict gave an uninterested shrug. 'I have received a bullet wound before now.'

'So you have.' His godfather closed the door softly behind him before walking further into the bedchamber. 'What I should like to know is how you managed to prevent this one from being fatal?'

Benedict blinked. 'You sound disappointed that it was not?'

'Not at all,' the older man assured him jovially. 'After all, a relapse of your condition will be just as easily explained and accepted, I am sure.'

Benedict became very still beneath the bed-covers. 'Explained to and accepted by whom?'

'Any of your friends who are interested enough to ask.' The earl looked calmly about the bedchamber, his top lip curling with distaste as he saw the evidence of Genevieve's bathtub beside the fire and the damp towels that she had allowed to fall to the floor. 'No doubt the solicitous Duchess of Woollerton will now be amongst that select few?'

All of Benedict's senses were on the alert now as a dreadful—an unbelievable!—truth began to assail him. A truth he found so unacceptable that every part of him screamed out in denial. 'Genevieve has been kind enough to nurse me herself these past six days and nights, yes.'

The earl gave him a knowing glance. 'I believe we both know she has done more than nurse you this evening.'

Benedict's jaw tightened. 'I advise that you desist from making any further personal remarks in regard to Genevieve!'

'Like that, is it?' The older man eyed him derisively. 'She is a pretty little thing, I give you that.' His expression hardened. 'But far too intelligent than is good for either herself or you, I am afraid.'

The cold knot that had been forming in Benedict's chest now turned to one of ice. 'Whatever your business is with me, it does not involve Genevieve.'

All pretence of joviality left Dartmouth's expression. 'She became involved the moment she decided to interfere in something which does not concern her.'

Benedict's stillness was now one of readiness rather than surprise or shock. 'You are referring to her suspicions in regard to those two servants who left my father's estate so soon after the murders?'

The earl gave a weary sigh as he nodded. 'As I said, intelligent as well as beautiful. An unfortunate combination in this instance.'

Benedict looked at his godfather as if for

the first time, seeing past the jovial exterior he usually presented to society, the quietly steady man of politics he presented to the House, or the briskly efficient spymaster he had secretly been for the Crown for so many years.

'What happened to them?' he pressed softly.

Cargill shrugged. 'It was as your lady no doubt suspected: they are both dead.'

'You killed them?'

The older man gave an inclination of his head. 'I arranged for them to die, yes.'

'Why?' Benedict demanded harshly.

'Why did I arrange to have the servants killed? Or why did I kill your parents?' the older man prompted mildly.

Benedict's stomach dropped as his worst fear was realised. 'Did you kill my parents?'

'Of course,' Dartmouth confirmed unconcernedly.

Benedict's jaw was clenched so tightly he could barely speak. 'Then I wish you to answer both those questions.'

The earl shrugged. 'Unfortunately, from something I let slip in conversation, your father realised that I had been a double agent all those years and decided to confront me with it when I rode over from my own estate to see him one day that summer. The two servants?' He grimaced. 'They both knew that I had visited your father that day and I could not take the risk that a bribe would suffice in preventing them from mentioning it to you or anyone else.'

The ice in Benedict's chest began to melt and be replaced by a fury that was as hot as it was deadly. 'You killed four innocent people in order to hide your own treasonous activities?'

'You will be the fifth.' Dartmouth nodded. 'And your little duchess will be the sixth.'

Benedict's eyes widened. 'You have absolutely no reason to harm Genevieve!'

'Her intelligence, whilst commendable, is also her undoing, I am afraid. As such, I am sure it will not take her long, once she has recovered a little from the shock of your own sudden demise, to add two and two together and find the appropriate answer of four.'

Benedict's hands clenched into fists above the bedcovers. 'You murdering, treasonous bastard!' He still found it difficult to believe that this man, his godfather, and his father's longest and closest friend, had not only killed him but also his wife, along with two of their servants. And that he now intended to kill Benedict, and later Genevieve... 'Why?' he demanded again. 'You are as English as I, so why would you do such a thing?'

The earl looked bored by the conversation. 'My mother, however, was French. As for the other reasons for my actions? Our king is insane, and our Prince Regent—why, the man is nothing but a profligate and a womaniser!'

'And those are your reasons?' Benedict stared at the other man incredulously. 'You killed your closest friend, his wife, and two of their servants, because Prinny is extravagant and adulterous?'

'As I have said, my mother is also French and my allegiance lies with that country and its true ruler.'

'Bonaparte?' Benedict spat out the name disdainfully.

'Exactly.'

Benedict gave a pained frown. 'And does— is my Aunt Cynthia aware of your loyalties?'

'Of course. She shares them.'

'And condones your actions?'

The earl sighed his impatience. 'Of course.'

All this time, all these years, the two people that Benedict had thought of as part of his family had been lying and cheating and conspiring with the enemy.

'There has been enough talk, Benedict,'

Dartmouth bit out dismissively. 'It grows late and I am sure your duchess is eager to return to your arms. A pity they will be cold by the time she finds you,' he added unconcernedly.

Benedict's chin rose. 'And how do you intend to go about achieving that?'

'By persuading you to drink the contents of this vial in the tumbler of water at your side.' He held up a glass bottle he had retrieved from the pocket of his pantaloons. 'I assure you, your death will be swift and relatively painless, and give all the appearance of a seizure of the heart following your fever.'

'And just how do you intend persuading me into calmly drinking that concoction?' Benedict scorned.

The earl shrugged. 'Perhaps by promising you that I will spare your little duchess if you will drink it without further argument?'

'A promise I have no trouble disbelieving!'

Dartmoth's mouth tightened. 'Then I will take care of her demise first. A slit of the wrists, perhaps, or mayhap an overdose of a sleeping draught? I am sure that none will disbelieve it if I were to let slip in the right ears how…close the two of you have become in recent weeks, and that her suicide, after discovering her lover dead, was inevitable.'

'Why tell me these things now?' Benedict's eyes glittered with fury. 'Why not just put the liquid into my drink when I was not looking and be done with it?'

'And ruin what little fun is allowed to me?' the earl drawled. 'I have spent years, all of my life, hiding behind this façade, and you can have no idea of the relief, the sense of satisfaction, I find in being able to tell you the truth at last.'

'You are insane!' In that moment Benedict truly believed it to be the truth. This man, a man he had trusted all his life, a man his father had called friend, was nothing but a traitor to his country and a murderer of all the people Benedict held dear.

'Do you think so?' The other man appeared to give the suggestion some thought. 'I prefer to think of myself as a true patriot of France.'

'Even the French do not wish to see Bonaparte return as their ruler!'

'Sheep,' Dartmouth dismissed contemptuously. 'And ones who will return to the fold once Napoleon has been put back upon his throne.'

'Something you no doubt intend to see happen sooner rather than later?'

'Naturally.' The earl gave a calm inclination of his head. 'He is a man of order. A true leader of men.'

'And just as profligate and as much of a womaniser as Prinny!'

Dartmouth's nostrils flared with displeasure at this criticism of his hero. 'You are too young to appreciate the pressures of leadership and—'

'And you, I am afraid, are as insane as Benedict has already declared you to be,' Genevieve spoke softly from across the room.

Both men turned sharply to look at her, Benedict with a sense of dread, Dartmouth with weary resignation. A resignation that turned to a look of appreciation as he saw that Genevieve held a pistol levelled directly at his chest. 'I am sure there is no need for bloodshed, my dear,' he soothed gently.

A gentleness which Genevieve, having overheard Benedict's raised voice a few minutes ago, before then listening unashamedly to much of the Earl of Dartmouth's conversation with Benedict, did not allow him to fool her for a moment. This man, Benedict's own godfather and friend, was responsible for killing four people.

And he had come here this evening with

the intention of killing Benedict, before later killing her.

The earl was perfectly correct in assuming Genevieve would not want to live if Benedict were dead, but she had no intention of allowing him to harm so much as a single hair on the head of the man she had discovered she loved with all her heart.

'I do not intend to shed your blood unless I am forced to do so,' she bit out contemptuously, more grateful than she could say for the loaded pistol she had kept near her ever since the night Benedict had been shot, in fear that whoever was responsible might come back and try again. As he obviously had... 'I would much rather see you tried and convicted for your crimes, before facing the hangman's noose.'

'Vengeful little wench,' the earl murmured scathingly. 'Unfortunately—' a sneer curled his top lip '—I do not believe for one moment that you will actually pull the trigger.'

'Why is it that bullies such as you severely underestimate what I am or am not capable of?' Genevieve returned with all the pleasantness of a conversation taking place in her drawing room.

'Genevieve—'

'You have rid me of the bully from my own life, Benedict,' she answered without so much as taking her eyes off the rotund and insane Earl of Dartmouth, 'please allow me to do the same for you.'

In truth, Genevieve had never looked more magnificent to Benedict than she did at that moment: hair still in disarray about her shoulders, her eyes calm and steady, cheeks flushed, mouth set, body tense beneath the peach-coloured gown she now wore, with not so much as a tremble in her hands as she held the pistol pointed directly at Dartmouth's chest. In the other man's place, Benedict knew he would not be questioning her ability to pull the trigger!

'My dear Duchess—'

'Do not move so much as a muscle, Dartmouth!' she rasped now as that gentleman would have done exactly that. 'I should warn you that my brother, lacking in male siblings, took great delight in teaching me how to use and shoot a pistol with accuracy some years ago.'

'The brother who took his own life—'

'No, Genevieve!' Benedict cried out in warning as her finger tightened on the trigger of the pistol. 'He is merely trying to goad you into firing irrationally and then hoping to overpower you before you are able to fire off another shot. Come here to me, love,' he encouraged as he held his hand out to her. 'Give me the pistol and ring for Jenkins. Genevieve, please,' he urged gently when she made no move to do as he asked.

The fierceness of Genevieve's gaze remained fixed upon the Earl of Dartmouth for several long seconds, before the tension began to ease from her shoulders and she lowered the pistol slightly as she turned to him, which was when Dartmouth decided to make his move!

What happened next took but a few seconds, and yet it seemed to Benedict as if it all took place in excruciating slow motion.

Genevieve became aware of the earl's step towards her almost at the moment he made it. She turned back quickly, aiming instinctively, before squeezing the trigger of the pistol. There was a brief look of surprise on Dartmouth's face before a bloom of red spread across the front of his jacket and he began to crumble slowly to the floor.

Chapter Seventeen

'All this time you have been working for the Crown?' Genevieve looked blankly at Benedict as he crouched down beside the chair upon which she now perched so tensely whilst he tried to explain the sequence of events which had led up to this evening.

'*Believed* I was working for the Crown,' Benedict corrected. 'Who knows now how much of the information I and others gathered was for England or to be passed on to Bonaparte!'

Her fingers tightened about the untouched glass of brandy she held in her hand as she gave a shudder. 'I cannot believe I actually shot a man.'

'He is lucky that it was you who fired

the shot, love.' Benedict's jaw had tightened grimly. 'I would have aimed to kill rather than wing him in the shoulder.'

She gave a shake of her head. 'He deserves to stand trial for his crimes and have the full extent of his duplicity revealed.'

All had been pandemonium since Genevieve had fired the pistol, the sound of the shot bringing not only Jenkins, but several other of the household servants running up the stairs, eyes wide as they burst into the bedchamber to find their mistress on the bed being cradled protectively in Benedict's arms, a pistol at her side, and the Earl of Dartmouth lying in a pool of his own blood on the floor.

Jenkins had taken in the scene at a glance and quickly shooed the other servants out of the room, those few minutes' respite allowing Benedict the opportunity to release a shocked and silent Genevieve before easing gingerly out of the bed and quickly pulling on his shirt and pantaloons, Jenkins finding him crouched over the felled earl by the time he returned to the bedchamber, the bullet having pierced Dartmouth's shoulder rather than his heart.

Benedict had straightened to issue instructions for the authorities to be brought to the house and for someone to remain in the bedchamber with the reloaded pistol trained on the Earl of Dartmouth, whilst he took the still-stunned and white-faced Genevieve through to her private parlour and quietly explained his own years of working for the Crown under the guidance of his godfather.

The godfather who had slain Benedict's own parents, and their household servants, as a means of hiding his treason. The same godfather who would have seen to the disposal of both Benedict and Genevieve this evening for that same cause...

Until Genevieve had appeared in the room with the loaded pistol in her hand. Benedict would never forget how magnificent she had looked at that moment. Every inch the warrior that she undoubtedly was.

She looked up at him now with tear-wet eyes in her parchment-white face. 'I could not allow him to harm you, Benedict.'

'And I shall be forever grateful for it, love.' He moved up to sit on the arm of the chair where she sat and placed his arm about her shoulders. 'How did you know to bring a loaded gun back into the bedchamber with you?'

'My suspicions were first aroused when you revealed that you had told your godfa-

ther of your interest in locating your parents'
two missing servants. Enough, I am afraid,
for me to listen unashamedly at the door once
the two of you were alone in the bedchamber.'
She grimaced.

'And I will be eternally grateful that you
did,' Benedict assured her fervently. 'This is
probably not the time to tell you—no, this
is exactly the time to tell you!' he corrected
firmly. 'I know you are upset, that you will
need time to—to accept the events of this evening, but before the authorities arrive and we
are taken up with other matters, I want you to
know that I love you, Genevieve. That I wish
very much to ask you to be my wife—'

'You—must—not—say—such—things—
Benedict!' she warned emotionally as she
turned sharply to face him. 'I cannot— You
must not.' More tears cascaded down the paleness of her cheeks as she shook her head.

'You cannot what, love?' Benedict stood
up slowly. 'Cannot ever love anyone after
your marriage to Forster? Cannot love me?'
He gave a brief smile. 'We have time, love.
All the time in the world for me to try to persuade—to cajole and love you into loving me
in return.'

'Do not talk nonsense, Benedict.' She eyed

him impatiently. 'Of course I can love you. I love you already. I would not have made love with you earlier if I did not already love you. It is only that—'

'You already love me?' Benedict crossed the room in three long strides to take her hands into both of his, his expression one of elation before a frown marred his brow. 'I do not understand… If you love me, why do you not want me to tell you how much I love you in return, how much I long to make you my wife?'

'Because you are talking out of gratitude and—and honour. Because you believe I saved your life by nursing you after you were shot and stopping Lord Cargill from his attempt to poison you just now— Why are you laughing, Benedict?' She frowned her consternation as he did exactly that, long and loudly.

'"Gratitude and honour"?' he finally sobered enough to repeat. 'Dante Carfax saved my life once during battle—should I tell him I love and want to marry him, too? Rupert Stirling once stopped a malicious French countess from running me through with my own sword as I slept—should I love and want to marry him, too?'

'Now you are being even sillier than before.' She frowned at him reprovingly. 'And what did you do to this French countess that she wished to run you through with your own sword? More to the point, why was she able to do so as you slept?' she added suspiciously.

Benedict gave another shout of laughter. 'Jealous, love?'

Pea-green with it, if Genevieve was honest, and she usually was, no matter what trouble it caused her. 'You cannot tell a woman you love and wish to marry her in one breath and then talk of sleeping with French countesses in the next!'

'I was not sleeping with her, but in a bed-chamber in a cottage close to her estate,' he assured her warmly. 'And the countess wished to run me through with a sword because I had only hours earlier informed her that her husband was a spy and now an English prisoner.'

'Oh.' Genevieve blinked, her indignation not completely mollified by this explanation. 'Anyway, you cannot compare the actions of your two friends with my own.'

'No, I cannot,' Benedict agreed fervently as he gathered her clasped hands to his chest. 'Genevieve, I may not have realised—may not have wished to acknowledge, until six nights ago, that what I feel for you is love—'

'Gratitude.' She attempted to pull away from him, her heart heavy.

A pull Benedict easily resisted by holding all the tighter to her fingers. 'But I knew it when I heard the sound of the gun firing, and the bullet whistling, and knew that if I did not step in front of you it would pierce your heart and kill you and take you away from me for ever,' he finished firmly.

'I—you—' Genevieve looked up at him uncertainly. 'You realised *then* that you loved me?'

'With just as much force as that bullet entering my side.' He nodded determinedly. 'I already knew that I admired you for your fortitude and strength during those terrible years of your marriage, that with you I laughed as I have not laughed with anyone for years, that your body excites me in ways I had never imagined,' he added huskily. 'But they were feelings and emotions that, until I thought I might lose you, I did not recognise as being love. I cannot lose you, Genevieve. Ever. I love you. I will always love you. You are my Warrior Duchess.' He became silent as Genevieve slipped one of her hands free and placed gentle fingertips against his lips.

'Once I am your wife I shall be your Warrior Lady,' she corrected. 'If you will have me?'

'If I will have you?' Benedict groaned. 'Genevieve—my love, I want nothing more than to spend the rest of my days showing you, telling you, how much I love and want you!'

'As I will spend the rest of my days showing you, telling you, how much I want and love you, too,' she vowed huskily.

It was, Genevieve realised, more than she had ever hoped for. A man she not only trusted but would love for ever, as she now had absolutely no doubts that Benedict would love her.

'Why do you have that cat-who-lapped-the-cream smile upon your lips, love? And why is Sandhurst scowling across at you so disgruntledly whilst doing his damndest to look as if he is interested in the Earl of Ramsey's conversation?' Benedict eyed his wife of but a few hours suspiciously three weeks later as the two of them strolled amongst the guests at their wedding supper being held at their London home, their four closest friends, Rupert and Pandora Stirling, and Dante and Sophia Carfax, having stood up for them at St George's Church, in Hanover Square.

Genevieve met that suspicion with wide and guileless eyes. 'I really cannot say.'

'Cannot or will not?' Benedict prompted indulgently, only too well aware, after three weeks of sharing days of laughter and nights of passion with this beautiful woman, that she did nothing without purpose.

She slipped her hand into the crook of his arm. 'I merely mentioned to the Earl of Ramsey that I had seen his daughter Charlotte and Sandhurst alone together in the conservatory earlier, and that perhaps he might wish to talk to Sandhurst on the matter of his intentions towards his daughter.'

'Was that altogether fair to Charlotte Darby, when she has only recently had such a lucky escape from her previous fiancé?' Benedict glanced across to where the two men were still in conversation, Ramsey looking coldly determined, Sandhurst having a hunted look in his blue eyes.

Genevieve shrugged. 'I believe, his daughter having so narrowly escaped being married to a man who is now known to be both a cheat at cards and a bankrupt, that Ramsey will keep a diligent eye on the next man who wishes to become his son-in-law. As I have no doubts that Charlotte, being as you once remarked, of a romantic frame of mind, would very much enjoy being married to a man as handsome as Sandhurst.'

'A Greek god, as I believe you once referred to him…?' Benedict recalled disdainfully.

'Besides which,' Genevieve continued as if he had not spoken, 'Sandhurst would be a fool to refuse the opportunity to take an heiress such as Charlotte as his wife. And he is many things, but not a fool.'

Benedict arched dark brows. 'And are those the only reason for your…matchmaking?'

Her mouth tightened. 'Well, there is still the little matter of Sandhurst having once tried to play me for a fool.'

Benedict gave a shake of his head as he chuckled; he should have realised that his Genevieve would not allow that incident to go unpunished. 'So you have decided that his punishment for that is to be married to a romantic chit whose father will keep such a tight rein on him he will never be able to draw so much as another breath without Ramsey breathing down his neck?'

Genevieve smiled impishly. 'I believe the three of them will deal very well together, yes.'

Benedict smiled ruefully as he slipped his

arm about the slenderness of his wife's waist. 'Remind me never to get on the wrong side of you, love.'

'Oh, you never could, Benedict.' She beamed up at him. 'For, you see, I love you more than anyone or anything and I always will.'

His arm tightened about her waist. 'And I love you as deeply and for always. When shall we be able to escape this hell and be alone together, do you suppose...?' He scowled at their numerous wedding guests.

'Do not glower, Benedict,' she teased as she ran the lightest of fingertips down the tightness of his clenched jaw. 'And what do you suppose I was doing in the conservatory earlier?'

Benedict looked down at her hopefully. 'Looking for a suitable place of seclusion for the two of us to escape to, it is to be hoped?'

'How well you know me, my darling Benedict,' Genevieve purred seductively. 'I also asked Jenkins earlier to see to there being a downy blanket or two in there for the two of us to lie down upon.'

'And has he carried out your instructions?' His eyes glittered darkly.

'Come and see.' She took his hand in hers and the two of them slipped away to the privacy of the conservatory, where the bride and groom proceeded to show each other just how much they would enjoy 'loving and cherishing' each other for the rest of their lives…

* * * * *

A sneaky peek at next month...

HISTORICAL

IGNITE YOUR IMAGINATION, STEP INTO THE PAST...

My wish list for next month's titles...

In stores from 1st February 2013:

☐ Never Trust a Rake — Annie Burrows

☐ Dicing with the Dangerous Lord — Margaret McPhee

☐ Haunted by the Earl's Touch — Ann Lethbridge

☐ The Last de Burgh — Deborah Simmons

☐ A Daring Liaison — Gail Ranstrom

☐ The Texas Ranger's Daughter — Jenna Kernan

Available at WHSmith, Tesco, Asda, Eason, Amazon and Apple

Just can't wait?

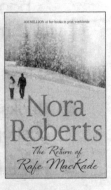